▲

THE CRITICS ARE THIRSTING FOR *THE VAMPIRE FILES!*

▼

"Good-natured fun . . . Elrod's got it down!"
—*Locus*

"Look out! From now on, every three months we'll be seeing Jack in a new adventure—the story of a vampire hero . . . so entertaining that three months may be too long to wait!"
—*Rave Reviews*

"Elrod's sharp vampire's-eye view of the powers of the undead goes a long way . . . Excellent . . . Intriguing . . . Tight and effective!"
—*Dragon*

"The pace is fast . . . intriguing . . . an updated version of the old pulp novels!"
—*Science Fiction Review*

"Well done . . . Original . . . Fleming makes a powerful and charming detective . . . You won't want to miss this series!"
—*Cemetery Dance*

"A pleasant addition to the growing number of vampire hero series . . . Entertaining!"
—*Science Fiction Chronicle*

"Builds to a frenzied climax leaving the reader almost gasping for breath. Be prepared to read the last half of the book in one sitting . . . Should satisfy even the most demanding adventure-lover's appetite for breathless, non-stop action and excitement."
—*Big Spring Herald*

"The twists and turns of the story are reminiscent of *The Maltese Falcon* or *The Big Sleep* . . . Excellent!"
—*Tarriel Cell*

Ace Books by P. N. Elrod

The Vampire Files

BLOODLIST
LIFEBLOOD
BLOODCIRCLE
ART IN THE BLOOD
FIRE IN THE BLOOD

The Vampire Files

BOOK FIVE

FIRE IN THE BLOOD

P.N. ELROD

ACE BOOKS, NEW YORK

FIRE IN THE BLOOD

An Ace Book / published by arrangement with
the author

PRINTING HISTORY
Ace edition / June 1991

ISBN: 0-441-85946-1

Ace Books are published by The Berkley Publishing Group,
200 Madison Avenue, New York, New York 10016.
The name "ACE" and the "A" logo
are trademarks belonging to Charter Communications, Inc.

PRINTED IN THE UNITED STATES OF AMERICA

10 9 8 7 6 5 4 3 2 1

For Mark,
for all the bandage work.

And a special thanks to
Dr. Lee for the
technical advice.

FIRE IN THE BLOOD

▲ 1 ▼

I WAS IN the process of tearing away the top half of Olivia Vandemore's silver-spangled evening gown when Escott abruptly opened the basement door and called my name.

"Are you down there?" His voice was necessarily pitched to carry through a brick wall.

"In a minute," I growled back.

The last fragile strap gave way under feverish, brutal hands. A terrible shriek of pure horror rushed from her perfect coral lips and echoed throughout the dank stone passages.

"Jack?" He was coming down the basement steps.

Her warm, white body writhed helplessly on the carved stone altar—an altar stained black with the blood of uncounted victims hideously sacrificed to slake the unholy thirst of . . .

"Jack?" He rapped a knuckle experimentally against the wall of my inner sanctum.

. . . Sabajajji, the Spider God.

I hit the period and debated whether to turn it into an exclamation point. A quick look through the other pages confirmed that I hadn't used one for some time now, and it seemed appropriate for the scene. The reader was going to be far more concerned with the upcoming description of Olivia's writhing body than my punctuation. I backspaced, tapped the apostrophe key, and rolled out the sheet, adding it to the stack of deathless prose next to my portable. Further excitement would have to wait until after I found out what the hell Escott wanted.

"I was working, you know," I told him, emerging wraithlike from the basement wall and solidifying. It'd taken a couple of months, but he'd finally gotten used to such stunts from me—at least on those occasions when he expected it. This time he'd expected me to be behind a bricked-up alcove in his basement, so it was hardly worth his notice.

"Sorry," he said, his nervous fingers absently jingling his key ring. He was wearing his hat and coat.

"Something up?" I asked, tying my bathrobe. I'd started writing as soon as I'd woken up and hadn't bothered to dress.

"I believe so. I may have a job for us and thought you'd like to come along and meet our prospective client."

This wasn't his usual method of work, which was being a private detective, though he preferred to be called a private agent. Most of the time he'd have some job already in progress and only asked me in if he needed extra help. I always tried to keep a low profile and rarely saw the client. The fewer people who knew about me, the better.

"I'm kind of in the middle of something," I hedged, reluctant to be dragged away from Olivia's impending sacrifice and last-second rescue. "Or are you getting a fishy smell off this one?" Sometimes he'd have me come along to watch his back.

"Such niceties of personal judgment are most difficult to ascertain, especially since I've had no actual contact with the client. I can positively state that the gentleman is determined, if nothing else, and possessed of some degree of consideration, in that he was kind enough to send his chauffeur over to make sure I did not miss his requested appointment."

I followed the cant of his eyes up the basement steps to the hall door. As he spoke, the doorway—the entire doorway—was blocked by the presence of a uniformed Negro. He was built like an industrial-grade refrigerator. Escott couldn't really say anything in so many words, but this was definitely one of those times when he wanted someone to watch his back.

"So, what's the client's name?" I asked, all interest now.

"Sebastian Pierce," he said.

"Never heard of him."

"He was quite a large noise in Chicago some twenty-five years ago. After making a fortune from various investments, he then retired to enjoy it."

"We should all be so lucky."

"And this is his chauffeur, Mr. Griffin."

Griffin nodded once at me. "Good evening, sir." The amused look on his face indicated that he'd noticed the pajamas and bathrobe.

"Good evening," I returned, and tried to look dignified in spite of the unconventional surroundings. Maybe Escott had told him I was checking the furnace. "What time's this appointment?"

"Eight o'clock. We can just make it if you hurry." Escott turned and trotted lightly up the basement steps, pausing only a moment at the top so Griffin could vacate the doorway. He hardly made a sound. Maybe Escott wanted me to cover him, but who the hell was supposed to cover me? I gave an inward shrug and followed. For the time being Olivia would just have to wait at the altar.

Escott and I started rooming together a couple weeks after the night I woke up dead on a Lake Michigan beach. He owned a three-story brick relic that had been a bordello in less innocent days. It had plenty of space and we'd both agreed that it offered me more privacy than a hotel. We shared the bills and I had two rooms upstairs with my own bath, but when writing, the basement was my exclusive territory. The intervening floors served as soundproofing, so the clack of my typewriter in the wee morning hours didn't disturb what little sleep his insomnia allowed him.

I'm up so late and only after dark because I'm a vampire.

Just like the folklore says, I drink blood for sustenance—usually at the Union Stockyards every other night, depending how active I am. The cattle there don't seem to mind. Human blood has its own special appeal, but like most people, I keep my nourishment separate from my sex life.

I don't have any aversion to crosses, garlic, or silver, though I do have a problem with wood and crossing free-flowing water. I can't turn into a bat or wolf, but can disappear, float around, and even walk through walls if required. Most of the time I use doors—it's less conspicuous.

During the day I'm stretched out on a fairly comfortable folding bed that has a layer of my home earth sewn up in a long, flat sheet of oilcloth. The bed is in Escott's basement, hidden behind a fire-resistant brick wall that he'd built himself. The tiny room beyond is located exactly under the kitchen, and Escott had thoughtfully fitted a trap into the floor there for emergencies. It was well hidden by his carpentry skill and a throw rug. I don't have a coffin. I hate coffins.

The room's pretty stark, but during the day I don't notice much of anything. It has an air shaft to the outside, electricity for the work light and radio, and a photo of my girlfriend Bobbi for decoration. My typewriter rests on a wide shelf attached to the wall. I enjoy the privacy when writing, but do my real living in my rooms on the second floor. There I keep my clothes and a comfortable scatter of magazines and books, and succeed in pretending that I'm no different from any other human. But the bed in the corner was for show only, and no mirror hangs over the dresser.

Tonight I picked out a plain dark silk tie to go with my second-best midnight blue suit. It was conservative without overdoing it, though next to Escott, I always look a little flashy. He feels the same way about double-breasted suits as I do about coffins and wouldn't be caught dead in one.

Escott and Griffin were in the parlor. Griffin was sitting on the edge of the big leather chair, his visored hat on one massive knee. He stood up smoothly as I came down. I couldn't figure his age, he had one of those thirty-to-fifty faces. Escott got up from the sofa and led the way out, locking up behind us. A minute later we were driving away in a shiny new Packard with Griffin at the wheel.

"Any idea where we're going?" I murmured to Escott, though there was a glass divider between the front and back.

He opened his mouth, shut it, and shook his head once, looking slightly embarrassed. "I asked all the usual questions, but Mr. Griffin deigned to answer only the most basic: the name of his employer and the time of the appointment."

"Nothing else, huh?"

"If his purpose was to inflict bodily harm upon my person, I think it would have happened by now. At least he had no objections to my request to have you along."

"If you feel so trusting, then why bring me at all?"

"I'm merely applying your own philosophy of not taking chances. Mr. Griffin did give me the impression that he wouldn't have been at all pleased had I refused his request to come."

He had a definite point there. I was much stronger than I

looked because of my changed condition, but Griffin was not someone I'd cheerfully go up against just to see what happened.

"My belated apologies for dragging you from your work. How is it progressing?"

"Just peachy." I had a fanciful mental picture of the editor of *Spicy Terror Tales* breathlessly awaiting my latest contribution to the slush pile. Several years of background in journalism notwithstanding, my literary career at this point had been anything but lucrative, so my partnership with Escott was a financial necessity. Vampires spend money like everyone else.

Griffin drove to a quiet street with only one open business at this hour, a bar called the Stumble Inn. He parked in front, got out, and opened the car door for us.

"You'll find Mr. Pierce at the last table on the left," he told us.

"On the left," repeated Escott, as though such meetings were normal for him.

Griffin gently shut the door, folded his arms, and leaned against the Packard, causing it to tilt a little. It was a freezing night, but he seemed to be as indifferent to the cold as I. He was breathing regularly, though, which meant he was human, after all. That was a relief.

We went inside. The bar lined one long wall and the man behind it had his ear pressed to a radio that was giving out with more static than program. The place had tables, but no booths, and as promised, only one customer in the back on the left.

He stood up as we came close, a tall, weedy-looking man with a lion's mane of wavy white hair, brilliant blue eyes, and a monumental nose. His handshake was dry and firm.

"Well, I thought there'd be only one of you, but I don't mind the extra company if it'll get the job done," he said in a soft, gravelly voice. "I'm Sebastian Pierce, which one of you is Escott?"

"I am Charles Escott, Mr. Pierce. This is my business associate, Jack Fleming."

"Pleased." He nodded at me, then turned back to Escott as we sat down together. "English, are you? Is that a London accent?"

"Yes."

Pierce found it amusing for some reason and asked if we

wanted a drink. I declined, but Escott said he'd have whatever Pierce was having, which amused him even more.

"Don't know as you'd like it, since it's only sarsaparilla. I got stinking drunk once in my life and swore never to repeat the experience."

"Sarsaparilla will be fine."

Pierce signed to the bartender, who brought over an open bottle and a glass, then returned to hunch over his radio.

"You think I'm some sort of lunatic, Mr. Fleming?" he questioned, reading my open-book mug correctly.

There were deep-set humor lines all over his face. It had been well lived in for the last sixty years or so, but they'd been good years. "I must know a hundred stories about what happens to the guy who walks into a bar and asks for what you're drinking," I said.

"Nonsense, you're only old enough to know two or three of those at the most."

I was in my mid-thirties, but looked a lot younger. I didn't bother to correct him and only shook my head a little.

"I happen to own this place," he said, moving his half-full glass around in smeary circles with long, flat fingers. On one of them, a huge ring made from chunks of cut-up gold coins winked happily in the dim light. "It's usually busier, but tonight I wanted some privacy, so Des here shooed out the regulars for the time being. Griff will make sure no one else comes in."

That was for damned sure.

Escott sipped his foamy drink without visible harm. "You mentioned a job, Mr. Pierce."

"Yes." He pulled out a photograph of a fancy-looking bracelet. It was covered in diamonds and some darker stones arranged in a spiral pattern. If the picture were life size the bracelet would be about an inch wide. "I was in Paris before the war and had this specially commissioned as a gift to my wife for our fifth wedding anniversary. It was and is unique, and as you can imagine, quite valuable, both in terms of hard cash and soft sentiment."

"What is it made of?"

"Diamonds and rubies on platinum. When my wife died some years ago, I put all her jewelry in the safe until our daughter came of age. Marian had her twenty-first birthday last month and took charge of it all, according to her mother's wishes."

"And this piece?"

"Has been stolen. I want it back, but quietly. I don't want publicity, and I don't want the police."

"Have you an idea who took it?"

"Oh, yes. Marian's best friend Kitty has a boyfriend. Now, Kitty is a little doll, but it's a sad fact that the sweetest girls can hook up with the most rotten men, and that's the case with her and Stan. He can put on a smooth kind of charm and generally fool those too young to know better, but it's all show. I've met his type before and they're always out for whatever they can get away with. Anyway, the two of them were over at our house for a Christmas party last week and I expect that that's when the bracelet was taken."

"But you've no proof?"

"Nothing I can go to the police with, but I wouldn't go to them, anyway."

"A week is a long time, Mr. Pierce."

"I only found out about it today."

"He may have pawned or fenced it by now."

"You think you'll be able to trace it if he has?"

"There are no guarantees, but we can try, if he is the culprit. Who else was at this party?"

"Myself, Marian, her current boyfriend Harry Summers, Kitty Donovan, Stan McAlister, and the servants who were working that night. They've been with us for years, though. It was Marian's maid who first told me about it."

"The circumstances?"

"Marian usually leaves the valuable stuff lying around on her dresser mixed in with the rest of her costume jewelry. I know it's careless, I've nagged her on it more than once, but in our house it was safe enough until now. Her maid was cleaning and straightening today and noticed that the bracelet was gone. She asked me if Marian had finally put it in the house safe. We checked, but she hadn't, so we went over her room again."

"Marian did not wear the bracelet today?"

"No, or in the last week, we're sure of that."

"And she has not noticed it's gone missing?"

"No. As I said, she's very careless."

"Has anyone else been in the house since the party?"

Pierce shook his head decisively.

"Could Marian have taken it herself?"

"If I thought that I wouldn't have to hire you."

"What made you choose me?"

"I didn't, you're Griff's idea."

"Indeed?"

"He said you came highly recommended by a friend of his, Shoe something."

"Shoe Coldfield?"

"I think that was the name."

Escott glanced at me, one eyebrow bounced, and a smile tugged briefly at the corner of his mouth. Coldfield was now a gang boss in Chicago's "Bronze Belt," but he'd shared some lean times on the stage with Escott in a traveling Shakespeare company years ago. Once in a while he threw some business in our direction, just to say hello.

Pierce continued. "Normally I'd ask Griff to handle something like this, but we thought it better to hire someone a little less noticeable for the job. Griff is a bit . . . tall, and McAlister knows him."

"And if Stan McAlister should happen to mention the encounter to your daughter . . ."

"I'll be accused of doing all sorts of things for her own good," he concluded with a sigh of long suffering, and shrugged. "She's my daughter, but I'm damned if I know what's going on in her mind all the time. She would accuse me of being too nosy or something. She likes to think she's very independent and bitterly resents any implication to the contrary. If you have, or ever have, children you'll know what I mean. All I want is to get the bracelet back. After that it's going into the safe until I'm gone, and then she can do what she likes with it."

"Assuming we're able to locate the bracelet, have you a preference for any particular method of recovery?"

"Since it was stolen, I thought you could steal it back. Stan wouldn't dare squawk."

"If he's fenced it already, we may have to purchase it—if it is still in one piece."

He grimaced. "I hope it is, or Marian's feelings or not, I'll have Griff fold the little punk in two the wrong way. The bracelet's insured for fifteen thousand, I'll go that high, but would appreciate if you could bargain things down to the lowest possible amount."

"We'll see what we can do. I unfortunately do not have any of my standard contracts with me."

Pierce pulled out a wallet and casually gave us each a hundred-dollar bill. It was a sumptuous retainer when compared to Escott's usual rate. "That's all the paperwork I think you'll need for now, Mr. Escott. If Griff trusts you, I can trust you. If the trust is misplaced, then Griff has ways of evening the score."

"Of that I have no doubts. We'll need a description of Mr. McAlister. In fact, I would like one of all the principals."

He was prepared and gave Escott a sheet of paper with names, addresses, and a list of McAlister's favorite haunts. He also produced another photo. "I took this at the party, it's a little harsh because I didn't get the flash right, but they're recognizable. That's my daughter." He pointed to a sleek brunette. "Fortunately for her, she took after her mother in looks. Unfortunately for me, she has my temperament and quite a lot of her own, besides. The handsome fellow next to her is Harry, and the two blonds are Kitty Donovan and Stan McAlister."

Escott carefully checked it over. "What does Mr. McAlister do?"

"Not very damn much, as far as I can tell. Stan has a taste for gambling and no inclination to work."

"Does Kitty work?"

"Yes, but mostly for amusement. Her parents left her with a comfortable trust. She augments it by designing hats for one of the big stores around here, custom stuff. She glues a few feathers and sequins to a strip of ribbon and charges a fortune for it. That's how she met Marian."

"What about Mr. Summers?"

"Harry's from a decent family. Not much money, but good people. Marian met him while he was working as a waiter at some party. He'd worked his way through school that way and now he's trying to start up his own business in radio repair, so I give him credit for some ambition."

"Does he also gamble?"

"No, Harry's pretty much of a tight fist with his money, which is sensible if you don't carry it too far."

"You think he does?"

Pierce nodded, amused again.

"You approve of him, though?"

"He's a cut above most of the losers Marian's brought home,

but I'm not taking it too seriously. She changes boyfriends as frequently as I change socks. She'll fasten onto someone else when she gets tired of going to the park and museums with Harry. They're free, you know.''

"Does Marian work?"

"Has hell frozen over lately?"

Escott almost laughed. "Where may I reach you?"

Pierce mumbled and growled a little under his breath, and reluctantly parted with his home phone number. "But don't call if you can help it, I'll check with you every evening at about five.''

We wound things up and left Pierce at the bar ordering another sarsaparilla. As Griffin drove us back home, Escott studied the party photo by the intermittent light from the street lamps.

"An interesting group, wouldn't you say?" he asked.

"I guess so. Funny how he's so leery of his daughter finding out about any of this."

"The extent that some fathers are dominated by their offspring would probably astonish you, and a man may go to absurd lengths in order to preserve the illusion of peace in his household."

"While disrupting others," I added.

"Yes, he did initiate this business in a somewhat unorthodox manner. At least it added a touch of interest to an otherwise commonplace case."

"That's what you figure?"

"This time, yes. The man didn't strike me as a fool. If he thinks McAlister took the bracelet, then it's likely to be true. We have only to find the fellow and verify things one way or another."

"Sure you need my help, then?"

"Most certainly. I could cover all of the places listed here alone, but it will go faster for your assistance. . . . Tell me, is Miss Smythe still headlining at the Top Hat?"

"For another month yet." Two weeks ago Bobbi had landed the star spot singing in one of Chicago's best nightclubs.

"Now, that is most convenient. It's down here as a place frequented by Stan McAlister."

I could see what he had in mind a mile off. "Aw, now don't go asking me to mix Bobbi up with this business."

"Miss Smythe need not be involved. All you have to do is

look the place over and see if McAlister is present. Don't you visit there each night, anyway?''

"Yeah, but only just before closing so I can drive Bobbi home. Her boss said no husbands or boyfriends during working hours for any of the girls, no exceptions. He thinks they take up valuable space.''

"He can't object if you're a paying customer. Mr. Pierce's retainer should be more than sufficient to cover your expenses for now.''

He'd made up his mind, so there wasn't much point arguing with him. Chances were, McAlister would be in some other joint and I could take Bobbi home as usual, with the added bonus of getting paid to catch her show. "Okay, I'll go have a look. What'll you be doing?''

"Checking some of his other haunts, and then I'll run by his hotel to see if he's in. If I find him, then I can sort things out right away.''

Griffin dropped us at home and drove unhurriedly away, the Packard's exhaust a thick, swirling fume in the winter air.

"How you plan to handle it?'' I asked Escott as I walked to my car and unlocked it.

"I'm leaving myself a wide range of options by not deciding that until I've met the man. If he's reasonable, I'll reason with him. If not . . .'' He spread his hands in a speculative gesture and walked away, taking the narrow alley between his building and the next so he could get his Nash out of the garage in back.

Since my suit was good enough for the Top Hat, I could start right away as well. The sooner we got the bracelet back, the sooner I could return to the typewriter and rescue Olivia from a horrible fate at the hands of the dreaded spider cult.

My mind was busy with permutations on the story's ending as I made a U-turn and followed Griffin's route out of the neighborhood. I was halfway to the club before I noticed the car following me. A couple of turns later and I was certain about the tail; not a new experience, but decidedly uncomfortable. For the time being I did nothing and drove to the Top Hat. As I parked, the coupe drifted past, looking for a spot of its own. It was a neat little foreign job I'd never seen before, driven by a woman who looked vaguely familiar. Maybe she was some friend of Bobbi's, but I didn't think so. I left my car, walked in the club entrance, and offered my hat and coat to the check girl.

The claim ticket was hardly in my pocket when the other driver charged through the door, looking a little breathless. She spotted me looking at her, pretended not to notice, and marched past to toss a wide silver fox wrap at the girl. She made quite a business of putting away her own ticket in her tiny purse and then pretended a vast interest in a placard advertising the club's entertainment. I hung around the lobby, not making it easy for her.

A noisy group came in and she used them as an excuse to glance around, but I was still looking right at her. She flushed deep pink and went back to fiddling with her purse again, this time pulling out a cigarette case. I crossed the dozen feet separating us and fired up my lighter. Startled, her eyes flicked up to meet mine. They were huge, very round, and a pure and lovely blue. Her thick sable hair fell back freely from cream-colored shoulders. They were bare except for two braided metallic straps holding up the silver sheath of her evening gown.

"Thank you," she said, and lighted her cigarette. She briefly locked eyes again, made a decision, and blinked prettily. "What's your name?"

"Jack. What's yours?"

She giggled, schoolgirl seductive, and shook her head, letting her hair swing a little.

I recognized her now and wasn't happy about it. Sebastian Pierce had been very insistent about keeping his daughter ignorant of his business.

"You always follow strange men around?"

"Only the ones I might like."

"That can be dangerous, Miss Pierce."

Her head jerked in surprise, then her eyes dropped. "So I've been found out. Are you going to tell Daddy?" She looked up from under her bangs, as appealingly as possible.

"Depends. Why don't you drop the high school flirt act and we talk about it?"

Now she did blink. I might as well have smacked her face with a wet towel. "You—"

"You're right, and if you're so innocent, you shouldn't even know such words."

She took another breath, held it, and indecision flashed over her face. She would either cuss me out or smile. I got lucky and she burst into laughter; the genuine article this time.

"Drink?" I gestured to the bar in the lounge, a smaller, quieter room away from the stage show.

"Why not?"

As we turned to leave, I heard the orchestra finish its fanfare and Bobbi's voice soared up, filling the next room. I couldn't help but pause, and it was a physical effort to resist the urge to go in and see her.

"Something wrong?"

I was a man in love and bound to turn sappy at any given moment. "No, not a thing." Marian Pierce latched on to my arm and led off in the wrong direction. Not that she didn't promise to be attractive company and was part of the job at hand, but she just wasn't Bobbi.

A waiter read the signs right, at least the ones Marian was giving out, and seated us in the back, behind a row of short palm trees. She ordered scotch and water. I ordered only the water.

"Trust Daddy to find another teetotaler," she said, pretending world-weary disapproval.

"I drink, but not on the job."

"Oh, are you working or something?"

"Would you have followed me if I weren't?"

She puffed on her cigarette and thought it over. "Actually, I was following Daddy."

"Any reason why?"

"No."

It was going to be one of those nights. "Then you started following me. Any reason for that?"

She smiled, trying to charm her way out again. "I liked your looks better than your partner's."

And maybe she thought she could more easily get around someone who seemed to be closer to her own age. "I'll be sure and tell him."

"No, promise you won't tell anyone you saw me."

"Daddy wouldn't like it?"

Her eyes went down. "Something like that. Why did he hire you?"

"Your father is a client, which means I don't talk about his business. You won't talk about yours, either. We're not going to get anywhere fast like this, Miss Pierce. One of us needs to go home."

"My name's Marian, but then if you're following me, you already know that."

"Why do you think I'm following you?"

"I really wouldn't know. Daddy . . . well . . . maybe he thinks I'm just a teeny-weenie bit too wild." She was back doing the vulnerable-little-girl act again. Any more of it and, job or no job, I'd leave to watch the rest of Bobbi's show. Escott could have my half of the retainer and good riddance to it.

"Why?" Impatience crept into my tone. It couldn't be helped, I was impatient.

"I can't really talk about it. But really, there's nothing to talk about."

"Well, that's too bad, then." I made to go and she caught my arm.

"No, please wait."

"For more runaround? Make up your mind, lady."

"All right. You can't tell me why you were hired, but can you tell me why you weren't?"

"Maybe."

"Did my father want you to spy on me?"

"No."

She sighed. "Well, that's something, at least."

"What are you hiding?"

"Nothing, but I do like to know what's going on around me. Daddy still treats me like a six-year-old." Her drink arrived and she put half of it away as though it were my glass of water. "How many six-year-olds can do that, Mr. . . . ?"

"Jack Fleming," I reminded her.

"That's a nice name. Why did you come to the Top Hat if you weren't spying on me?"

"My girlfriend works here."

"You would have a girlfriend, wouldn't you?" She pretended hurt. "Which one is she?"

"Let's never mind that."

Her face lit up with wicked mischief. "If you say so." She abruptly leaned over and fastened her mouth to mine like a lamprey on a fish. I could taste the scotch on her tongue. She fell back, looking flushed and triumphant, and finished the rest of her drink.

"Any reason for doing that?" I asked.

"Because I felt like it."

"That can be dangerous, too, you know."

"Oh, pooh, you're all right."

"Looks can be deceiving."

"That works both ways, darling. I could be a terrible vamp." She leaned back in the booth, crossing her arms to emphasize her cleavage.

"Then I'd better get out of here while my virtue's still intact."

"What?"

"Marian, you're a wonderful girl, but I have to be going."

"But why?"

"Uh-uh, we've already been down that street. I can't talk and you won't, and that makes for a dull evening."

She uncrossed her arms and moved in closer. I braced myself for another assault. This time I tasted the cigarette mixed in with the scotch. She released me, but didn't fall back. "It's about time you learned there's more you can do with your lips than talk," she stated, her voice husky and mature all of a sudden.

I showed my teeth and shook my head. It was safe enough to do this time; my canines hadn't lengthened by even a fraction of an inch. Like I said, she wasn't Bobbi. "Thanks, but maybe some other night, sister."

"Don't you like me?"

"Kid, you make a great first impression. I'm going to remember you for the rest of my life. . . ."

Then some bozo grabbed a fistful of my suit and yanked me from the booth onto the floor. What breath I'd drawn in order to talk got knocked out when I landed, not that he gave me much chance to say anything. Marian screeched a name, which I didn't catch, because the guy slammed into my ear with his knee. My head took a wild spin in the other direction, and I flopped out flat with the man towering over me like a building.

He got his balance fixed and carefully drew back one of his rough leather toes to kick my skull into the next county. I could disappear and let his foot sail through empty air, but this was the wrong place for that kind of fancy work—too many people and too many eyes. Just in time, I got my hand up and caught his ankle. He grunted at the initial shock and then gasped when I squeezed and twisted. He had to turn with it or suffer a green-stick fracture. Arms pinwheeling, he hopped once on his other foot and crashed into a waiter who had come up to stop the ruckus.

Both of them were on the floor in a sloppy football scramble. The guy that hit me started to hit the waiter, but I still had his ankle and gave it a sharp pull to remind him. He grunted out a very ripe curse, which upset some lady into calling for the manager at the top of her lungs. Another woman told her to shut up and a drunk said he would put ten bucks on the skinny guy in blue.

"Harry, how *could* you?" This from Marian, who had slid from the booth and was standing over us both.

Harry was in no mood to discuss motives and tried to kick me with his free foot. He hit my collarbone—hurting, but not breaking it—then he tried to slam sideways and get my other ear. I got my hand up in time again and twisted him pigeon-toed. He yelped, sat up, and tried once more to belt me, this time with his fists.

The waiter spoiled his aim by crawling out from under him just as another man was coming up. Together they tried to haul Harry away from me. I released my grip, still plenty mad, but content to let them handle him until it became clear they'd want help themselves. I got my feet under me, leaned over, and carefully pulled the punch I poked into Harry's gut. He only needed the breath knocked from him, not burst organs.

It worked. You can't fight if you can't breathe, and normal humans do need air on a regular basis. Harry stopped struggling with the waiters and rolled on his side, probably burning one of his own ears for a change as he scraped against the carpet. He made choking sounds trying to refill his lungs.

A man in a tux appeared, took the situation in with an experienced eye, and jerked his head toward the exit. The waiters picked Harry up and marched him away, presumably to throw him out. He didn't fight them, but his mottled red face was eloquent. If I wasn't careful, I'd be in for an ambush when I went out for my car.

"I apologize, sir, I trust you are not injured?" The tux was not a happy man. I told him I was fine, and then he apologized to the dozen or so people who had watched with varying degrees of interest. Two or three left, and the rest settled down to discuss the fight and wait for signs of more entertainment.

I straightened and dusted my suit, took Marian's arm, and made a decent exit myself as far as the lobby before stopping to square off with her. "Okay, who was he?" I already knew, but had appearances to keep up.

"Nobody important. Are you all right?" Her face was bright with excitement.

"Give me a name."

"Just some guy I used to date."

I kept looking at her.

Exasperation superseded the excitement. "Harry Summers," she snapped. "Is nosiness a part of your profession? No, forget I asked, the answer's got to be yes."

"I always like to get the name of anyone who sucker-punches me."

"Harry's got a jealous streak a mile wide. I'm really very sorry." Her apology was light, just words she was expected to say. Her mind was on something else.

"I think you should run along now, the management is figuring that we're bad for business."

She saw the tux talking with another tux and both were looking our way. "I'm not worried about them."

"I am. I don't want my girl to get canned because of this."

"They wouldn't do that," she said with the airy confidence of the unemployed rich.

"Don't bet on it."

"Then come with me. I know a very quiet place that Harry doesn't—"

"Excuse me, sir." It was the second tux and he knew me by sight if not by name. He'd seen me pick Bobbi up at the stage exit often enough.

"Never mind, I was just leaving."

"I think that would be best, sir."

I redeemed my hat and coat, Marian got her fox wrap, and we left with as much dignity as we could muster. It wasn't much; Marian started giggling before we were out the door.

"Did you see the look on Harry's face?"

"Yeah, we could sell tickets."

"My car's right over here." She steered me off to the left. I went along, keeping an eye out for Summers. Marian opened the passenger door, slid in first, and patted the leather seat for me to join her.

"Uh-uh. Time to say good night."

She shook her head in amused disbelief, then realized with a shock that I was serious. "But I want you to come with me."

"Not tonight, sweetheart." I shut the door on her. She flopped across the seat to try and open it again and, failing that, she rolled down the window.

"Jack, I *said* I want you to come with me."

"And it's the nicest thing I've heard all evening."

"But—"

"Marian, to tell the truth, you're just too much woman for me." I backed away and walked fast, putting a line of cars and a lot of darkness between us before vanishing into thin air.

Distant and muffled, I heard her door open as she charged out to chase me down. She called my name a lot, growing more and more frustrated as the minutes passed. I simply waited and floated free until she finally gave up. It took a long time, and even then she didn't go to her car, but back into the club. The clack of her heels faded and I returned to solidity again with relief.

I was crouched next to a Rolls and a Caddy and straightened with care. No one was in immediate sight, which was lucky. Pulling my vanishing act in a public place was strictly for emergencies only, but Marian more than qualified. As far as I was concerned, she was about as welcome as a case of warts—and as hard to lose.

Belatedly, I remembered that I was supposed to be looking for Stan McAlister. Maybe he was somewhere in the club and Marian had been putting up her best smoke screen to distract me. It would mean that she was in on the bracelet business, but nothing much would surprise me about that girl.

I'd been distracted, all right, but if McAlister was here, I'd find him. I started to go around to slip in by the stage entrance and had to stop cold. Harry Summers was coming across the parking lot straight for me, looking like a bulldozer on legs.

2

HE STOPPED ABOUT five feet short of me and glared, breathing hard. With wavy black hair and a strong, square jaw, he was matinee-idol handsome, but his hands were big and he looked as though he wanted to fasten them around my neck.

I was tired of him and he'd already put scuff marks on my suit. My conscience didn't chafe too much when we locked eyes and I told him to calm down. He was plenty upset, but soon stopped puffing so much, and the red mottling finally drained out of his face. He was unaware of what had happened; one minute he was ready to tear into me, and the next we were walking up and down the parking lot having a smoke like old friends.

"What was the donnybrook about, Summers?" I asked in a reasonable tone. "You must know I'm not interested in Marian."

Summers rumbled a curse and wearily leaned against a car, shaking his head. "I dunno. Something just comes over me when I see her look at another guy. She's crazy and she only makes me crazy. I wish I'd never met her."

I could sympathize. "You can't pick fights every time she looks."

His face was sour. "She was doing more than that with you. I saw it. Christ, the whole room saw it."

"Her idea, not mine."

"Then what were you with her for?"

"She didn't give me much of a choice. I'll level with you, Harry, I'm doing a job for her father and she only came on like gangbusters hoping I'd tell her about it."

"What's the job?"

"I can't say."

Like a lot of people, he ignored that fine point and pressed on. "Does it have to do with Marian?"

"Not really. What's she want to hide from her old man?"

He shrugged. "Me, probably."

"Something the matter with you? Pierce seems to think you're okay."

"Only because Marian doesn't let him look too close."

"Got a past, huh?"

Summers nodded. "Cops had me on a couple of assault charges."

What a surprise. "Like what you pulled on me tonight?"

"Yeah. Sorry. Nothing much came of it. I did some time and got out, but the records are there for anyone to find. Pierce won't think that that's okay."

"Tell him about it and see."

"I don't think it's worth it. Marian's flighty, she'll probably drop me for someone else after this. She doesn't forgive much of anything when she's crossed."

"She'll have to learn sometime or lose a lot of friends."

"With her dough, she can always buy more," he said bitterly.

I didn't gainsay him or offer advice or anything stupid like that. If he wanted to feel sorry for himself that was his business, doubly so if it had to do with Marian.

He tossed away his cigarette. It was only half-smoked and continued to smolder long after it bounced off the sidewalk. "I know I'm out of my class with her. She's as much as said she goes with me because I did time. I'm not the tough she thinks I am, all I got is a bad temper. But it makes her feel like she's breaking the rules herself. You know how that makes *me* feel?"

He didn't really want an answer, so I kept my mouth shut.

"She's got everything now and will have more of that when her dad goes. Maybe I'd have a chance if she didn't have so much."

"You don't want a rich wife?"

"The money doesn't matter to me, it's hers. I'd be working my own way no matter what. What it is . . . I dunno, it just gets between us somehow. Like with this.'' He gestured at the lavish front of the club. ''I wouldn't come to a place like this in a million years, but she's here and she expects me to be here, so I come.''

''No taste for the high life?''

''Too much of a good thing. I love strawberry ice cream, but I don't eat it till I'm sick. Marian would, and she'd insist that everyone else do the same.''

The more I learned about Marian, the happier I was at ditching her, but Summers was genuinely miserable. He saw her faults and still wanted her, which could add up to a bleak future. We can't always choose whom we're going to fall for, and I felt sorry for the guy.

''Guess I'll be running,'' I said.

''Wait . . .''

''Yeah?''

''If you see her, tell her I said I was sorry.''

I looked up at the brightly lit entry doors to the club. Marian was just starting to come through them. Her step was brisk and she wore a determined look on her delicate face. ''Right, but maybe you should tell her yourself. See you around.''

I ducked down among the cars before he could stop me again. In the general darkness, she might not have been able to spot me from the club. A second later, nobody could see me at all, and I floated off with the wind. When enough distance and time passed, I went solid and kept walking until I reached the rear of the building. At the top of some wooden steps was a metal fire door that could only be opened from the inside. I had to sieve in around the door, using the extremely thin space between its dense metal and the jamb.

No one seemed to be around. I materialized under a dim red exit light and ditched my nearly forgotten cigarette in a bucket of sand hanging on the wall. I rarely smoked the things anymore; my lungs didn't like them, but they made useful social props.

The band blared away in front of me, masked off from the backstage area by a silver curtain. It was flimsy enough to see through when the lights were up on the other side. A dozen girls wearing strategic bits of tinsel and tap shoes were trying to beat holes in the dance floor, an encouraging sight, because it meant Bobbi would be in her dressing room. I didn't waste any more time.

She said "Come in" to my knock. This time I turned the knob and walked through like a normal person. Bobbi was at the dressing table checking her makeup, a glowing oasis of platinum blond sanity in an otherwise screwy evening.

In the light-lined mirror she saw the door open and shut all by itself. Her wide hazel eyes blinked once in puzzlement, and then she broke into a smile.

"Jack!" She turned around so she could see me and opened her arms. I did what I could to fill them, half lifting her from the padded satin chair she'd been perched on. We were pretty incoherent for the next few minutes until she insisted on coming up for air.

"How's the show going?" I asked.

"Pretty good for a slow night. What are you doing up here so early?"

"On a job for Charles. If you have time, I'll tell you."

She glanced at a clock on the dresser. "I got five minutes."

"Okay." I gave her a very quick rundown on things, including Marian's attack on my lips, and the follow-up with Summers. Bobbi looked my face over and pursed her own lips critically.

"You run in rough company, buster. I didn't notice before, but that is definitely not my shade." She grabbed a cloth and briskly wiped my mouth. "The little tramp," she muttered. "Good thing you confessed or I might have clobbered you myself."

"What's to confess? I was just an innocent bystander. She was the one who got all the ideas, and then her boyfriend added a few of his own. He could have busted my eardrum."

Bobbi tossed the cloth on the table and swung around to sit in my lap. "Which ear?"

I pointed. She kissed it and tugged at the lobe a little with her teeth.

"Does that hurt?"

"Keep doing that and you won't make it out of here in time for your cue."

"Ah, nuts," she complained, and stood up to smooth her dress. She was wearing some kind of sparkly black thing tonight. Everything important was covered, but it looked as though it had been painted on. "I get a thirty-minute break after this set. Will you still be here?"

"Sure. If I watch out for your boss, you think I can see the show?"

"If you're careful and stick backstage. The girls won't say anything to him, but tell them to keep their mitts off you."

"Yes, ma'am."

I followed her out and hung close as she wound her way to the stage. A dozen breathless leggy girls in rustling tinsel clattered past us. One of them gave out with a wolf whistle and the others laughed. Bobbi looked at me with mock jealousy.

"They must have noticed the tie," I whispered. "Real silk." I waved the end at her like Oliver Hardy and she playfully swatted it down.

The band started another fanfare. She pecked my cheek and made a smooth entrance to welcoming applause. The lights went out except for a single spot centered on her. It sparked off her gown and turned her hair into a molten blond jewel. My heart ached, she was so beautiful. I forgot about looking for McAlister, hiding from the management, and any other complications the world had to offer. Bobbi was singing and that was all the world I needed or wanted.

After the show, behind the locked door of her dressing room, Bobbi peeled out of the clingy gown. "I love having a live audience, but it's so hot under that light. Radio work is much more comfortable."

I reclined on an old chaise lounge that was jammed up against the wall, admiring the view. Bobbi rarely used underwear with her working wardrobe, maintaining that it spoiled the lines. All she had on now were her stockings, knee garters, and heels. All I could think was, *Wow*.

She hung up the gown, turned on a little fan, and stood in front of it with her arms raised, which did interesting things to her breasts.

"Maybe I should go outdoors for a minute, that would cool me off," she mused.

"Or heat up half the city."

"Is it warm in here to you?"

"Yeah, you could say that I'm feeling a little hot and bothered."

"I can open the door to create a draft. . . ."

"Don't you dare."

She dropped her arms and sauntered over to sit next to me on the lounge. "It's not fair, I've got my clothes off and you—"

"My hat's on the rack," I defended. "The way I'm set up now, I don't have to take 'em off."

"But what if I want to touch your skin, too?" One of her hands wormed under my coat and started plucking at my shirt-tail.

"Uh . . ." Now I really was too distracted to answer. She got under the shirt and ran her nails up my back, which made me squirm. I caught her arm and did a thing or two to return the favor. We had to keep the laughter down; the walls weren't that thick. Her other hand successfully unbuttoned my coat as she began crawling all over me.

It was absolutely wonderful.

Bobbi craned her neck in the mirror to get a look at her throat. "Good thing I'm wearing a high collar tonight," she said, her finger lightly touching the small red marks there.

"Is it bad?"

"It's never bad with you."

"I mean, are you hurt?" Since our method of reaching a climax required my breaking her skin in a very vulnerable area, her comfort was of serious concern to me.

"What we do never hurts, you know that. I was talking about the hickey around it. It'll fade in an hour or so, but not before the next show starts."

"Next time I'll show a little more restraint."

"Uh-uh. I like things just as they are. Besides, it gives me an excuse to buy more stuff like this." She shook out a red satin gown and let it slither down over her body. Watching Bobbi get dressed was as absorbing an activity as watching her strip. There aren't many girls around with that kind of talent.

Someone knocked at the door. "One minute, Bobbi."

"Gonna stick around for the rest of the evening?" she asked, touching up the powder on her nose.

"I'm *supposed* to be here to look for McAlister. Maybe I can slip out front, do a quick gander, and come back."

"What if you find him?"

"The one weak point in all my plans," I confessed with mock drama.

"That and getting spotted by my boss. He'll know all about

the lounge ruckus and be in a wonderful mood. You stay back here and I'll ask around for you. Someone's bound to know this fella. Clubs like this thrive on booze and gossip.''

"Well, I . . .''

But she only smiled and winked and flashed out the door, locking it behind her. She wasn't trying to keep me prisoner, only make sure no one else got in. That mirror over her table reflected nearly the whole room, and neither of us wanted to borrow trouble.

The band already had the next fanfare going and Bobbi made her cue just in time. I relaxed back on the lounge and listened to her distant voice through the intervening walls. Throughout her set, I pleasantly speculated over how many other couples had used the same lounge for their own romantic interludes. I had plenty of time to think about it, but when Bobbi finally came back she had news.

"I talked with Gloria—''

"The hat-check girl?''

"I was hoping you hadn't noticed her.''

"What'd she say?''

"McAlister was here for a while and then left.''

"What time?''

"I'm getting to that. He was here when you arrived and didn't leave until after the ruckus. Looks like little Marian was trying to keep you two apart.''

"Why do you think that?''

"Marian came back after you lost her in the parking lot and made a beeline to McAlister's table off the dance floor. Tina was running the drinks in that section, but neither of them wanted anything. They had their heads together for a bit, and the next time she looked he was gone. Gloria said he got his coat, stiffed her on the tip, and took off. She saw Marian walk past a minute or so later.''

"Charles ought to have you as a partner instead of me. McAlister's probably halfway to China by now.''

"Maybe, but chances are, he'll stop to pack first. Where does he live?''

"He's got a flop in a hotel . . .'' I fumbled out my notebook, where I'd scribbled the address. It wasn't far; if I hurried I might get there in time to watch his dust settle. "Gotta go, sweetheart. If I'm not back by closing, get a ride with one of the girls.''

She laughed when I kissed her and wished me luck.

* * *

The Boswell House was a cheap residence hotel in a tough neighborhood that hadn't quite made it to being a full-fledged slum, but was trying all the same. No clerk at the desk challenged me when I walked into the dusty lobby and looked around. The stairs were on the right; ancient wooden things full of more creaks and pops than an old man's joints. I double-checked the lobby to be safe, then went semitransparent and floated up over them, guiding myself along with a ghostly hand on the banister. In this form I could see and hear what was going on, but it could scare the willies out of anyone spotting me.

Either the timing was good or for once my luck was holding. I went solid just as a leggy gal in a bright kimono emerged from the room next door to McAlister's. She had carroty hair and hard eyes and looked at me looking at her for exactly two seconds before spinning on her bare heel to go back into her lair. I must not have been the man of her dreams, after all.

A moment of listening at McAlister's door confirmed that he wasn't at home. The door was locked, but no problem.

The small room beyond wasn't much: cheap, battered furniture at the edges, and a Murphy bed taking up most of the space in the middle. It hadn't been made in a couple of weeks; that, or he was an incredibly restless sleeper. I figured he slept alone, since I couldn't think of a woman born who would voluntarily lie down in those stale sheets. I lifted the end of the bed and closed it up into the wall to give myself a little working space.

Escott had taught me how to poke and pry without leaving signs, so I went through everything, taking my time. Chances were, he'd be back before I was finished, and then I could tackle him about the bracelet.

His clothes were still in the wardrobe and bureau, which was good news. A dented metal suitcase was tucked under the spindly legs of a washstand. Unless he had plans to buy clothes along the way, he hadn't skipped town yet.

I'd just lowered the bed again to check under the mattress when the stairs outside warned me that someone was coming up; a man, by the sound of his shoes. He was going slow, but the old wood announced his progress like a brass band. I eased the bed down the rest of the way and vanished.

He took his time at the door and then opened it slowly, as

though he expected a problem was waiting for him inside. He clicked on the light, waited another moment, then closed the door up again. He made a quick circuit of the room, brushing right past me. He stopped in his tracks.

"Jack? Are you here?"

A clipped English accent. Escott.

I materialized with some relief and squinted. After working in the dark for so long, the room lights seemed painfully bright to my sensitive eyes. "Yeah, I'm here. How'd you know?"

He looked relieved as well. "I felt a sudden cold spot cut right through my coat. When that happens I am inclined to think you must be lurking nearby. Have you been here long?" He pocketed a worn leather kit that held a number of lock picks and skeleton keys. It explained the excessive time he'd spent at the door.

"Long enough for a search."

"Is it clean?" A fastidious man himself, he couldn't help wrinkling his nose at the place.

"Figuratively speaking, yes, but we may have a problem. . . . " I told him about my little square dance at the Top Hat with Marian and Summers and Bobbi's news on McAlister.

"Dear me, but Miss Pierce has thrown a spanner into the works by her misinterpretation of her father's actions. If McAlister is the guilty party with the bracelet, he'll have the wind up by now."

"Which is why I got over here. Bobbi figured he'd stop long enough for his clothes."

"I may put Miss Smythe on a retainer," he murmured. "I've just come from a betting parlor McAlister frequents. It seems we're not the only party looking for him."

"He lose big?"

"Almost two thousand dollars—"

"Ouch."

"—to a bookie anxious to take it from McAlister's hide if the money is not immediately forthcoming."

"Let's hope he stops here first."

"Indeed. If he's carrying the bracelet with him it could be lost to our competition to cover his debt."

"Want to wait here for him?"

"It's much warmer than the street below, though we should shut off the light." He relocked the door.

When he was settled in a wobbling chair, I hit the switch. The darkness washed comfortably over my eyes and they adjusted easily. The dim gray illumination coming from the room's only window bounced off the mirror hanging over the bureau and caught the edge of Escott's face.

"Can you see all right?" he asked.

"Just fine."

"Then perhaps you might answer a question for me."

"What?"

"Why do you need a light in your workroom if you can see so well in the dark?"

I'd wondered about that myself. "I think it's because the place is so totally sealed up."

"The darkness is absolute then?"

"Like a . . . cave." I nearly said "tomb" and changed it at the last second. "In most places there's always some kind of light available, like what's here now. It's more than enough for me to work with, but that room is the exception."

"What about your hearing?"

"You talking about the car that just pulled up out front?"

He nodded. We waited and listened. I heard a lot more besides the slam of the car door outside. Some guy was snoring two rooms down, and above us a happy couple were having an athletic engagement. The showgirl in the kimono must have been reading. I concentrated on the lobby below and picked out the clack of a woman's high heels quickly coming up the stairs. She paused at the landing and again just outside, then a key slipped into the lock and turned. Escott hastily vacated the chair and was crowded next to me behind the door.

It opened slowly and she fumbled for the light. She surveyed the room only a moment, killed the light, and left. When the door was closed, I quietly told Escott I was going after her, and vanished. I swept past her down the stairs and out the building, then materialized. She was just coming out as I came in, and I made sure we bumped into each other.

She was tiny, not much over five feet even in her heels, and despite the bulky lines of her coat I could tell the rest of her was built along the same scale. She automatically looked up when we collided, and I had a pleasant view of big blue eyes limned with golden lashes and a fringe of golden hair escaping the edges of her hat. Sebastian Pierce had said she was a little doll and he'd been perfectly right.

I stopped her as she started past. " 'Scuse me, but aren't you Stan McAlister's girl?"

"What?" She blinked at me, properly confused.

"Kitty Donovan?"

"Yes, what do you want?" She must have been concentrating heavily on something else. Her mind had to visibly shift gears to this new distraction.

"My name's Jack, I know your boyfriend." It was an exaggeration, not an outright lie, so I was able to get away with it.

"Oh . . . well . . . how nice," she said, a little blankly. I could have told her I was Teddy Roosevelt and gotten the same response.

"Are you looking for him, too?"

At this, her big eyes went very round and she broke into a kind of frozen smile. "Looking for him? Why, yes, but he's not here tonight."

"He's not? That's too bad . . . I really needed to talk to him. Do you know where else he might be?"

She shook her head. "No, I just thought I'd drop in and see, but no one's home."

"Isn't this kind of a rough place for a nice girl like you to—"

"I don't think it's really any of your business," she told me brusquely. She started to duck past. I caught her arm. "Lemme go or I'll scream my head off."

"No, you won't. You need to know why I'm looking for him."

She was ready to question that, but let me lead her back into the lobby. I kept a loose hold on her arm, as though to steady her. She unsuccessfully tried to shake my grip.

"You lug," she grumbled. I didn't argue with her.

Escott was just coming down the stairs. I nodded at him and he joined us, politely removing his hat when I introduced Kitty Donovan to him.

"A pleasure," he said, bowing a little. She didn't expect his accent or such a high polish on his manners; neither of them went with the neighborhood.

"What's this about?" she asked.

"We're friends of Stan and we're looking for him," I said. Her lips curled in cynical disbelief. "I'll just bet you are."

Escott stepped in. "He was at the Top Hat Club earlier to-night, do you know where he might be now?"

Eyes guarded, she shook her head. I was pretty sure she was telling the truth, but Escott wasn't satisfied. He cocked an eyebrow, indicating a lounge area off the lobby. It was just slightly more private and out of immediate line of sight from the door. We walked her in. I sat next to her on a couch and Escott took a chair in front of us.

She was scared now and trying not to show it. "Listen, if you are Stan's friends, he won't like what you're doing."

"We're doing nothing, Miss Donovan, only waiting until such time as Mr. McAlister returns."

"He's not here. I was just up in his room, see?"

"Perhaps I do. I think you have us mixed up with two other fellows. My word of honor, we are not working for Leadfoot Sam."

"Leadfoot Sam?" I echoed.

"Mr. McAlister's annoyed bookie. I believe he earned his colorful appellation due to his driving style during Prohibition."

Kitty was all anxious attention. "What about Leadfoot?"

Escott tried a reassuring smile that she wasn't interested in. "Nothing about him—at least as far as I'm concerned. We are not his agents."

"Then who are you working for?"

He pulled out his investigator's license and she studied it for a longtime. "We're on an errand unconnected to Stan Mc-Alister's debts and only wish to obtain some information from him."

"I'm sorry, but I can't help you, and I really have to go now." She started to stand, but I gently pulled her back.

"We require but a few minutes of your time," he continued.

"But *I* don't want to be here. Now, let me go or I'll scream the house down."

"Kitty . . ." First I got her full attention, then stepped up the pressure. Her eyes seemed to get bigger and bluer as I held them with my own. She was on her way to slipping under when the entry door opened and a dapper-looking guy with straw blond hair walked in. He distracted me and, worst of all, he distracted Kitty. Her eyes shifted over and she gave out with a little gasp, then drew breath for a full shout.

"Run, Stan! They're after you!"

He whirled in a flash and was out the door before she finished. Escott charged after him and I started to move, but Kitty made a tackling dive for my legs. She was tiny, but more than enough to trip me. I crashed backward into a chair and flipped up and over, feet flying in a clumsy somersault. The floor was wood and awfully damned hard to land on.

When the room stopped spinning, I slowly crawled upright. Kitty had recovered and stood facing me. She dug into her purse and brought out a gun, slipped off the safety, and leveled it on my heart.

"Aw, now, kid, don't do anything I wouldn't do."

Her hand was shaking, but there was a grim set to her mouth. "Back. You stand right back."

I raised my hands to show cooperation. She carried some kind of .22 automatic and knew how to use it or she might have forgotten about the safety. The five bullets it probably carried wouldn't kill me, but getting shot hurt like hell, and my suit had been through enough rough stuff for one evening. There were other ways to take care of her.

"Kitty, we don't want to hurt Stan. We just want to ask him a few questions."

She shook her head and told me to move back. I could try hypnotizing her again, but she looked too nerved up to easily respond. It would also be necessary to get closer and she'd already made a firm decision to keep me at a distance.

"Gonna keep me here all night?" I asked. "What will the management think?"

"Wha'd'ya think I'll think?" A middle-aged man who looked as tough as the rest of the place came around the check-in desk. His hair was sticking up in different directions and he wore a drab bathrobe over his shorts and undershirt. He carried a massive shotgun that made Kitty's .22 look like a water pistol.

Before I could answer, Kitty cut in. "I'm Stan McAlister's girl. This guy and his friend outside were trying to kidnap me."

"Is that what all the noise is about?" His unfriendly eye caught sight of the overturned chair. From his expression, you'd have thought it was his grandma's priceless antique.

"This is a misunderstanding," I said. "My partner and I are—"

"Trying to kill Stan," she blurted. "Please, mister, could you hold him here while I get away?" There were tears and a crack of fear in her voice. Whether they were real or not was anyone's guess, but the man was willing to buy it.

"Sure, little girl. You take off. He won't get out of here for a while." He hefted both barrels in my direction and looked confident.

She whispered out her thanks and was gone.

"Look, mister, my partner and I are detectives."

"Uh-huh. Got any proof?"

I hesitated. Technically I was just along for the ride; Escott was the only one with a valid license. The hesitation was enough to bolster any doubts and the man took a firmer grip on the stock. Outside I heard an engine gun and the whine of wheels as Kitty's car tore down the street. I wondered what had happened to Escott.

"What I said was on the level." I lowered my arms as though they were tired. It didn't seem to bother him.

"Yeah, yeah."

"She just got a little nervous, is all."

He shook his head in patronizing disbelief.

"Now, I don't happen to have my license with me . . ." I started to reach inside my coat.

He dropped the disbelief for a scowl, renewing his grip on the gun.

"But I do have my wallet . . . so maybe we can make a deal?" I opened one side of my coat so he could see where I was reaching.

He licked his lips. "Okay. Double sawbuck."

"Single."

"Double or nothing, buddy."

"Okay, okay." I pulled out the wallet and fumbled around with it, walking toward him. The change in my posture and attitude worked. His hold on the shotgun went slack as he came forward. His attention was on the money, but at one point he looked up at me.

His mistake.

A few minutes later he was peacefully snoring back in his office and I was outside looking for Escott and McAlister. Kitty was long gone, of course, and there was no sign of her fleet-footed boyfriend. The street was empty and black and the infrequent glare of tall lamps only deepened the shadows they were meant to relieve. It looked cold and was beginning to feel cold, even to me.

A distinct gasp and cough caught my attention and drew me to the alley running between the hotel and a closed coffee shop. The bundle of clothes lying in the middle of it was Escott, curled on his side, trying to remember how to breathe.

He stifled a groan as I helped him sit up. The only visible damage was a cut above one eye.

"I almost had him," he complained.

"What stopped you?"

"His blackjack."

It seemed like a good excuse to me.

"He thumped me and broke for his car."

"Round one to Stan, then." I got him out of the alley and folded into my Buick. He groaned again at this, since Stan had also booted him in the stomach for good measure.

"If this keeps up, I shall certainly consider raising my basic retainer," he said, hugging the damaged area.

"You go right ahead. Kitty got away, too. She had a gun and the manager's sympathy."

He didn't seem too upset. "Straight on, then. There's still a chance we can salvage things."

"How so?"

"I'm speculating she will head directly for her own home."

"Yeah? You got a crystal ball?"

"Hardly, but seeking a place of safety after receiving a bad fright is a very strong instinct. If she should follow that pattern, then we'll have the opportunity to question her without interruptions."

Escott gave me the address from Pierce's notes. I got the car in gear and we took off.

Kitty's home was in a nice block of modern apartments in a nice part of town. We parked on the curb out front next to a has-been of a car. I'd hardly stopped when Escott was out and pulling off one of his gloves. He put one hand on the old car's hood to see if it had been running recently, and his lips thinned with satisfaction.

"Stan's?" I asked.

He opened the door and checked the registration, then nodded. While I nervously watched the street for beat cops, he did something under the hood to make sure it wouldn't start.

The apartment entrance required either a key or that visitors
buzz. I saved us some trouble and slipped through to open the
door for Escott. Kitty lived on the second floor at the end of a
carpeted hallway. After trying her door and finding it locked, I
did the same thing again, but slowly. Still invisible, I checked
the room beyond to ascertain that no one was there. It was very
small, probably no more than an entry with a coat closet. I re-
formed and spent a moment listening, but picked up nothing. I
clicked the lock back as softly as possible and let Escott inside.

He already knew to be quiet and his manner was calm enough,
but I could hear his heart thumping like a drum. He enjoyed this
sort of work.

The living room was new looking, the furniture comfortably
plump, but not fussy. A low table displayed drawing pencils, a
battered sketch pad, and a stack of fashion magazines. Escott
flipped a few pages of the sketchbook. It was full of stylized
drawings of heads, all tilted to show off the crazy hats they wore.

The first bedroom was a work area. A couple of card tables
in the middle were covered with a colorful scatter of ribbons,
feathers, netting, lace, velvet, and similar junk. In the corner
stood a small black sewing machine, and stacked next to it were
different kinds of hat blocks. A wall full of shelves held samples
of the finished product. Most of them looked awfully strange to
me, but were probably just the thing for Bobbi to go crazy over.

Escott went down the short hall to the other bedroom and I
followed. It was done up in pale blues with an eye for comfort,
especially the central furnishing.

"That's a pretty big bed for such a small lady," I said. It
looked nearly double the regular size, filling most of the room.
I'd seen something like it once in a movie and had thought things
like that only existed in Hollywood.

"Agreed." He went over to one of the nightstands and opened
the top drawer, immediately pulling out several packets of pro-
phylactics. "Well, well."

I shifted uncomfortably. The girl was entitled to some privacy
and I didn't feel right about invading it on such an intimate level.
Escott dropped them back and shut the drawer with hardly a
raised eyebrow. To him it was simply information. He collected
it in the same absent way other people collect string. He checked
the closet and bath and came back right away, shaking his head

to indicate they were empty. That left only the kitchen at the other end of the flat.

The dining room was clean and uninteresting. The door from it to the kitchen was shut. I listened and this time heard the faint sound of someone breathing within. Just as I touched the door-knob I jerked my hand back as though from an electric shock.

"What is it?" asked Escott.

It was unmistakable, but I drew another cautious breath just to be sure.

"Jack?"

I swallowed with difficulty, because my mouth and throat had gone bone dry. "Bloodsmell," I whispered.

He started to say something but caught the look on my face. He nodded, understanding, and slipped his glove back on to open the door.

A lot of different images crowded my eyes: gray-speckled linoleum, shining steel cabinets, white curtains with red trim. The trim almost seemed to accent the red pool at our feet.

Kitty Donovan had pressed herself into a corner formed by the steel cabinets. Her hands gripped their edges on either side with white fingers. Her mouth hung slack and her eyes were too big to be real, as though they'd been painted on her face. She was staring at Stan McAlister, who was sprawled on the floor in front of her.

He was on his back. His coat and shirt had been unbuttoned, their pockets turned out, and the contents scattered. There was a nasty bruise on his temple; bad enough, but whoever had hit him had wanted to be sure of things. The blood had oozed from at least a dozen wounds in his chest and one in the neck, where the carving knife was still embedded.

Kitty looked up at us, shivering violently from head to toe. Her lips moved, but only a soft hiccuping came out of them. Her eyes fastened once more onto McAlister's body, then abruptly rolled up in their sockets. With an audible sigh, she dropped gracelessly forward in a faint.

3

I MOVED TOWARD her but Escott stopped me. His face was drawn and his lips had thinned to the point of disappearance.

"Mind where you step," he said in a low, carefully level voice.

He wasn't trying to be funny; he looked as sick as I felt. I nodded and took my time getting to Kitty. She'd just missed hitting the mess from McAlister's throat. I scooped her up and Escott followed as I took her out and put her on the oversized bed in the back.

"Still wearing her coat," he murmured. "She must have walked straight in and found him."

"I'm glad you don't think she did it."

"Of course, she could have knocked him out first and then killed him as he lay helpless. The physical evidence is against that theory, though. Except for this"—he removed one of her shoes and examined the smear of blood on its sole—"she is quite clean. The killer would most certainly have had at least a spot or two on his hands."

He sounded pretty clinical until I realized that the cold detachment was his way of being able to handle the whole horrible business. He was still pasty white and his fingers twitched with more than his usual nervous energy.

"I have to make some phone calls. If she comes round, keep her back here and don't touch anything that will hold a print." He carefully placed the shoe on the nightstand. Almost as an afterthought, he swiped his gloved fingers over the drawer handle, and left.

Her skin was clammy and blue at the edges. I pulled the bedspread up and tucked it around her slight body. There seemed no point in reviving her; she'd be awake all too soon and have lots of talking to do for the cops. She was still out when Escott returned a few minutes later.

"Our employer is not at home and no one knows where he is. I should have liked to have given him some warning about this, but it can't be helped now, the police are on their way. I rousted the manager of this place. She's downstairs waiting to let them in."

"You call Lieutenant Blair?"

"Yes. He'll be thorough, which means you might not wish to be here. If this ends up in court . . ."

"I'll stick around. Tell him that I was waiting out in the car while you followed the girl inside. They won't call me into court if I wasn't here to see anything."

"And your presence now?"

"I got tired of waiting and followed you in—after you found the body. The only problem is Kitty, she saw us both."

He hardly glanced at her. "I doubt that she will be in a condition to remember, but if so, then it is something you can remedy easily enough. Now, before Blair shows up I want to check things again."

McAlister's looks hadn't improved while we were gone. Escott picked his way around the kitchen as though the pool of blood were part of a mine field. He'd once mentioned that he suffered from squeamishness; apparently it was under control tonight. I couldn't bring myself to go in, and hung back in the dining room, out of the way.

"Seepage rather than splashing," he said to himself in a voice that sounded borrowed. "He must have already been dead for this one." He indicated the blade in McAlister's throat.

"What about his stuff?" My own voice was thin.

He surveyed the scattered debris from the turned-out pockets. "His wallet—if he carried one—is missing. Perhaps we are meant to think the motive was robbery."

"Maybe it was, but for the bracelet."

"Which is not here, unless it's under him, and I've no wish to move him and see. Only we and Mr. Pierce know of it as being a possible motive for this terrible thing, yet these multiple wounds indicate . . .'' He squatted on his heels, staring hard at them.

"What?"

He shook his head. He would talk when he was ready. He stood, casting around for something else to study, fastening his eye on the stove and a heavy iron frying pan there. Instead of sitting square on a burner, it was tilted half-on and -off. Escott peered at it closely, keeping his hands well clear.

"Is that what smashed his head?" I asked.

"I believe so. It more than qualifies as a blunt instrument and is the only likely object in the room."

"What about his blackjack?"

"Yes, there's that, but I really don't see him as cheerfully handing it over for his killer to use. Also this was done very quickly. We weren't more than ten minutes behind Miss Donovan, and McAlister was less than five minutes ahead of her."

"So the killer must have been waiting here for him."

"Unless Miss Donovan is the killer."

"But you said—"

"I know. It is most unlikely, given her actions to aid him at the Boswell House, but it is just possible."

"You don't really think . . ."

He shrugged. "All permutations must be equally considered, especially the unsavory ones. Perhaps you can settle things one way or another when she comes round."

"You can make book on it."

"Yes, that's another factor to consider," he mused.

"What?"

"Leadfoot Sam, the bookie."

He quit the kitchen and I led the way back to her bedroom. The bed was empty, its spread tossed aside. The shoe on the nightstand was gone. A corner window with access to the fire escape was wide open and the thin curtains over it seemed to shiver from the icy air drifting inside. We both darted over, but she was nowhere in sight.

Escott allowed himself a brief and entirely American-sounding obscenity. "She'll make for her car."

"I'll go find out."

He didn't argue. To save time, I vanished on the spot and hurled out the window, using the uncompromising metal gridwork of the stairs as a guide to the ground. Re-forming, I heard a motor kick over and rushed around the building in time to see her taillights flare and dim as she took a sharp corner out of the apartment parking lot.

My car was on the other side of the place, of course. I was halfway there when the first of the cops rolled up and stopped. I waved at him in a friendly, hurried way, but he wasn't buying any. He'd been called to the scene of a homicide and spotted a man running away; it was more than enough to inspire his hunter's instinct. He was out and shouting for me to stop.

I didn't know if he had his gun in hand or not and had no inclination to find out. Quickly swerving under the deep shadow of a couple of trees, I vanished again, and kept going. He was still beating the bush when I bumped against my car and slipped inside. I was feeling pretty smug as I started up the engine. The feeling lasted until a prowl car roared in from nowhere and screeched to a halt right in my path. The first cop ran up, half crouching so he could see inside the driver's window. He did indeed have his gun in hand and it was pointed right at my chest. I decided not to move.

He bellowed at me to get out and I obliged. While he and his friends went through the farce of slapping me down and putting on the cuffs, Kitty Donovan speeded merrily away into the night. I might have eventually been able to hypnotize my way out of it, but there were too many strikes against that gambit. The three of them were distracted and hostile, it was too dark for them to see me very well, but most of all I was just too dust-spitting mad to talk coherently.

A couple of unmarked cars rolled up and a medium-tall man in a belted leather overcoat emerged from one of them. We hadn't seen each other in several months, but I knew him right away. A young forty and dandy handsome, Lieutenant Blair was one of the best-dressed cops in Chicago, if not the rest of the state. He walked up slowly, studying things, and especially me. A broad smile of recognition appeared under his carefully groomed mustache.

"What have you got here?" he asked, addressing the cop who had a proprietary hand on my shoulder.

"Caught him running away, Lieutenant." The cop briefly described my capture.

"Uh-huh. Why were you running away, Mr. Fleming?"

"I was chasing someone."

"And who were you chasing?"

I didn't know how far Escott wanted to go in protecting his client's privacy. "Better ask Charles about that, I only came along for the ride."

Last fall, in order to avert a problem, I'd hypnotized Blair, planting the idea in his mind that we were friends. It had worked very well, but by now time and circumstances had eroded my suggestion down to almost nothing. Blair wasn't a bit amused with me.

"If you'd like to go for another ride, I'm sure we can arrange it."

The cop took a firmer grip on me as though to follow through with the threat, and that's when Escott made what I can only describe as a timely entrance. There were some smudges of grime on his clothes, indicating he'd also used the fire escape to exit the building. He was only slightly breathless, enough to give the impression that he was in a hurry.

"Lieutenant Blair, thank you for coming so quickly." He shook hands with Blair and at the same time got him walking back toward the apartments. He immediately launched into a succinct outline of his version of the evening, keeping me safely in the background until the last. Somehow he managed to avoid mentioning Pierce's name or how we broke into Kitty's flat.

". . . when we saw that she'd escaped out the window, Jack naturally went after her," he concluded.

"Naturally," he agreed, his tone bordering on sarcasm. "And just why did the young lady go out the window?"

"She was probably frightened out of her wits."

"Where would she go?"

Escott shrugged minimally, using one hand and an eyebrow.

As our parade reached the entry doors and the lights on either side of them, Blair noticed the souvenir Escott sported from McAlister's blackjack. "You been in a war or something?"

"Only a small skirmish, hardly worth the resulting headache."

Escott's offhand and deprecatory manner amused Blair long enough for him to have the cop release me. He had more important things to do than to push around the hired help. By the time we turned to go into the building his mood had gone sour again. It spread to the rest of the group, with the exception of the middle-aged woman in a bathrobe who let us in. For her, it was a toss-up between terror and curiosity. Murder can do that to people.

The next couple of hours were spent sitting on Kitty Donovan's overstuffed sofa watching a parade of cops turn the place over. Her neat little life was twisted inside out as they took photographs, dusted for prints, and collected anything that could be remotely connected with Stan McAlister's death.

Things wound their way down and the number of investigators thinned and left. Without ceremony or stir, McAlister was carried out in a stained and creaking wicker basket. Escott watched, his face carefully blank. One of his hands rested on the power switch of a table lamp next to his chair and he idly flicked it on and off until one of the cops told him to cut it out. He stiffened a little, not from the cop's annoyed order, but from some internal start. His pale gray eyes fixed on me, but he had no chance to say anything. Blair came over and started asking questions again, the kind Escott couldn't answer. I'd once been on the receiving end of one of Blair's interrogations and knew Escott's reticence would not be welcome.

A description of Kitty Donovan and her vehicle had been issued so the prowl-car boys could get in on the hunt. Blair hadn't made it any too clear whether he wanted her as a witness or a suspect. He'd listened to everything we could tell him, but had reserved judgment on our conclusions.

With the passage of time and the scarcity of facts, Blair's patience lessened in direct proportion to his growing temper. His olive skin got a few shades paler and his dark eyes were bright from all the internal heat. Push him too far and he'd explode. Escott didn't look very worried about it.

Blair abruptly stopped the questions when a muscle in his jaw started working all on its own. I thought the volcano would go off then and there, but he still had it well in check. His voice was smooth, almost purring. "Very well, Charles, I can admire your business ethics, but it's getting late and I've other work to do. I may need to call you in for more questions at any time, though, so I want you to hang around the station just in case anything new occurs to either of us."

"Are you charging me with anything?"

"Don't tempt me."

Escott had been carefully neutral since Blair's arrival and continued to hold on to it. He nodded, ruefully accepting Blair's terms, and I wondered what he was up to since he was fully capable of talking his way out of the situation. "Would you like to have my assistant accompany us?" he inquired politely.

"No, I would not. Your assistant can just get the hell out of here."

One corner of Escott's mouth twitched. Blair missed it or he might have reconsidered his snap decision. "Very well," he said, with only a hint of exasperation. "Jack, I was wondering if you'd look after my car before going home. I wouldn't want any pranksters bashing in the lights." He handed me the keys.

"Yeah, sure."

One of the plainclothesmen hustled him out.

"What's this about his car?" asked Blair.

"Nothing, Lieutenant," I said. "We had to leave it in a rough neighborhood, is all."

"Near the Boswell House, by any chance?"

"Yeah. What about it?"

"Just stay away from the place. My men are going over it now and you could get swept up and taken in along with anything else they find over there."

I shrugged, all innocence. "They won't even see me . . . I promise."

Escott had parked his Nash under the doubtful safety of a street lamp a little distance from the hotel. No one had bothered it; the weather might have been too discouragingly cold for anybody to try. I checked inside and found his notebook in the glove box, opening it to the last page. The paper with all the information on McAlister dropped out. Maybe that was what he wanted picked up, but I wasn't so sure. I put it in my own notebook and took a look at his lights, front and back. The whisper of city dust on them was undisturbed, so he hadn't left any hidden messages under the glass.

Half a block down were three cars too new for the area. One was a black-and-white, another unmarked with a tall aerial, and the third a slick-looking Cadillac. I sat in the Nash and waited until the cops finally came out, and drove away.

The driver waiting in the Caddy stayed put, but I wasn't much worried about him, figuring his employer was busy visiting some girlfriend. The street was dead quiet when I got out and walked across to the hotel.

The manager was awake again and had thrown on some clothes. He stood at the front desk narrowly watching a tall woman using his phone. Maybe he thought she'd walk off with it.

"Ten cents," he said when she finished.

"A nickel or nothing," she snapped.

"That's a business line. While you're calling for a cab, I could be losing money."

"Like hell." She dug into her handbag and stuck a cigarette in her freshly painted mouth. I stepped in and lighted it for her. She glanced up and nodded a brief thanks. The last time I'd seen her she'd slammed a door on me. Her eyes had lost a lot of their hardness and were puffy and red. She'd tried to disguise the lines with a layer of powder and almost succeeded. Her carroty hair was covered by a close-fitting black hat and she'd replaced the kimono with a dark dress and coat. The stuff looked expensive, but slightly shabby with age or a lot of wear. At her feet was a large suitcase.

"Moving out?" I asked.

"What's it to you?"

"Ten cents," repeated the manager. He concentrated on her, ignoring me because he didn't remember our earlier encounter at all. The suggestions I'd planted earlier were still strong in him. I fished out two nickels and tossed them on the desk.

"Hey," said the woman. "Don't do me any favors."

"Life's too short to spend time arguing, besides, I want to talk with you."

"Hey!" she protested as I took her elbow and steered her away from the desk. "I don't want to talk to you. Lemme go or I'll call a cop."

"You're too late, they just left."

She stopped fighting me, suddenly curious. "Who the hell are you, anyway?"

"A friend of a friend of Stan McAlister."

The name meant something to her but she pretended it didn't. "Who?"

"Your next-door neighbor."

"That lug. Well, he ain't my neighbor anymore. He ain't nobody's neighbor now. The cops—the cops said—'' She broke off with an involuntary shudder.

"Yeah, I heard what happened to him."

"You a cop, too?" she demanded.

"No, I'm here for a friend of a friend. Remember? Why are you in such a hurry to leave?"

"That's my business. Why are you so damn nosy?"

"Because Stan got himself and my friend into some deep trouble tonight."

"I'd have never guessed with all the cops around."

"Are they why you're leaving?"

"So what if it is? I don't like cops, it ain't a crime. Look it up."

"I believe you. Look, I'm only trying to dig out some information on Stan."

Her hard eyes lowered in sulky thought. "What kind of information?"

"What people he saw, how he made his living, that kind."

She shook her head. "I can't help you."

"Not even for some extra cab fare?"

"I don't know nothing worth that much. A place like this, it don't pay to get curious about anything."

I could believe that. "You ever talk to him in the hall?"

She almost laughed. "He talked to me."

"What about?"

She looked at me pityingly. "What do you think? Mugs like that are always on the make, but I wasn't interested."

"He have a girlfriend?"

"Yeah, there's always some noodle-brain around who'll fall for his kind of line."

"So he brought 'em here?"

She nodded and drew heavily on her cigarette, affecting boredom, but I could almost smell the fear rolling off her.

"You see any of them?"

"I'm not the housemother here."

"He have any other kind of visitors?"

Her eyes were less hard now than tired. "I already told all this to one of those goddamn cops. I don't know nothing, which means I can't say nothing. You want to know about the guy, ask the management."

"I will, but you're better looking."

She put on a thin, disillusioned smile. "Nice try, kid. Maybe some other time."

"Hold on—"

"I can't, my cab just pulled up."

"You hear of anyone called Leadfoot Sam?"

A little noise came out of her throat and she shook her head. She was plenty scared. "Please, I just wanta get out of here."

"I'll walk you out."

Her mouth dropped a little, but she was grateful for the release. I carried her heavy suitcase and put it in the trunk for her.

"Where will you go?" I asked, holding the door as she climbed in behind the driver.

"Anyplace where I can get an unbroken night's sleep. Hey, you don't have to do that."

I passed a five to her and shut the door. "Yeah, I know."

She rolled down her window. "You nuts or something?"

"Probably. Sweet dreams."

Her mouth worked and her teeth started chattering from more than just the winter air. She rolled the window up and the cab drove away. I waited till it made the corner then went back inside.

"What's her name?" I asked the manager.

"She's too old for you, sonny," he leered.

I quickly decided that manners and charm would be a total waste on him. Since there were no witnesses around now, I opted for my usual shortcut, and had him talking like a mynah bird in a very few minutes.

The guy said the woman's name was Doreen Grey and that she called herself an actress. A lot of girls called themselves actresses. I shrugged and passed it off. Life was tough all over. I skipped her and asked about McAlister and got some answers.

He'd moved in about six months ago and paid his rent on time, usually putting in a little extra on the side. He did the kind of entertaining that the management was content to ignore as long as the tips were good. He had a lot of different lady friends; Kitty had been only one in a long parade.

I told him to catch up on his sleep and went to McAlister's room to see what the cops had left. It was about the same as before, but with the drawers pulled open. The bed looked dirty and depressing. I didn't like to think of Kitty ever being in it.

Perhaps their assignations took place in her own room. The supplies stored in her nightstand lent some hopeful credence to that.

Escott's apparently idle play with the table lamp came to mind. I turned on the one overhead, once again wincing at the brightness. Two more lamps flanked the bed. I checked them over but found nothing odd. They were as cheap as the rest of the furnishings and had no hidden crannies for concealing expensive bracelets. They even worked. Their combined brightness made the dingy little room even more depressing. I shut them off and stared at the walls, trying to figure out what Escott had seen.

Across from the bed was the bureau and its mirror. As I ran an eye from one wall to the other, I noticed the crummy prints hung up for decoration. They had been left a little crooked on their wires by the cops; I'd been careful to leave them straight. They served to remind me that the mirror had been bolted to the wall. It was about the only thing in the place that might have been worth stealing. Because mirrors give me the creeps, I'd pretty much ignored it before, with my eyes purposely not focusing on its reflection of an empty room. I crossed over for another look. At each corner a bright new screw held the mirror's frame fast in place.

I gave one edge a tug and the whole thing snapped free with a sloppy crunch. The mirror was a fancy one-way job to hide a hole in the wall. The hole went right through the lath and plaster to Doreen Grey's room.

And I'd given her cab fare.

After indulging in a quarter-minute of intense self-recrimination, I put the mirror down and slipped through the wall to look around. Doreen's room was an appropriate reverse of McAlister's, except the bureau had been pushed over a few feet. There were three faint dents in the bare floor beneath the hole, probably where she'd set up the tripod. Normal room light wouldn't have been sufficient for her photography, but she'd seen to that by giving McAlister some extra-bright bulbs to leave on during the show. They'd had a nasty little racket going, either for blackmail or pornography, but I could admire the planning involved.

None of it was any too good for Kitty. If McAlister had tried putting the squeeze on her, she'd have plenty of motive for killing him. She was a little doll, cute and demure looking as you please, but I was beginning to have serious doubts—the kind that send people to death row.

I shook out of them and finished searching the room.

Doreen hadn't missed a thing. Her wastebasket held wads of soggy tissues, indicating she'd suffered a bout of genuine grief for her partner's demise, but the rest of the place was clean. I speculated that both she and McAlister had lived ready to pull stakes and leave on a moment's notice. With the kind of business they'd worked, it would have been a necessity.

She could be on her way to Timbuktu by now and only the cops had the resources to find her—unless I got smart and called the cab company.

I went downstairs and borrowed the business phone. It was getting late and things were slowing down. They didn't have much trouble finding the driver who'd just picked up a fare from the Boswell House address. He showed up again about five minutes after my call and I went outside to meet him.

"Where to?" he asked when I got in.

"Noplace."

He threw a suspicious glance up to the mirror, missed me, and turned around. "What's the scam, then?"

"The woman you picked up here, where'd you take her?"

He hesitated.

"My intentions are honorable," I said, and pulled out a couple bucks for him to see, as if money could indicate a man's honesty.

He shrugged. It wasn't his business. He gave out with a street name and some general directions on how he got there.

"This another hotel?" I asked.

"Nah. It's a rough patch like this, stores and things. She paid me and stood in the street till I drove off."

"No hotels, apartments, stuff like that?"

"Nope."

"Were any of the stores open?"

"Nah. There was a bar doing business down on the far corner, but it looked like a lot of walking for her to do with that suitcase. She didn't want any help with it, I'm glad to say. That thing looked fifty pounds if it was an ounce, and my back's bad enough."

"Here, get yourself some liniment." I gave him the two bucks in lieu of a regular fare and got out. He shook his head, but

grinned as he left. Crazy customers like me were always welcome. The exhaust had hardly settled when I heard the thunk of
a car door as it slammed shut just up the street. A big bald guy
stood next to the Cadillac I'd noticed earlier. He smoothed down
the vast lines of his overcoat and started walking toward me.

He seemed harmless enough, at least at a distance. I was
alone and not too worried about being able to take care of myself. As he drew near I started having second thoughts.

He was closer to being seven feet tall than six, with a massive,
muscled body under the coat. He wasn't naturally bald, but
shaved his head. He carried his hat in hand and swung it up in
place as he came closer. I settled my own more firmly so it
wouldn't fall off as I looked up at him. He stopped about a yard
away and regarded me with a calm, confident eye.

"I want you should come with me," he said in an even,
unhurried voice. He could have said something about the weather
and it would have sounded the same.

A dozen smart-ass answers to that one popped into mind and
just as quickly died away. He wasn't a cop, because I never heard
of a cop driving a Cadillac. That left two other possibilities and
I didn't think he was some kind of overgrown hustler.

"You work for Leadfoot Sam?" I asked.

He smiled, not showing his teeth, which was a relief. As it
was, he was more than enough to scare Boris Karloff, let alone
a solitary vampire.

"I hope it's not a formal occasion," I said, walking with him
back to the Caddy. He didn't bother to enlighten me as he held
open the rear door. I climbed in, sitting behind a gum-chewing
driver who looked only mildly interested in what was going on.
Sleepy eyed, he put it in gear and we rolled away as soon as the
big guy had settled in.

It did occur to me early on that I could have turned down the
invitation. I wanted to chase after Doreen Grey and get the details about her racket with McAlister. On the other hand, Leadfoot was another source of information, and he was going out
of his way to make himself available. His method was unorthodox, but for the moment not too threatening.

The drive was short; we stopped at an all-night drugstore less
than a mile away. My escorts took me around to the back entrance, used a key, and walked me in. We stood in a cluttered
storage and pickup area, full of crates and all kinds of bottles.

"That you, Butler?" a man called from farther in and down.

"Yeah, Sam," answered the big guy, ducking as he came through the door. He carefully shut and locked it. The driver hung back and Butler urged me in the direction of a rusty spiral staircase.

I wasn't too sure the steps would hold our combined weight. They protested a little, but not alarmingly so as we trudged down to a dry, dusty room stacked with more crates. A metal-shaded bulb hung low over a table that must have been assembled from pieces, since it was too big for the stairway opening. A long, weedy man in his late thirties lounged in a chair at the far end with his feet up on it. He wore two-tone shoes, plaid pants, and a flowered vest. He wasn't following a fashion so much as trying to set one of his own.

Off to one side, he'd placed a straw hat, brim up, and was tossing cards at it with tremendous concentration. We had to wait until he'd finished out the deck. When the cards were used up, he stared at the hat with regret, then turned his attention to us. He had a narrow face, weak chin, and rather wide, innocent eyes. His brow furrowed, as though he were trying to remember something.

"Who's that?" he asked Butler, staring at me with sincere puzzlement.

"He was at McAlister's hotel. He put Doreen in a cab, goes into the hotel. I see lights come up in McAlister's room. The lights go out and he comes out. He calls a cab, but don't leave in it, just talks with the driver. I thought you should maybe want to talk to him, too."

"I'm Sam. Who're you?"

"Leadfoot Sam?"

He was a study in blank astonishment. "You can't be. *I'm* Leadfoot Sam. Butler, take this man away, he's an imposter." Then he roared out with a room-filling laugh and Butler grinned.

I didn't know whether to join them or bolt out before it got worse.

"You're a killer, Sam," said Butler.

"That's right." Sam stopped laughing and stared at me meaningfully. "And don't anyone forget it."

If his game was to disconcert me, it was working. Lunatics always leave me unnerved.

He pointed at a chair. "Sit."

I looked to make certain he wasn't talking to Butler and walked over to take the chair. It was a plain wooden job with a worn chintz pad on the seat that didn't seem to belong there. Sam was blank eyed again, so I lifted the pad to see what was under it. He was visibly disappointed when I tossed his hidden whoopee cushion onto the table.

"Get us something to drink," he told Butler.

Butler located a crate and wrenched off the lid, nails and all. He pulled out a flat bottle of booze and set it down between us. Sam unscrewed the cap to let it breathe.

"No glasses," he apologized. "But this stuff should kill off most anything catching." He offered me the first swig.

The last time I'd swallowed something other than blood, I'd ended up heaving it into a gutter. Once again, I was trapped by the demands of social ritual.

He misinterpreted my hesitation and took a quick drink to show that it was all right. I accepted the bottle, put it to my lips, and held my tongue over the opening, pretending to drink. The drop of booze I did taste was bitter and burned.

"Is it that bad?" He really seemed concerned.

"I'm not used to the good stuff," I hedged.

He laughed, a single barking explosion. "Good stuff! Sonny, this is what we had left over after Roosevelt made it legal again. It's been sitting down here for—Butler, how long has it been sitting down here?"

"A long time, Sam."

"A long time."

I tried to look impressed. "You use to run this yourself?"

"I don't remember the cargos so much as the driving. It was a goddamn long haul from Canada to here, and you wouldn't believe the hours."

"Gave you a good name at any rate."

"Yeah, it gave me a good name. Now what's yours?"

I started to say Jack the Giant Killer and thought better of it, not being too sure of Butler's temper. I opted for my middle name and the name of my favorite radio hero. "Russell Lamont."

"Pleased to meet you, Russell Lamont." He took his feet off the table to lean over and shake hands. "You a cop?"

"No."

" 'S'funny, 'cause I'm getting a cop smell off you."

I showed him an old press card and covered up the name with my thumb. "I'm a reporter. Is that close enough to cop to get the smells mixed?"

He didn't like it, but was still too curious to throw me out. "How about telling me what your interest is in Sam Mc-Alister?"

"He's a friend of a friend."

Sam shook his head, his narrow shoulders slumped tragically. "Aw, that's not nice, Jack. You come down here, drink my booze, and then fib. Shame on you."

"That's the best I can do unless there's something in it for me."

"What'd'ya have in mind?"

"Information on McAlister and Doreen Grey."

"Gonna write a big story and name names?"

"Nah, I just want to help some kid out of a jam."

It was the truth, but he didn't want to believe it. "Ever think that *you* might be in a jam?" His eyes flicked to Butler, who was still looming somewhere in the back.

"Nothing I can't handle."

That was a barrel of monkeys to both of them. I smiled, too, just to show them I was a good sport. I was still smiling when Butler appeared behind me, gripped the seat of the chair, and steadily lifted it and me to the ceiling.

"You sure about what you can handle?" asked Sam.

Butler bumped the chair up and down a few times so that my head brushed a ventilator conduit.

I couldn't help but smile again. "You should rent him out to carnivals. He'd make a great ride."

Sam nodded once, Butler grunted acknowledgment, and without further ceremony, threw me and the chair across the room.

4

I'D BEEN MORE or less ready for that one and went partially incorporeal the second he released me. Semitransparent and considerably lighter in weight and mass, I was able to twist around and gain control of my fall. The arrested spin wouldn't look natural, but I was banking on the visual confusion of my blurred movement to cover up the stunt. The bad light shining in their eyes would help.

The chair clattered as it hit first and skidded out of the way. When my feet swung under me I went solid again and landed upright on the concrete floor with only a mild jolt. My hand flailed and struck the far wall as I recovered balance, but it was much better than having my whole body smash into it.

As though nothing unusual had happened, I made a calm business of straightening my clothes. Under all the show, I was plenty mad and needed the time to cool down before turning to look at them.

Leadfoot Sam and Butler were rooted in place and openly gaping. Sam's fingers splayed out flat on the table in preparation to jump in any given direction. When I didn't move, he groped blindly for the bottle and drained away a healthy amount with a desperate swallow. It was terrible stuff; his eyes began to water. Butler came around the table, his mouth still open, and he studied me good and hard. His shaven head swiveled back to Sam.

"Did you see . . . ?"

Sam had no answer. Both of them had touched something

totally outside their experience. When the world gives you that kind of a lurch it's hard to know what to do. After a long, long moment, silent except for their harsh breathing and thundering hearts, Sam gave out with a brief laugh. It sounded nervous and artificial compared with his previous efforts. Whatever control he thought he had of the situation was lost, and that sick little exhalation was his response to the painful truth.

I came forward and leaned my hands on the table. Sam sat back in his chair, unconsciously putting distance between us.

"Tell Butler to take a break," I said. I used no influence on him; it wasn't necessary.

"Yeah." Not an answer or a question, the word came out of him all on its own, a meaningless sound. The jokes and threats were gone now. He was afraid.

Butler sensed it and didn't want to move. I fixed on his eyes and told him to relax. Some of the sap went out of him. Without further hesitation, he turned and trudged up the spiral stairs. Somewhere above a door closed, leaving me and Sam alone in the basement.

Sam's hands were under the table and I could guess why. He'd be packing a gun the way a shop girl carries her face powder; it was part of the daily uniform. I pretended not to notice and let him keep it if it made him feel better. I didn't feel like going to the trouble of taking it away.

"We need to talk, Sam."

He slowly nodded. I took my time picking up the chair and bringing it back to the table. It was a tough old hunk of wood and hardly showed any new scratches as I put it right and eased onto it again.

"Where you been tonight, Sam?"

The question was plain enough, but not what he'd expected. "I been around."

"Around where?"

"The Hot Spot."

"What's that, a bar?"

"Yeah."

"Anybody see you there?"

"Anyone who wants to bet on the game that's coming up."

"How long were you there?"

His answer left him well covered for the time of McAlister's murder. I was disappointed.

"Where was Butler?"

"With me."

"Now tell me about Stan McAlister."

He'd lost some of his fear and was almost comfortable. "What about Stan?"

"I know you were after him."

"He owes me money. What'd'ya expect?"

His use of the present tense wasn't lost on me. He hadn't heard the bad news yet, that or he was wasting time as a bookie when he should have been acting in the movies. "I don't expect someone like you to take bets on margin."

He was a little embarrassed. "It happens to the best of us."

"How'd it happen to you?"

"We were having a few drinks and I was just drunk enough to do it. I went over the records later, saw that he owed me big, and got Butler to start looking for him. I got a lot of people looking for him, but he must have heard about it because he's lost himself good this time."

"You got any people with a grudge on?"

"Say again?"

"You or your people want to bump him off?"

"Huh? Why should I do that? If he gets bumped, I can't collect my two grand. I'm not so rich I can shrug off that kinda loss. Is someone after him? Is that why you're asking all this?"

"You could say that. Who wants to kill him?"

"Not me. You ask around."

"I'm asking right here. What do you know about his business? Who'd he come in contact with?"

"How the hell should I know? I just take their bets; I don't care how they get their money. Why don't you ask him?"

"I can't. C'mon, Sam, give me a name."

"There's Doreen Grey."

"Uh-huh, who else?"

"He's seeing a little blond named Kitty, but I don't remember if she had a last name."

"What do you know about her?"

"Only that she's cute as a button. He takes her around, shows her the sights. I think she's too clean for him, but he's had others like her before."

"Yeah?"

"You know the type, girls that like to slum. They look peaches and cream on the outside but inside they got a taste for . . . well, Stan ain't exactly rock bottom, but he's pretty close."

"You don't like him?"

"I don't give a damn one way or another about him. He's a customer. All I want is the money he owes me." Most of his confidence was back. "Your turn: what's your game with Stan?"

"I already told you, I'm trying to get some kid out of a jam. You gonna call Butler down for another tumbling act?"

The reminder put him off a little, or so I thought. "Nah, I don't need to do anything like that. What kinda jam?"

"Nothing you need to worry about."

"Just trying to be friendly. You been asking a lot of questions and I been giving you the straight dope, so you at least give me one thing: where's he hiding?"

"He isn't. Tell me about Doreen Grey. If you've got Butler watching for you, why didn't he bring her in?"

"Huh? Doreen? She wouldn't know anything. She hangs around Stan, not the other way around."

He sounded so certain that I briefly wondered if McAlister himself had even known about the trick mirror—but only briefly. "She a girlfriend?"

"Her and a dozen others that think they are."

"You mean he's a pimp?"

"No, nothing like that, though I wouldn't put it past him. He's just got a way with him and women. I wish I could figure it out, I'd bottle it and retire rich and happy."

"Is Doreen Grey her real name?"

"Grow up, kid. Women like her never had a real name."

"Women like her?"

"She's a hustler, or was. Calls herself an actress or model. Do I have to tell you what kind of acting?"

"Does she do photography?"

"I heard she sits on both sides of the camera. She's got a little studio for all the dirty work."

"Where?"

It was on the same street where the cabbie had dropped her off.

"This studio got a name or number?"

"I dunno. A place like that doesn't advertise to the general public. It's over a grocer's, second floor, you can't miss it."

"You know a lot about it, ever been there?"

He only grinned.

I felt I'd gotten all the information I was going to get and stood up to leave.

"Uh-uh," he said. "You stay right there. We're not finished."

"It's getting late, Sam. I gotta go."

He brought his hands above the table. One of them held a fistful of black revolver. He was smiling all over his face again as he leveled it on me. "Not just yet, you don't."

I sighed, trying to be patient. "Okay, what is it?"

"Tell me where Stan is."

"With the cops."

"The cops? What for?"

"He was in the wrong place at the wrong time."

"Cut the crap and tell me what's going on."

If he'd been more polite, I might have answered without thinking. There was no reason not to tell him about McAlister's death, but I have an inherent dislike of being pushed around, and he'd pushed me plenty already.

"You'll read it in the morning papers," I said, and moved to go up the spiral stairs. Behind me I heard the soft double click that meant he'd thumbed back the hammer.

"Hold it, Lamont, not unless you want one right now."

I paused and looked at him. "Brother, I've already had more than one. All they do is put holes in the suit and make me mad."

"Think you're tough?"

"Let's put it this way . . . do you really want to end up the evening with a hunk of dead meat on your hands?"

"I don't have to kill you," he pointed out.

"Yeah, you're too late for that," I muttered. He was getting on my nerves with the thing.

"You step back here and sit like a good boy."

That tipped the scales for me. He needed a lesson. I turned, made sure he was watching, and vanished. When I re-formed, I was right behind him. It only took a moment, not nearly enough time for him to understand what he'd just seen or to begin to react to it. I wrapped one hand over his mouth and clamped another around the revolver. The idea was to prevent it from going off by keeping the barrel from turning, but I'd forgotten that by cocking it, it had already turned. But the gun didn't go off when his finger twitched. The back of my thumb was between the firing pin and the bullet.

Ouch.

It wasn't nearly as awful as actually getting shot. The pain was best compared to a bad toe stubbing—brief, but of an intensity all out of proportion to the area involved. I knew now why they called it a hammer, since the firing pin had neatly nailed itself into me. My hand jerked away, taking the gun along, and I had to release my hold on Sam. I shoved him across the room and pried back the hammer to free my thumb from its painful trap. I must have looked like an idiot standing there alternately shaking my hand down and sucking the side of my punctured digit.

Then Leadfoot Sam gave me something else to think about when he caught his balance, turned, and broke out a nasty-looking switchblade. In his confusion over the last few seconds, he must have forgotten that I was the one with the gun. I still held it loosely in his direction and was grinning at him. Actually it was less of a grin and more like a show of teeth. My fangs weren't out, but the effect was just as satisfactory, if I could tell anything from his flinching reaction.

"Hold it, Sam. Start thinking twice."

He did, with his wild eyes fastening on the revolver in an interesting mixture of rage and fear. His next move might be to call Butler down, but I didn't want any more witnesses. He needed distracting.

"See this?" I broke the cylinder open, pushed the extractor rod, and let the bullets drop out. He stared, wondering what the gag could be. I turned the gun upside down to get a firm hold on the grip and cylinder, then gave them each a hard twist in opposite directions.

The metal groaned quietly and snapped. I knew I was strong enough to damage the thing, but was pleasantly surprised at this development. I tossed the two pieces on the table. Sam stared, his jaw dragging the floor again. I was still grinning.

"Sam?"

He appeared to be very sick.

"Do you know what evil lurks in the hearts of men?"

He made a sick little sound in his throat.

"Well, *I* do." At that, I reached up and flicked my index finger hard against the bare bulb of the room's single light. The glass shattered with a dull pop and plunged us into total darkness.

The sick sound began to descend into a prolonged whimper.

"So you watch yourself from now on . . . because that's what I'll be doing."

I couldn't see him—our complete insulation from outside light prevented that—but I could hear his heart banging away, and by now I could clearly scent the fear smell rolling off him like a tide. He'd recover soon enough, maybe even convince himself he'd been tricked, but he'd never forget it. I didn't care, as long as he gave me a wide berth from now on.

Dematerializing, I swept past him, making sure he got thoroughly chilled. Some spine-tingling laughter would have been appropriate, but I didn't trust mine to be sinister enough for the occasion.

Once up the stairs, I bumbled my invisible way out. Butler and the driver were still in the back storage area, quite oblivious to what had been going on in the basement. I didn't bother with them and seeped through the door into the rear alley, where the Caddy was parked. The keys were gone, but Escott had once taught me how to do a neat hot-wire job. I figured after all the trouble I'd been put through, they owed me a ride back. Neither of them made it out of the building in time to see me driving away.

I'd spent long enough on my forced detour and went straight to Doreen Grey's studio. The general location was a short cross street with T intersections at both ends. Down on the corner the bar was open, but everything else was dark. A single grocery store with hand-painted signs obscuring the dusty windows took up space in the middle of the block on the left side.

I parked the Caddy some distance away and walked. Next to the grocery door, narrow stairs led up to the second floor. On the vertical part of each step someone had carefully painted advertisements for the businesses within. None of them had to do with photography.

Nothing to do but bull on and hope that Sam's information was as square as he claimed. The stairs brought me to a long, dim hall lined with doors at regular intervals. The hall went through the width of the building and ended with another identical opening at the far end that served the next street over.

I checked each door and its sign. Two of them were empty

and for rent, and one of them had no sign at all, only a number painted onto the aging wood. It was sufficiently different from the rest to invite closer inspection. Listening, I could pick up no sound from the other side. With no change in my posture I sieved through, solidified, and straightened in an unlighted room. The darkness was thick even for me. A little seepage from the hall around the base of the door was barely sufficient for my eyes to use.

A table and some old chairs constituted the room's total inventory, unless you counted the dust in the corners. As a reception area, it was stark and discouraging. Opposite the entry door was another, firmly closed. I listened here as well, then passed through.

The room on the other side was as pitch black as my basement hiding place. Since my change, true darkness for me was rare, so this was not a comfortable thing to experience—especially when my ears told me I wasn't alone. I held perfectly still. If I couldn't see them, they certainly couldn't see me.

Odds were that the single set of lungs and swiftly beating heart belonged to Doreen Grey. She'd probably heard my footsteps in the entry and was scared to death.

"Doreen?" I asked, hoping to put her at ease.

My voice seemed very loud in the claustrophobic blackness, but not so loud as her brief, terrified scream and the gunshot that followed.

The muzzle flash fixed an image of the whole room in my eyes. I got a general impression of the layout of the furnishings and a specific one of Doreen crouched in a corner holding a pistol in my direction. Her eyes and mouth were wide open, her arms held stiff and straight. All that crowded onto my retinas to be sorted out later, since a split second after the shot I was too busy ducking to think about it. Bullets don't cause me any permanent damage, but I don't enjoy getting hit.

"*Doreen!* It's me—the guy with the cab fare!"

No second shot came.

"What?" Her voice sounded as shaky as I felt.

"I was at the Boswell House—cab fare—remember?"

"Wha-what do you want?"

"Talk, that's all. Put down the gun."

"No."

A sensible answer—if I were really dangerous to her. She was about three yards to my left and I was flat on the floor with no other cover within reach. Not having all the time in the world to talk her out of her fear, I opted for a more direct method and vanished.

I floated toward her, extending invisible arms until we touched. She was already shivering and gave out with a violent shudder at this freezing contact. I got very close, positioning what would be my hand over hers and her gun and making sure my thumb was well clear of moving parts. It might go off, but this time the noise didn't matter.

A good thing, too. She shrieked like a crazy woman when I re-formed holding onto her like a lover. She was ready to kick and fight till doomsday so I pried the gun from her hands and quickly backed off. Suddenly released, she stumbled away and scrambled for the door, sobbing all the way. She wrenched it open and escaped to the reception room while I was taking the gun off cock and slipping on the safety. I caught up with her again in the second she spent fumbling to unlock the outer door.

She screamed and kept on screaming when I slipped an arm around her waist to pull her back. I put a hand over her mouth and tried to talk her into calming down. Eventually she did—not from my efforts, but from simple lack of energy and oxygen. Her legs stopped thrashing and caved in. Propping her up seemed like too much work, so we both sank to the floor. I held her firmly but took away my hand so she could breathe.

She collapsed against me, still sobbing. Not knowing what else to do, I cradled her and told her everything was all right and hoped it would get through. When she seemed settled, I reached up with a questing hand and flicked on the overhead light. It hurt my eyes until they adjusted to the brightness.

"You okay?" I asked. A dumb question, but every opening can't be clever.

The sobbing had diminished to irregular hiccups. She twisted around to see me.

"Remember me now? I'm one of the good guys."

She shook her head in denial and struggled to find her feet. I let her go, being between her and the nearest exit, and stood up as well. She backed away to the opposite wall and turned to stare. There wasn't much of a show to see, all I did was dust off my knees and straighten my hat.

"How'd you get here?" she asked, her voice thick.

"I talked to your cab driver and he told me where he dropped you. Your former landlord gave me your name. Mine's Jack."

"What do you want?"

"Only to talk. I'm not going to hurt you."

She still wasn't ready to believe me. She kept her back to the wall and walked crab-wise to the other door and slipped into the next room, hitting the light. I followed and watched her pace nervously around, her eyes on the floor.

"Looking for this?" I held up her automatic.

She stopped dead cold, her heart racing fit to break.

"Take it easy, darling. I'll just keep it for the time being." I made a business of returning it to my pocket. "Why did you try to shoot me?"

"I didn't know . . . know that . . ."

"What? That I wasn't Leadfoot Sam? Why are you afraid of him?"

"Because it's stupid not to be."

If I'd been sitting alone in the dark, scared shitless from listening to approaching footsteps, I might have done the same thing. I could handle someone like Sam, but Doreen didn't have my unnatural advantages.

"It's a nice little gun. Did Stan give it to you?"

"It's mine."

"This place, too?"

"Yeah—yes."

A plain backdrop nailed to the ceiling covered one wall. Several different light stands were aimed at it. A stack of pillows cluttered the floor next to a dressing screen. Another closed door interrupted the rear wall. I checked it. The room beyond was a washroom converted to a darkroom, its single window made lightproof with a thick coat of black paint.

"Where's your camera?"

She didn't answer, but her eyes darted to her suitcase, which was parked by the pillows.

"What about your photos?"

"I don't have any."

"A photographer with no photos. C'mon, Doreen."

"Look, you just get out of here."

"It's too late for that." I circled around and shut the inner and outer doors.

She kept plenty of distance between us and ended up against

the backdrop. A photo of her now would not be too flattering. Her carroty hair was in every direction and her clothes were thoroughly mussed about. Both knees on her stockings sported ladders. She became conscious of me looking at her and abruptly retreated to her purse to find a powder puff. While she repaired things, I brought two chairs from one side and set them down facing one another.

"Park it here, Doreen. It's time for a heart-to-heart."

She closed her compact with a decisive snap. "Is it?"

"Uh-huh. It's either me, the cops, or Leadfoot Sam. Take your pick."

She didn't like any of the choices. "Who are you, then? Why are you here? I don't know anything."

"Have a seat and we'll find out."

Her jaw settled into firm defiance. The tears and panic were gone and she was ready to deal with me. She glared, waiting for my next move.

Every little bit helped.

It took longer than usual. She was on her guard and I didn't want to overdo the pressure. This was different from the simple suggestions I'd shot at Butler and the hotel manager. A give-and-take conversation was more complicated, requiring greater subtlety and care on my part.

"You can relax, Doreen," I whispered.

After a long, long moment the tension leached from her posture.

"No one's going to hurt you."

Her lips parted and her eyes went glassy.

"Relax . . ."

Her face softened as her lids drooped and closed. She was asleep on her feet and as vulnerable now as she ever would be. I could get the answers I needed. All I had to do was come up with the right questions and listen.

While I thought on where to start, I noticed her body as though for the first time—her long legs and crown of fluffy red hair. I became very aware of her beating heart and the blood surging through it. I recognized the feeling stirring within me, but this time its irresistible intensity was startling.

Hunger.

Or thirst.

For a vampire they're much the same.

The red life I'd taken and exchanged with Bobbi was as deliriously fulfilling as any sex I'd ever experienced as a living man. The blood I drank from animals gave me the joy of pure energy and strength greater than I'd ever imagined. Now I was facing a combination of the two: to have human blood in quantity—and to take it from this woman.

The temptation was a very solid, thriving thing and much more difficult to put off than on other occasions when I'd faced it with Bobbi. I had always taken care with her and found it easy not to overindulge for fear of hurting her. The difference this time was the woman herself. She was a stranger to me, unimportant, nothing more than a small-time blackmailer and hustler.

Someone no one would miss.

Her scent filled my head. Human flesh, a trace of cheap perfume, salt from the dried tears on her face, and beneath them all, the bloodsmell. The rest were like bits of flotsam floating upon its deep river. I licked my lips, my tongue brushing against my lengthening canines. To drink from that dark river . . .

I caressed her neck with the backs of my fingers; first one side, then the other. Lightly. Softly. She was utterly fascinating. It was as though, turn in turn, she were hypnotizing me.

Eyes shut, she responded with a slight tremor and sigh. I knew well how to give pleasure. She would love me for what I was capable of giving and doing to her. Because of the influence I was exerting she would not be able to help herself.

My arms wrapped protectively around her, pulling her body close. She swayed and rested against me, her heart quickening. Her head went to one side, exposing the tender white column of her throat. I tasted it with a slow kiss. The big vein pulsed rapidly beneath my lips. My mouth yawned wide, my teeth gently brushing over the thin barrier of her skin. We were both trembling. The blood suddenly welled up, pouring through me like scarlet fire as the first shock of ecstasy took us.

She would love me and I would love her. I *was* loving her.

Her heart fluttered against my chest. Her breath was full and warm as it whispered over my neck.

I had wanted her, I was taking her, and she was loving it. I drank from her and drank deeply. She was an endless fountain of shimmering strength.

Not endless.

It didn't matter. She clung to me; she didn't want it to stop. Besides, no one need ever know.

No one but me.

Conscience invaded craving. They mixed, separated, and tore through my brain like summer lightning.

I would love her to death.

I drew back, as though it were part of our love dance. She sighed again, turning it into a protesting moan. Two threads of blood trickled down her neck from the wounds I'd made.

To death.

But no one need ever . . .

Teetering.

I wanted her badly, more than anything else I'd ever dreamed of wanting.

To death.

I backed off until we ceased to touch. It helped. It helped more to picture her limp and heavy in my arms, her skin gray, her heart silent. I had killed before, but not for this, not for the convenient satiation of hunger.

The room was heavy with bloodsmell. I forced air from my lungs and did not replace it. I backed off another step.

The fusing of desire and appetite was nothing new and had conquered stronger men than myself. The absolute power I had over her—over anyone I wished—was an awful, frightening thing. I retreated from it, seizing on the quickest escape with a desperate will.

My body dissolved and floated free, tumbling a little from the inertia of its last faint movement. I remained in that state until the fever ebbed away and the grip of hunger eased and finally released me. Still, it was a very long time before I re-formed, and then only after I'd pushed far away from her. I drifted through the thin partitions of wood and lath until I stood in the outside hall of the building.

Air, icy cold and bitter, cut at my throat and lungs. I drew a second painful breath and a third. It was glorious. I felt like a swimmer unexpectedly breaking the surface after being sucked to the bottom of a whirlpool. My legs still shook, but eventually everything settled down as the world started spinning along its usual course.

I stood and stared at nothing, and tried not to feel what I was feeling.

I felt it, anyway.

Terror.

She could have died. I'd come that close to going over the edge with her. And I still wanted to finish what I'd started. My hunger was quiet, but not yet sated, and tugged at me to return to her.

Was it because of my changed condition, or had this always been within me? Was I a rapist or an animal fulfilling a physical need?

Or both?

I'd had lapses of temper and of sanity and had used them against people; I'd never before had such a lapse concerning hunger or had ever been so close to killing because of hunger. Until tonight I'd regarded myself as being a man with a condition that could be controlled—that *was* under control.

That safe and comfortable image was altered now, and I wasn't sure of anything anymore. I only knew I was scared.

And inside me, her blood fused with my own.

She was standing in the same spot when I returned, her face closed and defenseless with sleep. I made myself look at her, to see *all* that she was, all that I'd nearly destroyed. Her name was Doreen. She had a right to feel and learn and love, to choose for herself. She had a right to live.

She was human. I was not.

I went to the darkroom and wet my handkerchief under the tap there and used it to clean her throat. The marks were small and hadn't bled much. She might not notice them. I drew her collar up a bit, then touched her cheek, not with desire, but with a caring that had been missing before.

"Wake up, honey."

Her eyes flickered open.

"You okay?" I wasn't sure if she would remember anything.

She nodded. One hand came up to touch the spot on her neck where I'd kissed her, then fluttered away in confusion. "I think . . . I mean . . ."

I searched her face for the least sign of awareness of what had happened. The only thing I could see was puzzlement. I should have been relieved, but was just too emotionally hammered out to feel much of anything. Shoving my hands firmly in my coat pockets, I turned my back to her and took a few aimless steps. "There's a bar down on the corner. You think it's still open?"

"Yeah, it'll be open."

"I thought maybe I could buy you something." It was half statement, half question.

She accepted the offer with relief and gratitude. It went double for me.

She wrapped up tight and we walked across the street to a place with no name that I had noticed. Socially, it was somewhere between the Top Hat and the Stumble Inn. I bought a couple drinks at the bar and carried them to a booth in the rear, where we sat opposite each other. She put half of hers away in one needy gulp and fell back to catch her breath.

"All right?" I asked.

"Yeah. It was getting pretty cold up there in the studio."

"Cold?" I was worried about how much I'd taken from her.

"They practically turn the heat off at night. I guess the idea is to discourage tenants from doing what I was trying to do. They got ordinances against taking a flop in a joint zoned for office space."

"You have no place else to go?"

"I figured it'd be okay for one night, then I could look for another hotel."

"Tell me about Stan."

Her face clouded and started to crumple. "I can't."

"Yes, you can."

Our encounter must have left a few positive aftereffects somewhere in her mind. Either that or she really did want to talk. I kept my supernatural influences to myself and waited her out.

"It's just—the stuff I've done . . ." Tears ran out of both eyes and she blindly pawed the contents of her purse.

I gave her a clean handkerchief. I usually carried an extra. "It's all right, Doreen. I've seen a thing or two."

She brought the snuffling under control and cleared her throat by draining the other half of her glass. "Stan was the one with the ideas," she explained, finally jumping in.

"Like that fancy mirror in his room?"

"Yeah. He was already doing stuff, but only in a small way. He'd get love letters and use them—that kind of thing."

"Rich girls?"

"Not rich. He wasn't in that crowd, but he did go for ones

that had money of their own and a reputation to keep. He could spot a spoiled brat looking for thrills a mile away, then move in and take them. He'd get enough money from them to live on, but not so much that they'd scream for a lawyer or cop. Stan was careful not to push too hard. If it looked like she'd kick up a fuss, he'd back off and find someone else easier to deal with.''

"How did you two get together?"

"He needed a photographer."

"And . . . ?"

"He heard I did artistic photos, so he came around and asked if I was interested. He had everything all worked out about the hotel rooms. A place like the Boswell don't have any kind of house man, so it was easy to set up. We just moved in and I started taking pictures."

"He didn't mind being photographed?"

She smiled crookedly. "No, he enjoyed it. When he wasn't playing Prince Charming for the girls, he was just about the vainest creature on God's green earth. He used to flip through the prints I made, get himself pretty worked up . . ." She began to blush. I was glad that she could still do it.

I smiled wanly. "I know what it's like, Doreen."

"I guess we all do."

"What happened with Kitty Donovan?"

"She was just another mark."

"You get pictures of them together?"

"No. She liked her own place better. Stan never could get her into that hotel bed."

I was happy to hear it. "Then why'd he stick with her?"

"Because of the people she knew. She was his ticket into the good places and the people with real money."

"Like Marian Pierce's crowd?"

"Yeah, she was part of it. Stan thought she was ripe for picking, except he couldn't get past that crazy boyfriend of hers." The smile melted away. "Oh, God, I can't believe he's gone."

I was fresh out of handkerchiefs and gave her the drink I'd bought as window dressing. "You loved him?"

"I didn't have any reason to, so I guess I did. That'd explain all this, wouldn't it?" She gulped down a sob and got control again. "Look, would you tell me what happened to him? I couldn't ask the cops."

"And they didn't tell you?"

"Why should they? I was listening while they were in Stan's room. The way they were talking about him . . . I put it together that he was . . . was dead. I couldn't say anything, either. I was afraid they'd take me in if they found out about the racket we had going. It was horrible."

And what I had to tell her was no comfort. I kept it short. "Stan was killed at Kitty Donovan's place. Someone knocked him out and stabbed him. It was quick. He wouldn't have felt much."

She put her head down in her hands, moaning. I left the table to get another drink.

"Trouble?" asked the bartender.

"Death in the family."

He was sympathetic and pushed my money away. "On the house."

"Thanks."

"After this one, get her home, make her sleep."

"You know her?"

"She's been in a few times for a beer. She won't be used to the hard stuff. It'll hit her like a brick pretty soon."

"I'll watch out." I went back to the booth. "Doreen?"

She raised her head with difficulty and blew her nose into the sodden linen. "I'm . . . I'll be all right."

"Sure you will."

"Do the cops know who did it? Do they know why?"

"They're looking for Kitty."

"That little girl scout? She couldn't do anything like that."

"I don't think she did. You knew him. Who wanted to kill him?"

She shook her head and kept on shaking it. "Leadfoot Sam, maybe. Stan owed him a bundle. That's why I got out while I could. I didn't want him learning about me and Stan or he'd try and muscle it out of me. I don't have that kind of money, but he wouldn't believe that."

"I talked with Sam earlier."

"You . . . " she blinked against the tears with surprise.

I made a calming gesture. "He's not so tough once you learn how to handle him. Anyway, he doesn't know what's happened and I figure that that's the truth. He can't collect money from a dead man, so he's not really a suspect with me. Can't you think of anyone else? One of your clients?"

"Jeez, I just don't know. There were plenty of 'em sore as hell or hurt or embarrassed, but not enough to kill. He was careful, I said."

"Did he ever call one in?"

"What'd'ya mean?"

"The photos, did he ever use one and blow things for the girl?"

She was genuinely astonished. "Not that I know of. He only threatened, it wouldn't do him any good to push it that far. He'd just hold it over their heads. They'd either call his bluff or pay off. Almost all of them paid off. He knew how to pick and choose. If they didn't pay, he'd just let it go and find someone else to work on."

"Did he always take money?"

"Brother, that's all he would take."

"What about jewelry?"

"Too much trouble to hock or sell. He left that for them to do." She finished off the drink. "Y'know, maybe it was that crazy boyfriend of Marian's."

"Why do you think so?"

"Stan said the guy was nuts, even took a swing at him once."

"When and where?"

"I dunno. One of those fancy places. Stan ducked in time and laughed about it later. He said all he did was have a dance with Marian, then the guy comes in and goes berserk."

I could believe that. "When did this happen?"

She leaned her head on one hand, mussing her hair. "I dunno, I dunno. I'm too tired to think. Will you just take me back?"

"Did Stan have any hiding places?"

"Huh?"

"Where'd he put his valuables?"

"Noplace."

"He must have stashed things somewhere. What about the bank? Did he have a safe-deposit box?"

"No, nothing like that. He carried everything with him. Not that he ever had much."

I remembered McAlister's turned-out pockets. "Wasn't it risky?"

"Safer than leaving it at that fleabag hotel. Stan had a gun, too."

"All the time?"

"Of course."

Whoever had clobbered and stabbed him hadn't given him the chance to use it. "It wasn't on him."

The news didn't matter much to Doreen. Her head had slipped down onto her arms again. Those three doubles were having their effect.

"C'mon, honey. I'll get you home and put you to bed."

"You'n what army?" she mumbled, more than half-gone. I got her to her feet, waved a good-night to the bartender, and walked her out. The cold air revived her a little, but she leaned against me, as much for comfort as for warmth. We staggered up the stairs to the studio and I steadied her while she fumbled out the key and gave it over.

The entry was dark as before, but we'd left the light on in the inner room. Now it was off.

"Whatizzit?" she asked crossly when I wouldn't let her go in.

I signed for her to stay quiet and listen. The whole building seemed to be listening. Except for her own heart and lungs, I heard nothing. I went inside. When I turned on the light, she followed, tiptoeing unsteadily.

There weren't that many places to search, but the place had been thoroughly turned over. Her suitcase was open, the contents scattered, the pillows gutted, a file cabinet gaped in one corner. The darkroom was in the same shape.

"What did you keep here?" I asked.

She was too far gone to answer right away. "Photos, negatives, chemicals, nothing important. No cash."

"Maybe they didn't want cash." I checked some of the prints from the file cabinet that now lay on the floor. Girls striking different poses wearing little more than a provocative smile was the predominant theme. I recognized the backdrop and pillows.

Doreen knelt by her suitcase and methodically shoved the clothes back inside. She tenderly turned over the smashed remains of her camera, then left it on the floor. "They got all my negs."

"What was on them?"

She sniffled, found a dry handkerchief among her things, and blew her nose. "What'd'ya think? Stan's gone and now I got nothing. Absolutely, goddamn nothing. I'm leaving this town before they take even that away."

''To where?''

She shrugged and began to shuffle photos into a pile. I bent to help her, but a creaking floorboard in the entry caught my attention. I didn't have time to do more than straighten and turn before Leadfoot Sam walked in on us.

5

DOREEN LOOKED UP, blanched, and joined me in staring at him. The first to move was Sam. The second he recognized me, his hand jumped to his overcoat pocket and smoothly pulled out a gun. It was another revolver, identical to the one I'd twisted in two. Maybe he got them in sets.

"No need for that, Sam," I said, taking a long step away from Doreen. If he planned to start shooting, I wanted her to be well clear of me.

"Shut up and hold still."

I held still. His voice was even enough, but the short nose of the revolver trembled, and he was nearly as white as Doreen. I'd made quite an impression on him earlier, but it hadn't been as effective as I'd hoped.

"Hands up and out."

I complied. It gave him a shade more confidence, which gave me more time to think. I could risk things and try controlling him with a quick suggestion, but he looked too nerved up yet for anything fancy. The wrong word from me and we'd all end up feeling sorry for what happened.

"Thought you had me going, huh?" he finally said, with just the barest hint of desperation.

"Going?"

"With that crap you pulled earlier off that radio show. You think I don't know a con trick when I see one?"

"Can't blame a guy for trying," I said sheepishly.

Given half a chance, people have a remarkable capacity for self-delusion, and if I could tell anything from the relief on his mug, Leadfoot Sam was proving to be no different from the rest. He'd really needed me to say something like that. Never mind that my generality was pretty meaningless, I had vaguely agreed with whatever explanation he'd invented for himself, and now all was right with the world. He relaxed by a single degree and smiled a thin, superior smile.

"It was a good one, wasn't it?" I asked, as though I'd been caught fair and square.

"How'd you do it?"

"I'll show you sometime. It works better in the dark."

He didn't take to that particular bait by obligingly turning off the lights, nor did he put away the gun. His eyes flicked away from me only once. "Hello, Doreen."

She'd sobered up quite a bit in the last minute and was probably wondering what the hell we were talking about. "Hi, Sam. What're you doing here?"

"I came to collect on a debt."

"What debt? I don't owe you anything. I don't owe anyone anything."

"Sure you do, sweetheart. You were partners with Stanley, weren't you?"

"I hardly knew—"

"Can it. I've just been over to Stan's room and found that sweet little racket the two of you had set up there. You must have raked in plenty. As I see it, partners are responsible for each other's debts."

"But, Sam . . ."

"Shut up. And you, Lamont—if that's your name—were you holding out on me so you could have first crack at her?"

"Holding out?"

"You never told me about Stan getting knifed, or did you do it yourself? Is there a picture of your girlfriend somewhere in Doreen's photo collection?"

"You're full of beans."

"Maybe you forgot to tell Doreen about it like you forgot to tell me."

"I see you still managed to find out."

"Oh, yeah, after a ton of time and trouble. The cops don't exactly give that information away to the public, you know." He turned a sour face on Doreen. "And what kind of line has he been feeding you, sweetheart? What do you know about this guy, anyway?"

She said nothing, but he'd gotten the wheels turning in her head—in the wrong direction as far as I was concerned.

"He's not here to get his picture took, is he? What's he want from you?"

"He don't—doesn't want anything," she said.

Sam shook his head sadly. "The world don't work that way, Doreen. You oughta know that by now. Everybody wants something. What'd he come to you for?"

She licked her lips, her tone guarded. "He was just asking about Stan, is all. Who mighta killed him, like that."

"And you never thought he mighta done it himself?"

She hadn't, and turned her doubts full onto me.

"Don't let him rattle you, Doreen," I said out of the side of my mouth. "Remember, I'm one of the good guys."

"Sez you," put in Sam.

"How about you tell us who did the redecorating here?" I asked, wanting to change the subject.

"I only just got here. Pin it on someone else, Lamont." He bent an eye on Doreen. "Is that the name he gave you? Russell Lamont?"

Her answer was easy enough to read. I'd lost her trust, at least for the moment.

"And what makes you a better bargain, Sam?" I countered.

His attention switched back to me. "Doreen knows what to expect from her old friends."

"Like a shiv in the throat?" I ventured.

"We'll see." He backed up to the door and whistled. A moment later a man that I recognized as Sam's driver walked in. He was followed by Butler, who had to duck his head slightly to miss the lintel. He took in the wrecked room, Doreen on the floor by her suitcase, and finally focused on me. He then raised the kind of smile you don't want to see in your worst nightmares.

"You took Sam's car," he stated flatly.

I said nothing, since it's pointless to argue with facts.

"Where is it?" Sam asked him.

"Just down the street. It seems okay."

Sam glared at me. "You better hope it is, or that'll be another one I owe you.'' He nodded at the driver. ''Take her back to the joint. We'll follow in the Cadillac.''

Doreen balked. ''Where?''

''Just a quiet place so we can talk, sweetheart. If you're good, I'll buy you an ice-cream soda. You and I are going to cut a deal over Stan's outstanding markers.''

''I don't have any money, Sam.''

''Not yet, you don't . . . but you will. I'm just gonna make sure I'm around for my share.''

''Please,'' she said to me. ''Don't let him.''

Sam centered the gun on her. ''All we're gonna do is have a nice talk, Doreen. You kick up a fuss and I'll show you how mean I can get if I try.''

''It'll be all right,'' I said. ''Go on, sit tight and wait for me.''

She looked at me as though I'd gone crazy and only needed a straitjacket to make it official.

''I'll come for you.'' I hoped she'd believe me.

Sam and Butler laughed at this. The driver hauled her up and dragged her out the door. The laughter did wonders for her confidence, but I was at last able to relax. With Doreen out of the way and relatively safe, my choices on how to handle the situation had increased considerably. The only thing I really had to worry about now was how to keep my suit in one piece.

''Ready to get down to business?'' I asked once they were long gone.

Sam pretended to be impressed. ''He still thinks he's a tough guy. Look him over, Butler, find out why he's so tough.''

Butler approached, keeping out of Sam's line of fire, and slapped at me with big hands. I didn't quite fall over. He found Doreen's automatic right away. ''This must be it.'' He grinned.

''Is that it?'' Sam asked me.

''As far as you're concerned,'' I said.

He shot me a wary look and told Butler to continue. He pocketed the gun. My notebook, pencil, keys, and wallet were extracted and examined, the latter catching the most interest.

''It sez he's Jack R. Fleming.'' Butler squinted at my New York driving license.

Sam nodded, as though he'd known all along.

''He's rich, too.'' He held up Pierce's C-note.

''Put it back,'' I said softly.

With high good humor, Butler shook his head and stowed the bill away with Doreen's pistol. "Now what, Sam?"

"Now you teach him not to be so nosy. But go easy, Butler. I don't want to put him to bed with a shovel."

Butler looked me over, trying to decide where to start. He was a man with total confidence in his own physical capabilities and was probably taking my lack of fear for bravado. Right away I could tell he didn't like the smile I was showing him. He matched it with a nasty one of his own and followed it up with a fast punch.

He'd had some fight training in his past. Because of his height and massive build I'd been expecting a slow roundhouse-type swing that could be blocked with a raised arm. As it was, I only snapped my head out of the way just in time. His fist brushed my chin, but he caught me flat footed with a lightning follow-up left that went straight into my stomach.

I doubled over and staggered with all the talking breath knocked out of me, falling backward over the ripped-up pillows. It was a soft landing, more or less. Butler stood away from the swirling feathers and waited for me to recover. I held a hand to the sore spot until it faded, and stood up, stepping clear of the mess. He totally missed the fact that I was not gasping for air or showing any of the other usual symptoms of such an attack. In fact, all I did was grin, and that really put me on his good side.

He had the height and reach on me, but the grin made him forget about those advantages and move in close. I let him back me up to a corner, left it till the last possible instant, and went transparent just as he struck. His fist tickled through my ghostly midsection and connected solidly with the wall behind me. The resulting howl of pain from him was almost deafening.

I immediately went solid again. If Butler had noticed me flickering on and off like a bad light, he was too occupied with his injured hand to think about it. Leadfoot Sam couldn't have seen much; I'd taken care to shift so that Butler's body blocked his view of the incident.

Butler tried another left. I was moving fast myself and his anger and pain were working against him. I caught his wrist in my right hand and returned his gut punch with interest with the left. He folded up like an old wallet. As soon as I let go of him he hit the floor and stayed there, gulping and gasping.

Sam knew his number was up because I was looking in his direction and still grinning. He showed his own teeth in a sticky grimace and raised his gun to fire.

"Aw, Sam, now do you want I should break this one in two as well?" I took a step toward him.

He made that sick little sound deep down in his throat once again and bolted for the exit. I flashed invisibly ahead of him and got to the entry first. He slid to a stop on his heels just inches away from me. While he was dancing to get his balance back, I popped him a light one on his chin. He dropped like a sandbag.

He was fairly stunned but made a halfhearted attempt to lift the revolver. I took it away from him, this time without puncturing my thumb. Grabbing a wad of his clothes in my free hand, I dragged him into the studio, dumping him on the floor next to Butler, who was still nursing his bruised gut. Sam's long bones thudded on the bare wood. His arms came up protectively.

"Sam?"

It took him a minute, but he eventually opened his eyes.

"Watch carefully, 'cause you musta missed something the first time around." I opened the cylinder, emptied out the bullets, got a good grip, and twisted as hard as I could.

Sam whimpered when it snapped.

"Next time it'll be your neck. You understand that now?"

He nodded a lot. I froze on his eyes and stepped up the pressure just enough for him to feel it. I wanted him good and scared.

"From now on you stay out of my way. You're gonna lay off on Doreen, too. You don't talk to her, you don't even think about going near her. You leave her completely alone. You got that?"

His jaw sagged. I knew I'd finally gotten through to him. I put the two pieces of his gun in each of his hands. Butler didn't fuss at all when I picked his pocket and retrieved my hundred-dollar bill and Doreen's automatic. I walked out, pausing long enough in the entry to flick off all the lights.

Somewhere behind me, Leadfoot Sam moaned miserably in the abrupt darkness.

Sam's remark about buying Doreen a soda hadn't been lost on me. Within a quarter hour I took the Caddy out of gear, cut the motor, and coasted to a stop across the alley entrance to the drugstore. A fresh-looking Ford stood next to it. Doreen and the driver were probably waiting inside for Sam and Butler to return.

A dim light gleamed in a single rear window of the building. I set the brake and got out. The place was silent, which could be good or bad.

I slipped inside the back way and went solid, listening hard. The easy whisper of soft breathing finally drifted to my ears from the direction of the spiral staircase. Sniffing instinctively like a hunting animal, I picked up a strong stench of booze and the heavy, familiar tang of bloodsmell.

The stairs led down to pitch darkness. I was reluctant to enter it and investigate; the hair on my nape was already on end. It was my own fault, since I'd shattered the overhead bulb myself.

I swallowed dryly, went transparent, and slowly coasted along the twisting metal rail into the basement. At the foot of the steps I was solid again with my nerves running on full. The breathing from a single set of lungs continued with the undisturbed regularity of sleep. I took a chance and lit a match. The burst of yellow fire flared and settled, revealing the room pretty much as I'd left it, except for the man sprawled senseless on the floor. He gripped a flashlight in one hand. It was on, but the batteries were exhausted.

His clothes were sprinkled with liquor and shards of brown bottle glass, and there was a hell of a bump and cut on his forehead. He was the driver who was supposed to be watching Doreen. She must not have expected me to return and had aced him herself when she got the chance. I couldn't blame her, but it was an unexpected nuisance. First Kitty and now Doreen . . . it was really my night for losing people.

I searched the rest of the store, but she was long gone. I left him to sleep it off, got in the Caddy, and drove quickly back to the studio. It was empty. Sam and Butler had pulled themselves together and left, hopefully for good. They were probably busy right now finding the driver in the drugstore basement.

Doreen's clothes were still scattered all over the place. I packed whatever I could find into her suitcase, then carried it away with me as I went to pick up Escott's car. Before leaving, I left a note for her hanging prominently from a slightly dented tripod. Chances were that if she had the moxie to smash a bottle over a guy's head, she'd eventually return to pick up her things. My note had Escott's office number and directions to call him for the stuff. I still had some questions for her and no doubt so would Escott after he'd heard about the evening's events.

His Nash had come to no harm sitting on the street, but I decided to take it home and pick up my more expendable Buick later. Though his concern for the safety of his car had only been a blind to get me here in the first place, it could do no harm to follow through with the ruse. Lieutenant Blair was a detail-minded man and I wouldn't put it past him to check up on me. I wondered if Escott had managed to talk his way out of his spot. If anybody could, he was the one to do it. I'd find out later; I had an errand to run now that I didn't dare put off.

The Stockyards were cold and quiet. The cattle huddled in their small pens and only rarely did one of them vocalize their collective misery at this late hour. The time was ideal for me, with no human eyes to watch as I crouched by an animal and sucked blood from a vein I'd opened with my teeth. It sounds pretty bad, but as Bobbi had once pointed out, I didn't have to kill in order to feed myself.

What had happened tonight, though, had shaken me from that confident complacency. I was running scared. The fusion of desire and appetite that I'd experienced with Doreen had nearly been too much to handle. After all these months, I thought I knew all there was to know about being a vampire, but circumstance and opportunity had proved me wrong, almost dead wrong, as far as Doreen was concerned.

I was *never* going to place myself or anyone else into that kind of a situation again.

The emotional temptation was easily avoided; all I had to do was swear off hypnotizing people. The intimate bond required for such deep hypnotic control was a two-way trap. Breaking free of the one I'd fallen into with Doreen had been one of the most difficult things I'd ever done. The next time, I might not be able to do it, therefore, there would be *no* next time. I would stick with simple and direct suggestions, nothing more.

As for the physical temptation, I was taking care of that by drinking deeply from a safe source. Usually I had only to drop by the Stockyards once every three nights, sometimes four, depending how often Bobbi and I got together. That would be altered to every other night. My hunger was inescapable, but easily remedied. To ignore it was to take chances with other lives.

I drank as much as I needed and more until the hot strength surged through and filled me with its red tide of life. Appetite and a shadowy mental bond that I barely understood had contributed to the incident; both would be under sharp control from now on. I only hoped that it would work.

Escott's office by the Stockyards was closed tight and deserted, so I moved on and purposely took a route home that led past Bobbi's hotel. Her living-room window on the fourth floor was visible from the street. It was just after three A.M., but her lights were glowing. She always spent at least an hour winding down from her work at the Top Hat; this was an open invitation for me to drop in on her. Without thinking, I found a place to park and went inside.

I took the elevator up and exchanged meaningless pleasantries with the sleepy operator. He opened the doors and I walked out as I had done a hundred times before. The doors slid shut behind me and the thing descended back to the lobby again.

I was halfway down the hall when I realized I absolutely could not go in to see her, at least not tonight. The truth of it was that I was still uneasy and Bobbi was perceptive enough to be able to spot it. She would want to know what was wrong and this wasn't something I could talk about.

Especially to her.

What I was capable of doing and what I had done frightened me, but mixed in with the fear was a large chunk of guilt. It wouldn't matter much to Bobbi that I'd fed from Doreen as if she'd been one of the cattle in the pens. The simple fact was that I'd been with another woman. As I saw things, it was more than enough to destroy our relationship.

No, going in to see Bobbi tonight would be another big mistake. I needed time to settle down. Tomorrow night would be soon enough. I punched the button and waited for the elevator to return. The operator didn't ask questions about my change of mind, which was just as well.

The hotel lobby should have been deserted at this time of the morning. The night clerk often napped on the office sofa, and Phil, the hotel detective, usually hung out in the radio room when he wasn't making his rounds. Both of them were now at the front desk with two other men I didn't know and there was something about their collective posture that caught my attention.

Phil was a leaner. He leaned against pillars, chairs, tables, whatever was handy, and rarely put his weight on more than one foot at a time. Now he stood straight and alert with his hands at his sides and a look on his face that was no look at all. He'd blanked out all expression and not once did his eyes flick over to me, though he was certainly aware of the elevator doors when they opened.

The clerk was a slightly younger man whose name I'd never bothered to catch. He was also standing straight, with his hands in front of him on the counter as though he needed it to keep his balance. His eyes were wide and flashed briefly on me as I emerged into the lobby.

It was subtle stuff to pick up within the space of a couple seconds, but enough to make me pause.

One of the two strangers slowly turned his head in my direction. The other continued to face Phil and the clerk and didn't move. My pause became a full stop. Something was wrong, but I wasn't sure what to do about it.

The one looking at me took his time. He had a dark, unpleasant face with an expression to match, and both his coat and overcoat were unbuttoned. It was very cold outside and I could think of only one reason why a man would not bundle up against it.

The hair on my nape began to rise as he broke away and walked over. I waited for him.

"That your Nash out front?" he asked.

He already knew the answer, so I nodded. "Who wants to know?"

"Come with me and find out."

"You a cop?" I knew he wasn't and he knew I knew, and so on. It was part of the game we were playing. He shook his head. I checked on his partner, who was still watching Phil and the clerk. No one had moved an inch. "He coming, too?"

"Yeah."

"Then call him off."

"Rimik."

"Okay, Hodge," the other man answered.

He broke away from the desk, never once turning until he had enough angle and distance to cover us all. He wasn't showing any gun, you just knew it was there. The clerk was freely sweating now. Phil threw a silent question at me; I shook my head.

"You boys get on with things," I said. "Business as usual."

They had their own skins to keep in one piece, so no one said a thing as I walked from the lobby door under escort. It was an armed escort, but we were busy pretending that everything was normal.

As we stepped outside, a Cadillac with smoked-over windows pulled up. Its motor was so silent that all you could hear were the tires rolling over the pavement. These guys liked the classy cars, all right, but I was getting a different feeling from this bunch. They were as far removed from Leadfoot Sam as a tiger is from a tabby cat, and proportionately more dangerous.

I got into the backseat and Rimik climbed in next to me. Hodge sat in front with the driver. The car was in top shape; I barely noticed when we started to move.

Rimik was focused on the back of the driver's neck, but I had no doubt he was more than prepared to deal with any fast moves on my part. I kept my hands in the open and watched our route through the front window. I couldn't see out the side ones. There was a divider between the front and back, which was probably also opaque, but they didn't bother raising it. That could be good or bad. I was assuming the worse, but too curious to take action about it just yet. First I'd find out what they were after, then I'd think about getting away.

We drove over the river and into a familiar neighborhood, though I hadn't been through the area since last August, when I'd first arrived in Chicago. Nothing seemed to have changed, it was only colder and more empty than before. The cheap hotels and pawnshops gave way to long blocks of warehouses and inadequate lighting. The drive was half an hour of total silence. The last leg of it took us along a narrow street running between two huge warehouses built out over the river. We stopped at a side door.

Hodge was out first to cover things. Rimik signed for me to move.

"What's this about?" I asked, because it was time I showed some curiosity. I was also genuinely uneasy.

"Later," said Hodge.

The driver was ahead of us and opened the narrow door into the warehouse, then hit the lights. The place was still gloomy.

It was full of crates of all kinds and the sharp odor of new wood, excelsior, and machine oil. It looked naggingly familiar. The stenciled labels on the crates identified their contents as machine parts. That tripped the final switch in my memory. I fought down an involuntary shudder that had nothing to do with the winter air.

Hodge sat on a crate, Rimik stood and stared at me, and the driver went to the office I knew to be out front. He returned several minutes later, nodded once at Hodge, then leaned against the far wall and fired up a cigarette.

I looked at Hodge. "It's later. What's this about?"

"You'll find out soon enough."

"I'll find out now, or I'm walking."

"You can try, kid."

From out of nowhere, Rimik had produced a big bowie knife and polished it with a soft cloth. He was still staring at me.

"You take me out with that," I said, "and your boss might not like it."

"You'd like it even less, Escott," said Hodge.

That shut me up.

Their mistake was a natural one. While I'd been talking with Bobbi they'd searched the Nash and found its registration and Escott's name.

"Take off the coat," he told me after a moment.

"It's cold," I reminded him.

"We'll give it back."

Rimik put the knife within easy reach—his reach—and came forward. His action distracted me, so I hadn't noticed Hodge pulling out a forty-five automatic. These boys were moving as smooth as oil and I didn't like the kind of teamwork that that implied.

He leveled the gun at my gut. "Take off the coat."

I took it off. There was no sense in forcing them to put holes in it or the suit. A shoot-out might force me to do other things as well. I knew what they wanted and stood by for yet another frisk. Rimik found Doreen's gun right off.

"Déjà vu," I said as he put it on the crate next to the knife.

"What?" asked Hodge.

"Nothing. Just French for 'here we go again.' "

Rimik didn't bother searching my wallet or they'd have realized their mistake about my identity. They were looking for weapons, not enlightenment. He turned it back over with the other stuff, and I was allowed to put my coat on again.

"Who's your boss?" I asked.

Hodge answered readily enough. "Vaughn Kyler."

If he expected a reaction, he drew a complete blank. "What's he want with me?"

He carefully stowed the forty-five into its shoulder holster and let the edges of his coat and overcoat fall back into place. Unbuttoned.

"What does he want?"

He dug into a pocket for a cigarette and lighted it, paying no attention to my question. The temptation to make him answer was there, but I decided to wait. I had the time, and chances were his boss would tell me all about it. Right now they were playing a nerve game, but that only works if you can be intimidated. I sat on a crate and watched him smoke. Rimik picked up the bowie knife and slipped it into some kind of a hip sheath. I caught a glimpse of the gun under his coat as well. He was prepared for all sorts of weather.

Hodge smoked his cigarette down to a butt and tossed it accurately at a drainage grate in the floor. He looked ready to light another when we all turned in response to a distant noise from the office out front. The driver broke away from the wall, went into the office, and returned a moment later to usher in a new addition to the party.

He walked in without hurry, a medium-sized man in a vicuna overcoat with his hat pulled low. He paused in the penumbral area between the lights and checked things over before coming any closer. I had no problems making out his shadowed features, but he wasn't trying hard to conceal them. If he were really worried, he'd have taken more effective steps.

Every instinctive alarm God ever invented to help us survive the wide world had gone off inside me. The urge to vanish and whip out the door away from him was that strong; it was all I could do now to stay solid as he walked over.

His movements were as fluid and controlled as a dancer's. He had dark blue eyes and short black brows. His nose was long and fine lines led from it to a thin, hard mouth. His face was square, with dewlaps just starting to form, giving the illusion of a mournful look that was, indeed, only an illusion. The set of his mouth and stony eyes confirmed it. His pale skin was just a little puffy from soft living; he looked to be edging fifty. He had a fairly ordinary face, on the surface no different from a hundred others of the same general type. But there was something . . . abnormal . . . about the man behind it that made my flesh crawl.

My own mug was easy enough to read. What he saw there didn't bother him. Maybe he was used to such reactions.

He looked me over good and close, then wandered past to see Hodge. I turned as he went behind me, wanting to keep him in full view.

"What?" he asked in a low voice.

"Spotted him going into her studio," said Hodge. "He came out with a suitcase, then drove to the Stockyards."

My spine turned to ice. I hadn't noticed anyone following me.

"He drove to a hotel off the Loop and went in. We got him coming out."

"Suitcase?"

"We searched it while he was in the hotel. Nothing inside but women's clothes. Must be hers."

"Name?"

"Escott."

"No," I said.

They each looked at me as though I had snot on my face. I was to speak only when spoken to. Well, to hell with that.

"The name they took from the car is wrong. My name is Fleming." I'd thought of giving them a phony, but it would be too easy for them to frisk me again. "Are you Kyler?"

"Yes." He studied me. "Where's the woman?"

We both knew whom he was talking about. "I don't know."

"Why do you have her suitcase?"

"I'm keeping it safe."

"When do you expect to see her again?" His voice was low, almost gentle, and had a slight East Coast accent.

"I don't know. Why are you after her?"

He ignored that one. "What is she to you?"

"Just a friend."

"Where is she?" he repeated.

My mouth is dry. "I'd cooperate better if I knew more about what's going on."

He didn't answer right away. The silence stretched out as he focused on me. It was meant to make me uncomfortable and was working to some extent. If need be, I could handle him, but he gave me the cold creeps.

"Doreen Grey has something I'm looking for," he finally stated.

"What's that?"

"No one's business but mine."

"Why should I help you, then?"

"I need information, not help. I will pay for it, if that's what you want."

What I wanted was to know exactly why this ordinary-looking man was so frightening. I tried to read something, anything, from him and could not. Maybe that was the answer.

"How much?"

He assessed me, my clothes, and other details. "One hundred dollars," he offered.

"You must have spent that on the hired help just to bring me here."

"Two hundred."

"Save your money. Tell me what you're after and I might be able to do something about it."

Kyler wasn't used to such treatment. Rimik, who hadn't said a word since I'd come in, shifted restlessly, perhaps hoping for orders to start committing mayhem. Hodge snorted. My nerves were acting up as well. My lips had peeled back just enough for the teeth to show.

"He thinks he's hot shit," observed Hodge. "We oughta show him better manners."

"You could try, gunsel." I didn't know if he went that way or not. It didn't matter, all I wanted was to make him mad and see which way his boss jumped.

Hodge jerked as though I'd touched him with a live wire. He closed the space between us in one step, his fist up and swinging. I blocked it by raising my arm then backhanding him, all in one move. He staggered bonelessly into a crate, bounced, and flopped to the floor. He stopped moving.

Rimik brought his knife out in the first second and swept it past me in a short arc to get my attention. He centered it with the blade at just the right angle to gut me like a fish. I held my ground and checked on Kyler out of the corner of my eye. He just stood there, watching the show, so I probably had a few seconds' grace.

His stooge was feeling playful. He tried an experimental thrust with the blade to get me to dodge back, only I didn't. I shot my hand out and caught Rimik's wrist, but the man was wise to that one and fast. He yanked his whole arm down, slipped away, and flicked the blade back up again.

White fire ran along my forearm. Now I did fall back, clutching the part just below my elbow where he'd neatly sliced things open. A few drops of blood splashed onto the concrete, the rest soaked into my shredded sleeve.

I wasn't badly hurt, metal wasn't as harmful to me as wood, but I had to pause a moment to keep from vanishing involuntarily to heal. The bleeding would stop quickly enough without such a complication and the pain would pass; at least I wasn't in the part of the warehouse that was over the river or I might not have had a choice.

What I couldn't stomach now was the uneven hiss of air between Rimik's teeth. He was laughing at me. It got me mad enough that I made another start for him.

The knife flashed like miniature lightning just under my nose. He was still playing, trying to give me a scar to remember him by. And he was still laughing.

I lost my temper then, and picked up the first thing that was handy; it happened to be a crate the size of a small suitcase weighing about forty or fifty pounds. We were no more than six feet apart and he had no room or time to duck. The look of gawking surprise that flashed over his face just as the crate caught him full in the chest was most satisfying.

Two steps and I was standing over him, tearing the crate to one side. My fingers had just closed over the handle of his bowie knife when I felt something small and solid bump inarguably against my left temple. It was followed by a soft double click that I recognized all too well. My grip went slack; I stopped moving altogether.

"Stand still," Kyler ordered in his gentle voice.

6

I'D OVERLOOKED THE driver simply because he was the driver.

He'd thumbed the hammer back as a subtle warning to me. I wouldn't get another. All it needed now was a minimum amount of pressure on the trigger to go off. While I was very busy not moving, Kyler walked around just enough to check on Rimik.

"Lucky man," he said. Rimik was still breathing. "Chaven, take the kid over there." He nodded at another stack of crates that were too big to be thrown.

The driver, Chaven, bumped my temple again with the muzzle of his gun. I let go of the knife and straightened cautiously. He gestured in the direction he wanted me to go. I stepped away from Rimik's body and walked toward the crates. Two steps and I had to stop because the river below our feet was holding me back. Chaven put a hand in the middle of my back and pushed. It helped and got me past the point of no return.

"Turn around." Chaven had a voice like the edge of Rimik's knife.

I turned and was looking down the short barrel of his gun, noting that he favored a revolver over an automatic. Revolvers are simple tools, particularly the double-action type; there's no need to remember about the safety or chambering a bullet or clearing a last-second jam. All you have to do is pull the trigger and it goes boom. . . . In this case, it could go boom right through my skull. The shot wouldn't kill me, but it was an experience that I altogether preferred to avoid.

Now I knew how far Kyler was willing to go with things. He and his men were ready to kill, and kill casually for whatever they wanted. I was dealing with human garbage.

Chaven had a narrow, hatchet-hard face with no more emotion in it than the gun he held, so I watched his eyes. If he decided to do anything, I'd see it show up in them first.

"He's cold," Chaven commented to his boss.

Kyler hardly glanced up. "Only because he thinks I need him alive." He came over to stand next to Chaven and to look at me more closely. "Well, I don't."

The cut on my arm stopped burning and began to sting. I let my breath out slowly and drew another.

"Your last chance," he said, carefully spacing the words. "Where is the woman?"

I waited a moment before answering, just so that Kyler knew I'd understood him. "On the level . . . I don't know."

"Why do you have her suitcase?"

"For safekeeping."

"Then you expect to see her again?"

"Maybe. I don't know for certain."

"I will guarantee her safety. I will even pay her. She, at least, might appreciate some compensation for her time. She'll know me. She'll know I'll be fair."

"But I don't know you."

"I've already noticed and allowed for that, or you'd be dead by now. You're not stupid. Start asking around. You'll find out all you need about me and how I work."

I'd already gotten a pretty clear idea. Chaven still held his gun three inches away from my nose and his hand was very steady.

"I expect you to find her. When you do, tell her that if she leaves town before settling her business with me, she will regret it."

"I'll let her know."

"Do that, Fleming." Kyler's eyes froze onto mine. It was like standing in front of the cobra exhibit at a zoo, but without any protective glass in between. "Do it as though your life depended upon it."

Kyler returned Doreen's pistol—without the bullets—and had Chaven drive me to Bobbi's hotel, where the Nash was parked. It was another silent ride. I hugged my sore arm and bit my tongue to keep from asking him anything. They could learn a lot about me from the kind of questions I might have, and I didn't want any of them getting too curious. My best course was to keep a low profile; I was to be a messenger boy and nothing more.

Chaven pulled up next to the Nash, braking only long enough for me to get out. The Caddy glided away out of sight. I breathed a heavy sigh of relief, made sure the street was empty, and vanished.

It was swift and certain release from my pain. Through trial and a lot of error, I'd learned that going incorporeal speeded up the healing process. I floated around for a time and eventually sieved into Escott's car to rematerialize and take stock.

The bloodstains were alarming, but a little soap and water would clear them away. The seven-inch gash was already closed and had reduced itself to a nasty-looking red scar. It would fade soon enough. Too bad I couldn't say the same for my memory. He was out of commission for now, but one of these nights I planned to pay Rimik back in full, and take my time about it.

I considered going in to see Bobbi for a little cleanup and sympathy, but quickly decided against it. Kyler had made me paranoid. If his men were able to trail me from the studio to the Stockyards without getting spotted, they could still be on the watch. Walking back to the hotel might lead them to Bobbi, and I wasn't about to involve her in this mess.

Starting the car, I prowled around the streets. At this time of the morning, anyone following me would easily stand out. After half an hour of searching the mirror and seeing nothing, I felt reasonably safe and drove to Escott's office near the Stockyards. I parked the car, locked it, and walked away, going around the block to the next street over. Being reasonably safe isn't the same as being certain about it. I stood in a shadow-filled alley until the cold started to penetrate even my supernatural hide. Only one car came by, an old cab driven by a middle-aged man who looked both sleepy and bored. Not Kyler's style at all.

Vanishing again, I left the alley and felt my way two doors down the block, slipping inside the third one with heartfelt relief. The first thing I sensed after going solid was the rich, earthy aroma of tobacco. It was a small shop, jammed with all the usual paraphernalia needed for a good smoke. Escott owned a half interest in the place and used it for more than just keeping his favorite blend on hand.

I went around the small counter and up the narrow stairs. Woodson, the other owner, used the front section of the second floor for storage and never bothered with the back. The dust on the floor was undisturbed and I left it that way, choosing to float over it to get to the rear wall, where Escott had installed a hidden door. I didn't bother messing with the catch and just seeped through, re-forming in the washroom of Escott's office.

My eyes automatically skipped past the mirror as I walked into the back room, which was furnished with a few bare necessities. Once in a while his work kept him late and he wasn't above camping out here. His neatly made-up army cot was short on comfort, but adequate for an overnight stay. He also had a suitcase and a change of clothes on hand for occasional out-of-town trips. I opened the door to the front room.

Except for the blotter, phone, and ashtray, the top of his desk was clean. He was an extremely neat man, insisting on order and precision in every detail of his life, right down to the exact way his chair was centered into its well under the desk. I avoided moving it and sat in the other office chair.

I used the phone and tried reaching him at the house but got nothing. I dialed police headquarters and asked for Lieutenant Blair. He'd gone home hours ago. When I asked for Escott, they'd never heard of him.

He'd left no messages for me with his answering service. I wasn't sure if I should be worried about him or not. I decided not, and gave them a message for him to check his safe deposit box when he came in. It was what he called the hidden compartment he'd installed behind the medicine cabinet in his washroom. Now all I had to do was put something in it for him to find.

He had a Corona and a ream of paper on the top of his file cabinet. I brought them down and started typing.

It was a few minutes shy of dawn when I finally finished and put everything away. I tugged at the frame of the medicine cabinet and jammed the pages of my report into the narrow space there. Escott may have liked things tidy, but I was tired and in a hurry. I shut the cabinet fast before it could all fall out again and quickly walked through the wall to the tobacco shop storeroom.

Screened by a load of old crates and other junk was an especially long box that Escott had constructed for me as an emergency bolt hole. This was the first time I'd ever felt jumpy enough to want to use it. I slipped through and materialized inside its cramped confines. Like my cot at home, the bottom was lined with a quantity of my home earth in a flat oilcloth bag. It was secure, but far too much like a coffin for much mental comfort. Fortunately, the sun came up before claustrophobia overcame common sense, and I was asleep for the day.

There was no sense of waking for me, no coming up through the layers of sleep into full consciousness. When in contact with my earth, I'm either awake or not awake. It all depends on the position of the sun. I called my daytime oblivion sleep because it was a familiar word, not because it was accurate. Precisely at sunset the next night, my eyes opened, I remembered where I was, and wasted no time getting out. The box was useful enough, but I preferred being crammed into one of my steamer trunks.

In the tobacco shop downstairs a door opened and shut—either a late customer or Woodson himself closing things up for the night. He knew about the hidden door, but not about my long box or its supply of Cincinnati soil. Escott and I had figured that, like a lot of people, he'd be much happier not knowing.

No further sound came from below. I walked through to the rear of the office. On the radio that served as a nightstand was my typed report. In one corner stood Doreen Grey's cheap suitcase. Escott was lying on his army cot, a pile of newspapers within easy reach on the floor and a crumpled afternoon edition folded over his face. The deep regularity of his breathing told me he was in dreamland.

I really hated to wake him up. "Charles?"

The paper rattled. He was a light sleeper. He dragged the paper away and sat up. "Good evening," he said almost cheerfully. He did a beautiful double take. "Perhaps I should say good heavens. You look as though you've been busy."

"No need to be nice about it. We both know I look like something the cat dragged in. Can I borrow your razor?"

"Please do. Whatever happened to your arm?"

I'd omitted a few details about last night's activities from the report. "Kyler's boys play rough. Think your tailor can fix it?"

"Your arm?" he deadpanned.

"The clothes. My arm's fine." I peeled off my overcoat and

suit coat. The blood had dried and all but glued everything to the skin. It looked terrible, but the damage beneath was almost healed by now. As I scrubbed off in the sink, I could see that last night's angry red line was now a long, white welt. Eventually, even that would disappear, leaving no scar. "Did you get things straightened out with Lieutenant Blair?"

He added his paper to the stack on the floor and stretched a little. "Yes, after I'd gotten hold of our employer and informed him of the murder. It gave him quite a serious turn but he came down to headquarters himself to see to things. Mr. Pierce is a formidable fighter. I was very glad that he was on my side. He managed to keep me free from any legal difficulties."

That was a relief; I'd been afraid that Blair would have his license yanked for wanting to protect his client for a couple of hours. "I tried calling you. They have you down there all night?"

"No, it was Mr. Pierce who kept me so occupied. He insisted on buying me a late dinner to compensate a bit for the trouble I'd been to on his behalf, and then we got to talking."

"What was he doing while McAlister was getting murdered?"

His sharp gray eyes glinted with approval. "He maintains he was at the Stumble Inn for several hours, conversing with Des the bartender and cleaning out his stock of sarsaparilla. Pierce was terribly shocked at the news about McAlister, doubly so that the murder had taken place at Kitty Donovan's flat."

"The cops find her yet?"

He shook his head.

"What's Pierce think of her as a suspect?"

"He was partly incoherent, partly obscene, but wholly against the idea."

"What about Marian Pierce?"

"She was in the company of Harry Summers, who was trying to patch up a quarrel they'd had over you."

"Oh, brother."

"It seems you made quite an impression on both of them."

"That goes double for me."

"Which reminds me . . . Pierce went ahead and let his daughter know what is going on."

"I'll bet she was thrilled that I wasn't really following her like she thought."

"One wonders what activities she engages in to inspire such secretiveness."

"Smoking, drinking, and necking—those are the ones I witnessed, at least. I think she's just shy about having her daddy hear about them. He could take away her car keys. Have you heard from Doreen?"

"Not a word."

"Shit."

"But after such a harrowing evening, one can hardly blame her for wishing to keep out of sight."

"From Leadfoot Sam, you mean. She doesn't even know about Vaughn Kyler. If she leaves town before I can talk to her . . ."

"Indeed," he agreed. "I've made calls to one or two contacts I have. Since last night it has become common knowledge in Miss Grey's . . . ah . . . social set that he's looking for her. I daresay she'll discover that for herself soon enough. The police are also trying to locate her."

"Wonderful, just what she needs. How'd they get on to her?"

"I learned that they made another visit to the Boswell House and noticed the hole in the wall between the rooms."

After removing the mirror, I hadn't replaced it. They must have practically tripped over the mess. "What about her studio?"

"They searched it but discovered nothing of value, nor any clue to her whereabouts."

"But I left a note there with the office phone number on it."

He tapped the typed sheets on the radio. "So you said, but the police either ignored it, which is quite unlikely, or she got there before them and took it away."

"Or Kyler's men found it. They probably have the place staked out."

"And this one as well, if they troubled to trace the number down. You said they got my name from the car registration; I'm sure Kyler knows all about me and my little business by now."

I started to apologize or say something like an apology, but he cut it off.

"It's part of the job," he said with a dismissive wave of his hand. I'd forgotten that he enjoyed this kind of work. "I applaud your caution, but by now it may be superfluous."

"What do you know about Kyler?" I took it for granted that

Escott would have some knowledge of the man, and I wasn't disappointed.

"Vaughn Kyler, as you correctly deduced in your report, has taken control of the gang formerly headed by Frank Paco. Kyler is not his real name and I've not been able to find it out. He is well educated, thought to be intelligent, and in less than six months has doubled the earnings off the rackets previously directed by Paco. We may reasonably conclude from this that he is ambitious and perhaps not a little greedy."

"The guy's a snake," I grumbled over the running water.

"He also knows how to efficiently deal with any rivals. His chief competitors for his position, Willy Domax and Doolie Sanderson, have been missing since last August, along with half a dozen of their lieutenants. No one seems to be too anxious to speculate on their whereabouts, either."

"What about Frank Paco?"

"He's still in the sanitarium. Apparently he is not considered to be much of a threat."

I could believe that. The last time I'd seen my murderer, he'd been drooling like a baby.

"Despite this, Kyler has a high reputation in the criminal community. People may not like to deal with him, but by their standards he is fair. If he has promised safety and monetary compensation to Miss Grey, I have no doubt that she will get it."

"Yeah, that and what else?"

Escott shrugged. "Now as for *why* Kyler wants to speak with her . . ."

"I figure it's either some photos she took or has to do with that damned bracelet."

"Probably the latter. It's the only obvious thing of value in— I take it that she didn't have it?"

"Not that I know of." I concentrated very hard on scraping away soap and bristles.

"Not that you—did you not ask her?"

"She mostly talked about McAlister."

"And you never thought to ask about the bracelet?"

"I had other things on my mind."

He looked at me as though I'd dropped out of the sky from another planet. He almost said something, stopped himself, and was silent during the rest of the time it took to finish my shave.

Inside me, memory twisted like a sword in my gut. Part of me wanted to talk, badly needed to talk, but a much larger part wouldn't allow it. I rinsed and toweled off. Only inches away from me, the mirror reflected an empty washroom. The sword twisted a little deeper.

"What is it?" He could sense that something was wrong.

"Nothing," I lied, staring straight ahead.

Escott loaned me one of his spare shirts from the tiny closet and a suit coat that didn't quite match my pants, but was free of slashes and bloodstains. There wasn't much I could do about my damaged overcoat; going without one in the middle of a Chicago winter was more conspicuous than wearing it as is. I'd just have to bluff through any questions.

Not that I was planning on leaving the office. I wanted to stick close to the phone in case Doreen should try calling. She might have had to hole up for the day herself, and I was hoping she'd feel safer now that it was dark.

Escott left to get something to eat; I filled in the time by reading what his paper had to say about McAlister's murder. The reporter had done a fair job; most of the facts were straight, and the names spelled correctly. Mine had been excluded, which was a relief. It was an odd feeling, too, considering my days on the paper in New York, when I'd once fought tooth and nail for a byline.

Blair had issued a standard statement that his men were looking for a suspect, but he remained cagey concerning that person's identity. Miss Kitty Donovan, the tenant of the flat in which McAlister's body was found, was unavailable for comment.

I folded that section of the paper and tossed it onto the rest of the pile. They were full of the usual insanity. Some big brain was recommending that people start using the word *syphilis* in guessing games and spelling bees as a way of breaking down the taboos concerning venereal diseases. He had an idea that if people started putting it into crossword puzzles it would cease to be so shocking. In theory, it sounded like a good idea, but I had at least two maiden aunts who would have swooned in their high-button shoes at the idea. Once recovered, I was sure they'd have hunted the guy down and shot him on sight.

The other papers I left unread; I wasn't in the mood to bone up on the the screwy workings of the rest of the world. My own little corner of it was more than enough to keep me unpleasantly occupied.

The blank white walls of the office offered no distractions. Escott liked them plain and for just that reason: so he could think. I stared at them and purposely cleared my mind of everything but white paint.

It worked for nearly a whole minute and then I was lost in the problem of whether or not to talk to Bobbi. I rarely mentioned my feedings at the Stockyards, no more than anyone would normally talk about how they brush their teeth. How I had used Doreen was on the same level—that's what I was trying to tell myself, anyway. I was desperate for some grain of comfort, for any excuse that would let me off the hook. Nothing worked, though. I'd lost control and that was it.

No excuses.

So I put off thinking about Bobbi. I wouldn't be able to decide what to do until after I saw Doreen again, which could be never. The phone wasn't . . .

Wrong. The phone just did. Twice, as I stared at it.

"Hello?"

"Hi, lover."

That damned sword twisted in me again. This was the first time I'd ever felt uneasy talking to Bobbi. "Hi, yourself." I sounded artificially cheerful in my own ears.

"You weren't at home, so I thought I'd try my luck at Charles's office."

"Yeah, I'm holding the fort while he puts on the feed bag."

"When you didn't come back last night I got a ride home with Gloria."

"Yeah, sorry. Things got busy."

"Did you catch up with that guy?" Bobbi hadn't seen the papers yet.

I ran a nervous hand over the dark wood of Escott's desk. "Yeah, Charles and I found him."

"What happened?" Her tone turned serious. She'd picked up something from my own.

"Someone got to him first. Killed him."

"Oh, Jack . . ."

She listened and eventually some of the story came out. I needed to talk, but even then it was only a sketchy account, especially the business with Doreen Grey. Mostly I spoke of McAlister's death, which had bothered me more than I'd realized.

He was a nobody, a vain and disgusting little blackmailer, but his death was hardly a good ending for even his sort. Any pity I felt stemmed from the fact that I, too, had been murdered. It gave me a unique, if personally horrifying, insight into things.

"What about Charles?" she asked. "Is he square with the cops?"

"He seems to think so. He knows how to take care of himself and he's got a sharp lawyer. He only wanted to wait until he could talk with Pierce first, to let him know the investigation's changed from theft to murder."

"And you don't think the girl did it?"

I shrugged, which she couldn't see. "She didn't do herself any favors running out like that."

"On the other hand, she doesn't know you or Charles. She must have been too scared to think."

"She handled herself pretty well at the hotel."

"Yeah, but seeing her boyfriend like that . . ." Bobbi got quiet, retreating into her own memories. I knew they weren't pleasant ones. I instantly forgot my troubles.

"God, I wish I could be there to hold you," I said.

"I know."

We didn't say anything, but then talk would have been superfluous. I waited her out, eyes shut, listening.

After a long time, she heaved a sigh as though to clear her mind of the dust. "Maybe you can make it up to me later. Will you be coming by tonight?"

"If I can, baby. But if I'm not at the club by a quarter till closing, then you'd better hitch another ride."

"In other words, I'll expect you when I see you."

" 'Fraid so."

"Okay. If you can put up with my hours, I can handle yours."

"Fair enough."

I'd almost sounded normal toward the end, but after the last good-bye, the restless worry flowed back like a cold tide against my heart.

When Escott returned I was hunched over his radio trying to find something worth listening to—a futile effort in my present mood. I wound the dial back to his favorite station and shut the thing off.

Since the phone call, I'd managed to make one decision, and that was to go looking for Doreen. If I hung around the place much longer, I'd be climbing his blank white walls and talking to myself in three different voices. I was about to tell Escott, but he interrupted before I had the chance to draw breath to speak.

"Get your coat and hat," he said. "They've found Miss Grey. She's in hospital."

He dropped an evening edition onto the cot. It was folded open to a story on the front page. The headline read, "Shooting Victim in Critical Condition." The facts were slim. A woman had been found lying in a drainage ditch of a city park with three bullet wounds. The police were still trying to identify her.

"This could be anybody," I said faintly.

"I called someone I know there and got a description of her. It matches the one in your report."

"Oh, Christ." I stopped wasting time and grabbed my stuff and followed him down to his car. He couldn't drive fast enough for me. When we eventually got to the hospital, I hung in the background, letting him ask the questions at the front desk, then followed again as he headed off down a corridor.

We were used to working like that by now; he dealt directly with the public while I stayed out of the way and went unnoticed. It worked until we reached the surgical ward. We had another desk to pass and no one was allowed through except family.

Escott started to make explanations to the nurse in charge, but I interrupted. "Look, I need to see the woman who was shot. I think she might be my cousin."

The woman asked questions. Other people had been calling the hospital and making inquiries about her patient. She wouldn't say who. I gave her a song and dance about Doreen not turning up for work today and her general description. The latter seemed to make a difference. Her expression was grave as she went off to confer with her supervisor. Both returned with a doctor, who took us off to one side to hear things all over again. I'd always been a lousy liar; tonight it seemed to come naturally.

"If she is your cousin, you'll have to talk to the police," he told me.

"Fine," I agreed. Escott's eyes flickered, but he kept his comments to himself.

Under the eye of the supervisor and with the help of a large orderly, I was enveloped in a hospital gown that looked like a sheet with sleeves and given a cloth mask to cover my nose and mouth. This time, Escott had to stay outside and wait, but he was turning it into an opportunity. I glanced back before walking through the doors to the ward and saw him turning on the charm for the nurse at the desk. She didn't seem too cooperative, but he could work miracles with that accent of his.

The mask did not shut out the smell. It was always the same: a kind of death-sweet stink that I always associated with hospitals. The people who worked with it and the suffering that engendered it deserved Medals of Honor.

I was taken past a couple of beds loaded with silent human wreckage and shown a frail figure all but smothered under her bandages. A nurse stood close by, watching her breathe.

Until this moment, I'd held on to a vague hope that it would not be Doreen. As it was, I barely recognized her in this sterile setting. Her face was slack and colorless, the skin spread thinly over the sharp bones beneath. Only her carrot red hair stood out, a bright incongruity against the harsh steel and enamel fixtures. I put out a hand to stroke its limp strands.

"Is she your cousin?" asked the doctor.

If I said no I'd have protection from the dangerous curiosity of officialdom. It was also an easy escape from a responsibility I didn't want and could ill afford.

On her neck were the faint marks I'd left. Engulfed as she was with all the tubes and bandages, they were nothing, barely noticeable.

The doctor repeated his question.

"Yes," I said, hardly aware that I'd spoken.

He expressed sympathy and told me he needed information. I anticipated the first question. "Her name is Doreen."

"Last name?"

"Grey."

The nurse wrote it on the chart at the foot of the bed without any reaction. Maybe she'd never heard of the Oscar Wilde book. I gave Escott's office address and phone number for a place of residence and made a guess at Doreen's age. If I didn't know an answer I said so. She took down the meager scraps of fact and then the doctor led me back out to the hall.

Escott looked up. He was leaning comfortably against the desk facing the nurse and she had a smile on her face. Both sobered and straightened when I emerged from the ward.

"It's Doreen," I told him.

He also said something sympathetic. I didn't really listen. For the next half hour, as I ran the gauntlet of answering questions for a lot of people in uniforms, I didn't listen to much of anything.

The doctor in charge of her case was named Rosinski. He seemed to know his business and was reluctant to make any optimistic promises. From the way his eyes shifted and how he answered my own questions, I knew he wasn't holding out much hope of Doreen pulling through.

"Her lungs were punctured, and one of them collapsed," he said. "I take it as a good sign that she survived long enough for us to get her into surgery, but that's it as far as it goes. She was very lucky that the bullets didn't bounce around her ribs and cause more damage than they did."

"What kind of bullets?" I asked.

"Very small; twenty-twos. The holes aren't much, but they're enough to do the job. The main problem now is to keep her breathing and hope that pneumonia doesn't set in."

"Was there much blood loss?"

"Her pressure and volume were low when she was brought in—"

"But she's not harmed from it, is she?"

"No more than one would expect in such a case."

"What do you mean by that?"

"I mean that her blood loss is something we took care of early on. Right now, she's got other things to worry about."

"When will you know anything?"

Rosinski would only shake his head. "We'll both have to wait and see on that one."

Earlier, I'd let Escott know I was willing to run my end of things for the time being, so he'd gone off to tend some business of his own, giving me room to work. He must have kept tabs on me, though, since he turned up not long after the questioning ended.

"This is hardly the place I'd expect to find someone with your particular condition," he said in a subdued voice, taking a seat nearby.

"It's quiet," I mumbled, staring at the floor.

I'd found refuge in the hospital chapel. The silence of the small room helped soothe my inner turmoil, and I won't lie and say that I didn't use the place for its intended purpose. Doreen needed all the help she could get; I just hoped that God hadn't minded hearing a prayer from the guy who may have helped to put her life in jeopardy in the first place.

"All the same . . ." But he didn't finish whatever he might have said about the oddity of a vampire being in a kind of church, and shrugged the rest away. He could see I wasn't in the mood for it. "I had to call Lieutenant Blair."

"What'd he have to say?" I wasn't all that interested, but wanted distraction from the stuff inside my head.

"Little that may be repeated in these surroundings. He dispatched a man to be here in case Miss Grey should wake up."

"Yeah, I remember talking to that guy. He may have a long wait."

"What did you tell him?"

"Just that we were doing private work for Pierce and that we'd also wanted to question Doreen about McAlister's death. He took it all down and left it at that."

"Was he not curious that you are listed as her next of kin?"

"Yeah, but I told him she really didn't have anyone else to look after her. When we talked last night I got the feeling that she really was all alone."

"Alone," he repeated thoughtfully. "Obviously not."

"What're you thinking?"

"I was only speculating about who might have shot her."

"Kyler or one of his stooges."

"Are you so certain?"

"Something's telling you different?"

"The circumstances of her assault."

"What about them?"

"Can you recall what caliber weapons Kyler's men possessed?"

"Chaven was using a thirty-eight, Hodge had a forty-five."

"I learned that the bullets taken from Miss Grey were from a twenty-two . . . an experienced criminal might prefer a larger caliber."

"There're always exceptions. Kyler or Rimik could have been carrying the right size."

"True." He started to dig for his pipe, remembered where he was, and changed his mind. "But if one is planning to kill a person, a small bullet is a poor choice for the job."

"Unless you want to be quiet about it. Back in New York I filed more than one murder story on the subject. Put a twenty-two right up next to a person and it makes less noise than a popping balloon."

"It was with that in mind that I managed to arrange and make an examination of the clothes she was wearing."

I shook my head. Escott could talk a tree out of its sap. "She was shot from a distance, right?"

"Correct. It's very possible that the person who shot her was an amateur."

"Just because it was a small bullet?"

"Because she was not killed outright. Did Kyler strike you as the type who would plan a murder and then botch the job?"

He had a point there. "Unless he wanted to make it look like the work of an amateur."

"The major objection I see against that is the fact that she did not simply disappear as did others before her. That's his usual pattern."

"Like Domax and Sanderson?"

"Hmm. A disappearance simply raises questions that may never have answers. Leaving a body to be found may result in the same situation, but one is at least certain of the violence involved and may work outward from that point."

"Okay, if we take Kyler out of things, who's left?"

"The same person who killed McAlister."

"I can figure that, Charles, but who?"

He shrugged. "We shan't discover that sitting around here."

"And Doreen?"

"We can always call the nurse on duty for any news concerning changes in her condition."

"What're you planning to do?"

"To get out and ask some questions. I suggest we start with Vaughn Kyler."

I nearly choked. "Great. Might as well start at the bottom and work our way up. How do we find him?"

"We won't have to. My researches today were most rewarding. . . ."

"You found out where he hangs his hat?"

"Not quite, but I've an idea on where to start. Care to come along?"

"Lead on, Macduff."

Escott winced. "That's 'lay on.' "

"Sorry."

"The misquote doesn't bother me so much as your choice of play to misquote from."

Escott was not even remotely a superstitious man—except when it came to the theater. His particular quirk had to do with *Macbeth*, and he never would say why. I apologized again, respecting the quirk, even if I didn't understand it.

He shook his shoulders straight and drew in a deep breath. "Ah, well, perhaps our surroundings will cancel out any malign influences. We can hope so, at least."

"Amen to that," I said, and followed him out.

Not that I was taking his stuff too seriously, but I did insist on a quick stop back at the office to pick up his bulletproof vest and the Webley-Fosbery. Just in case. If we got close enough to interview Kyler, he'd probably be frisked and not allowed to keep it. On the other hand, if Kyler didn't want to see us, we would very definitely need some protection. I still had Doreen's automatic, but without bullets it wasn't much more than a weight dragging in my pocket.

Escott stowed his gun into his shoulder holster. With his suit coat and overcoat on top, it was invisible, even to experienced eyes. Now I realized why he favored single-breasted styling; they look okay unbuttoned and he'd left things that way to be able to get at his gun more easily.

We were all set to go when the low rumble of a motor drew my attention to the outside. From either end of the front window, we peered through the slats of the blinds to the street below. A flashy new Packard had parked just in front of Escott's Nash.

"It's Pierce's car," I said. "Wonder what he wants?"

He shook his head and watched with interest as Griffin lurched from the Packard and crossed the sidewalk to our stairwell. For a big man he didn't make much noise, even on those creaking boards. The door shook a bit as he knocked.

Escott let him in and offered a greeting.

"Mr. Pierce extends an urgent request that you come to his house immediately," said Griffin. There was a hint of humor in his eyes. He was very aware of the artificially formal tone of the invitation.

"Did Mr. Pierce state the reason behind his urgency?"

"I am not at liberty to say, sir, but you may rely on the importance of it."

Escott looked ready to toss the ball back again. It was entertaining, but I didn't feel like standing around all night just to watch. "C'mon, Charles. We'll follow in your car and take care of the other business afterward."

He'd been all wound up to tackle Kyler, so it was tough going for him to have to switch his intentions so abruptly. His curiosity was up, though, and that helped. A minute later and we were on the road in the wake of the Packard.

I expected Pierce to have a big place and wasn't disappointed. The grounds were well kept but informal enough so that the keeping wasn't too obvious. His house was a big brick monster that must have been stacked together by a piecework crew. It had a couple of turrets with flags, gables, and extensions out of the main building that looked like additions made by the architect after he'd sobered up. Ugly as it was, it looked friendly, and there were warm lights showing in the windows.

Sebastian Pierce emerged from the front door before Escott could set the brake and signed for me to roll down my window.

"I don't want the servants to know what's up," he said. "We'll talk in the guest house around back." Without waiting for a reply he trotted forward on his long legs and hastily slipped into the passenger side of the Packard. It was a very cold night and all he wore over his clothes was a bulky sweater.

Though much smaller than the main house and built of humble wood, the guest house was enough to do an average family proud. Its two stories were painted a fresh-looking white with dark trim. The porch light was on and a window shade upstairs twitched, indicating someone was waiting for us.

Pierce was out and striding up the walk as soon as his car stopped. Escott and I had caught some of his nervous energy and quickly crowded onto the porch. Griffin wasn't moving as fast but managed to arrive just as Pierce unlocked the door and ushered us into a tiny parlor. An arched opening on our left led to a large living room, where he settled us by the fireplace. There was a good blaze going and Escott peeled off his gloves, gratefully extending his hands toward it.

"Now where have they got to?" Pierce muttered, glaring at the empty room. Somewhere upstairs, a toilet flushed. He looked at the ceiling as though he could see through it and nodded with satisfaction. "Good. Excuse me and I'll bring them down. They're probably having a last-minute attack of nerves."

He darted from the room, leaving us to look at each other. Griffin's face was bland and not giving anything away. He removed his chauffeur's hat and asked if he could take our coats. Escott shrugged out of his and I did the same. Griffin had just hung them in a closet when Pierce returned with company.

Marian came into the room, looking troubled and sulky, the picture of a kid who had been caught red-handed at the cookie jar. She wore a dark collegiate sweater over wide trousers and sturdy walking shoes that had seen some use. Her sable hair was pulled back and sported a demure black ribbon; all she needed to complete the effect was a pair of Harold Lloyd glasses. It was quite a contrast to the sleek, sophisticated girl who'd tried to suck my tonsils out last night.

"Is she his daughter?" murmured Escott.

"Uh-huh. Guard my back, would you?"

He made a small sound that might have been a laugh.

A second person reluctantly walked in, urged on by Pierce.

"Holy cats," I whispered. "He's been holding out on us."

"Well, well," said Escott, his tone conveying agreement and delight. "Miss Donovan, how nice to see you again."

Kitty Donovan looked up from the section of carpet she'd been staring at. Her huge eyes went first to Escott, then to me. Her face crumpled, then seemed to swell from the pressure of all the emotion she was trying to keep in check. Then she broke down and burst into tears.

Escott quietly and eloquently sighed.

It was shaping into another long night.

7

PIERCE WAS RIGHT next to her and in the best position to offer a
shoulder to cry on, or at least the middle of his chest, which was
as high as she came on him. None of the rest of us leaped
forward to take the job so he patted the back of her head and
told her everything was all right and let her soak his sweater for
a while.

Not knowing what else to do, I shoved my hands in my pockets and tried to look someplace else. The girl wasn't crying just
to cry. The gusting, ugly sounds that came from her were the
raw stuff of honest grief. She was in pain and there was nothing
anyone could do but let her get through it.

Escott gave them a wide berth as he stepped over to whisper
something to Griffin. The big man nodded and left for the back
of the house, returning with a flat bottle and a shot glass. He
poured some amber liquid out and passed it to Pierce. Though
teetotaling himself, he apparently didn't believe in enforcing it
onto others. He put the glass to Kitty's lips and got her to drink.
She choked, hiccuped, and settled a little. Her sobs became less
frequent and softer, but she still hung on to Pierce. He steered
her toward the sofa and they sat down together. When she groped
in the pocket of her dress and pulled out a sodden handkerchief,
Pierce took it away from her and replaced it with a dry one of
his own.

She blew her nose a few times and said she was sorry.

"It's all right, honey," said Marian, echoing her father's

calming assurances. "You've been through the wringer. Nobody minds when a little water has to come out."

Kitty responded with something unintelligible and blew her nose again. Marian relieved Pierce of the shot glass and had Griffin refill it. Kitty finished her second drink more quickly and easily than the first, welcoming its deadening effect.

"Would you gentlemen care for anything?" asked Griffin, lifting the bottle.

Escott declined. He wasn't exactly a cop, but sometimes considered himself to be "on duty." This was one of those times. As ever, I politely shook my head.

"At least some coffee, Griff," said Pierce. "A nice, big pot and very strong."

"Sinkers, too?"

"Yes, if we have them."

Griffin left the glass and bottle within Pierce's reach on a table and I presently heard him in the kitchen clattering around with things.

Escott sat on the edge of an easy chair opposite the sofa. "I'm very glad you sent for us, Mr. Pierce. What exactly is it that you require?"

"Some help, of course."

"I'll do what I can."

Pierce gave out with a good-natured snort. "I certainly hope so, or I'll want that retainer back."

The corners of Escott's mouth briefly curled and he leaned forward, going to work with a benign expression.

"Good evening, Miss Pierce, Miss Donovan."

Marian shot him a brief, meaningless smile and went to sit on the sofa next to Kitty. Kitty nodded and dropped her reddened eyes.

Pierce said, "I've convinced Kitty that she needs to talk with the police. But first I wanted her to tell you what happened so you can find out who did kill Stan. I'm hoping you'll be able to get her off the hook."

"Your confidence in me is most flattering, but I can make no promises."

"If you tried to at this point, you'd be going out the door right now."

"Fair enough. Miss Donovan, would you please tell us all that you did last night?"

It was slow in coming. The girl was obviously uncomfortable with everyone looking at her. Pierce nodded encouragement and once in a while Marian patted her friend's hand.

"Stan and I had a date," she said in a flat, lifeless voice. "I was waiting for him at the Angel Grill. I was there extra early—"

"Why was that?" asked Escott.

"I had some displays to arrange at a department store and finished them sooner than I'd expected. I didn't feel like going home just to go right out again, which was all I would have had time for, so I went straight to the Angel. While I was there one of his friends came over, a guy named Shorty."

"Has he another name to go with that one?"

"Shorty was all Stan ever called him."

"Describe him."

"Well . . . he's short," she said unhelpfully.

I envied Escott's patience. He tried another tack. "What sort of clothes does he wear?"

She was on firmer ground here. "Cheap and awful. They're good enough for him to get by, but he doesn't clean them. He had egg stains on his coat, and he smokes cigars—he just reeked from them."

By working off of the girl's emotional reaction to the man, he was able to get a fairly complete description. One detail led to the next. He produced a notebook and took it all down, then asked, "What did he want, Miss Donovan?"

"He was trying to tell me that Leadfoot Sam was looking for Stan."

"Trying?"

"He didn't just come out and say it, he kind of talked around it, hinting. I put him off and tried to ignore him, but he kept hanging around as though he wanted something, and kept *hinting*. I finally got the idea that Stan was in trouble and that I'd better let him know so he could avoid it. Stan wasn't due for another thirty minutes and Shorty had scared me. He said that Leadfoot knew where Stan lived and might be waiting for him there. I couldn't just sit around after hearing all that, so I left."

"For the Boswell House?"

"Uh-huh. That's when I ran into the two of you."

He smiled to let her know all was forgiven. "Now, tell me exactly what happened after you left the hotel."

"I went straight home. I thought Stan might go there, too. When I saw his car on the street out front, I knew I'd guessed right, and went inside."

"Was your door locked?"

"Yes. I unlocked it, went inside, and locked it behind me."

"You were still nervous?"

"I was still scared."

He nodded, not blaming her for that. "Did Mr. McAlister have a key to your door?"

She didn't blush and said yes in an even tone.

"Is that the only way one can get into the building?"

"I think so."

"No unlocked back doors?"

"I don't know. You'd have to ask the manager."

"Very well. What did you do after you were inside?"

"I called for him, but he didn't answer. I thought he might be in the bathroom, but he wasn't. I checked all over and then I went into the kitchen. I don't remember much after walking in. I know I saw him, but that's all. I know I saw him, but I don't remember seeing him."

"You were in shock, honey," said Marian, squeezing her hand. "Don't let it worry you. You're better off not remembering."

"But it *feels* strange."

Escott continued. "What is the next thing that you can recall?"

"Waking up in my room. I heard two men talking down the hall—you two. I was scared. I thought maybe you'd done it. All I wanted was to get out, so I took the fire escape and ran and ran. I just couldn't stand it. I had to run."

"That's where I come in," said Marian. "She drove over here to see me, but I hadn't gotten home yet."

"Then Miss Donovan talked to one of the servants?"

Kitty shook her head, probably more than she needed to, but the drinks were working on her now. "I didn't dare. I took the back road in to the estate and put my car in the guest house garage. Then I came in here and tried to call Marian on the phone."

"How did you get in?"

"I checked under the doormat for a key and got lucky."

"What did you do when you could not reach Miss Pierce on the phone?"

"Nothing. That is, I couldn't do anything. I had to sit in the dark or someone from the main house might look out and see the lights. It was cold. I couldn't build a fire because of the smoke, and I was afraid to change the furnace setting. It's only high enough to keep the water pipes from freezing. But I turned on the electric stove in the kitchen and left its door open and that helped. Then I found some blankets and wrapped up."

Escott looked sympathetic. "So you stayed here until you could reach Miss Pierce?"

"All night."

"It must have been most uncomfortable."

"I don't remember much of that, either. I had a little brandy and it went right to my head. I just fell asleep at the kitchen table."

Considering the emotional strain and the fact that she'd missed dinner, it was no surprise, but I could almost see the sneer on the prosecutor's face if she brought that story to court. Real damsels in distress were few and far between, even if they looked the part as Kitty did.

Griffin returned just then with a tray full of cups, milk, sugar, and the long-awaited coffee. A plate stacked with donuts was on one side of it and on the other was a smaller plate with a neatly made up sandwich. He put it all down on the coffee table and handed the sandwich plate directly to Kitty. She accepted it with some confusion.

"Eat," he ordered in a stern voice. Wide-eyed because he was nothing if not impressive, the girl picked it up and took a bite. A second later she remembered to chew and swallow. Once the process was started, she had no trouble finishing.

The food almost turned it into a social occasion, and Escott had to wait as cups were filled and donuts were passed. I declined offers of both and hung back by the fireplace. My hands felt cold. They shouldn't have, since I was fairly indifferent to anything but the most extreme temperatures now. Maybe it had to do with the question I would have to ask her. It wasn't so much the question, but the method I'd need to use to get my answer.

"Not hungry?" Marian came to stand next to me, a coffee cup in one hand.

"I had dinner just before Griffin came for us."

She looked me over. "I'll bet you're one of those men who eats like a horse and never shows it."

"Maybe I am." I was uneasy with the conversation. She seemed the type to insist I have something and take a refusal as an insult. A subject change was in order. "I understand you and Harry Summers made up."

Her eyes were still fastened on me. Their pure blue color was just as lovely, but harder and colder, like a mountain lake with ice in it. It had probably been a bad move to remind her about last night. "Yes, Harry and I are all lovey-dovey again."

"I'm glad to hear it."

A hostile line appeared in the set of her mouth, then softened. "So's Harry. It was all his idea, after all."

"He said he was crazy about you."

"I know that. He only tells me so a hundred times a day."

"You could do worse."

"Like with you?" She smiled. It wasn't an especially nice one.

"Like with Stan McAlister."

She blinked, as though I'd smacked her on the nose.

"What did you tell him at the club?"

"Tell him? I don't know what you mean."

"Yes, you do. You were seen sitting at the same table and talking. He got up and left, then you did the same. What did you say?"

She blushed. Under her carefully applied face powder, it looked muddy rather than becoming. "Damn Daddy, anyway," she whispered, her teeth exactly on edge.

"Never mind that. What did you say?"

She put down her coffee cup because her hands were shaking. She was plenty mad. "All I did was say that I met you and that I thought Daddy had hired you to follow me."

"Why would that make Stan bolt the place?"

"It didn't. He asked me a lot of questions about the talk you and I had, and then he said that you weren't after me, but after him. That's when he left. I'd wondered why at the time, but now I know he was afraid because of the bracelet he'd stolen. He must have realized the theft had been noticed and that you were there to find him."

"Why would he talk to you, then?"

She looked puzzled. "Why not?"

"Since he stole the bracelet from you, I should think you'd be the last person he'd want to see."

"Not if he was trying to play innocent about it all. Stan only had to lie, you know. I'm sure he was good at it. He'd be able to stand up to me or even Daddy, but it must have all fallen apart for him the moment he thought someone was actually after him."

"Yeah, I guess it must. Did he say where he was going in such a big hurry?"

"No, but he had to have gone straight to his hotel. Kitty said that you and your partner scared him off."

"With some help from Kitty."

"Don't be so hard on her, she really loved him. She was expecting to marry him."

Oh, good Lord. "With your bracelet as a wedding present?"

She started to blurt out some kind of a retort and caught herself before any sound came out. She looked over at Kitty, a sick expression on her face. "Oh, my God, you can't mean it."

"I gotta look at things the way the cops would."

"But Kitty wouldn't do anything like that."

"Like what? Theft or murder?"

"Either one."

"Maybe you could be a character witness, but you'd better work on your delivery. Right now, it's not too convincing."

"You—" She bit the word off but I had a good idea about what she'd wanted to say. I'd been called worse. Name calling wouldn't have eased things for her; what she really wanted to do was to knock my block off.

"Who do you think did it?" I asked.

"Leadfoot Sam," she spat. "Whoever he is. Kitty knows a little bit about him. Not much, but enough to be scared."

"And if he didn't?"

"I'm sure I don't know, perhaps some one of Stan's other friends. He must have had others. Why don't you find that man Kitty told you about—Shorty—and ask him?"

"What about you?"

"I wouldn't know where to look."

"I mean did you do it?"

A soft laugh puffed from her. "Don't be ridiculous. Besides, I was with Harry."

"Then both of you were in on it, or maybe you talked him into covering for you. Or you're covering for him."

"Is that the best you can do? Why would either of us want to kill poor Stan?"

"I learned enough about 'poor Stan' last night to know that a lot of people might have wanted to kill him."

"Then go talk to them; I'm not part of that crowd." She swept back to the sofa to sit next to Kitty again. She glanced once at me with obvious distaste, then turned her attention to the others. Maybe she was hoping I'd just disappear as I had in the parking lot.

The short break had given her drinks time to really circulate into Kitty's system. She was a lot more relaxed when Escott resumed his questioning.

"Once you were able to get hold of Miss Pierce, what did you say to her?" he asked.

"I told her I was in a jam and to come see me here."

"Presumably without being seen to do it."

The girl nodded. "And then she got here and I told her everything that had happened . . . what I could remember of it."

"What time did this interview take place?"

"Sometime this morning," answered Marian. "Around ten or so."

"And when did you decide to mention it to your father?"

Pierce glowered at them. "They didn't."

"How did you find out?"

"My study window overlooks this whole area. When I saw Marian tiptoeing around in her own yard I had a feeling something was going on and came down to find out why."

"Which you did," said Marian, smiling as though chagrined at being caught. But her smile was a tight one and didn't reach her eyes. She clearly resented his checking up on her.

"Which I did," repeated Pierce. "And a good thing, too. These two innocents had some crackpot plan to hide Kitty out here until the fuss had died down, and then take off for Mexico. Lord knows what would have happened to them. . . . White slavers or worse."

Marian restrained herself and did not roll her eyes.

"Then you sent for me rather than inform the authorities," Escott concluded.

Pierce was scowling, but not too seriously. "I needed time to

hear her side of things and figure out what to do next. I talked
with my lawyer, but he's not a specialist in criminal law. Right
this minute he's doing what he can to find someone who can
help us.''

"Once he does and after he's had a chance to talk to Miss
Donovan as well, I think you should take her in as quickly as
possible to make a statement. It might look better for her."

"It might look better, but would it *be* better?"

"To be honest, I don't know. Legally, you are required to
do as I've suggested. There is a warrant out on Miss Donovan, and the longer you delay, the worse it can get. You and
your daughter could end up facing charges for harboring a
fugitive."

Pierce erupted from the sofa. The living room was really too
small for him to decently pace off his anger. He vented some of
it verbally, his colorful abuse aimed at the law in general and
the criminal court system in particular. "I've half a mind to go
along with your plan and put you on the next train out of town,"
he concluded, looking at Kitty.

"Then they would know I was guilty," she murmured. She
was almost in tears again from his outburst and was shaking
from the effort to keep them in. Marian was stone-faced bored.
Perhaps she was well used to her father's tempers.

"Of course you're not guilty." He started to add something,
then realized what shape the girl was in and put a lid on it. "I
just want to do what's best for you. It's about time someone
did."

If Kitty failed to notice what he said and how he said it,
Marian did not. She was as stone-faced as ever, but her big eyes
narrowed slightly.

"Miss Donovan?" I was adopting Escott's formal manner. It
seemed right for the question I had to ask.

She looked up at me, glad for a distraction.

"Just to set the record straight for us, did you kill Stan?"

Pierce started to erupt again, this time his anger directed toward me, but Escott stopped him. Escott knew what I was doing
and knew that I had to be careful not to let it be noticed. It
wasn't hard, since everyone was looking at Kitty, waiting to hear
what she said.

She didn't answer right away. I repeated my question, holding
her eyes. When she did answer, it was with a negative. It even

came out sounding normal—or as normal as a person could sound, given the circumstances.

I continued to concentrate on her. I wasn't seducing her, she wasn't seducing me. This was simple influencing to get at the truth. I had to remember that to keep myself steady, to stay in control.

"Do you have any idea who might have done it?"

"Leadfoot Sam," she said without hesitation.

I let up on the light pressure I exerted. The girl was unharmed and nothing else had happened. Memory and conscience still writhed inside like bloated worms, but I could ignore them for now.

"Why do you think that, Miss Donovan?" Escott asked, picking up the slack before anyone knew it was there.

She displayed no awareness of my mental tampering. "Because of what Shorty told me. But I don't know why or how it could have happened at my place."

I had an idea or two, but kept shut about them.

"Have you been here all day?" he continued.

"Yes."

"Alone?"

"Yes, except when Marian was here."

"When was that?"

"This morning . . . after ten, wasn't it?"

Marian confirmed the time.

He shifted his attention to her. "How long did you stay here, Miss Pierce?"

"An hour or so, maybe a little longer."

"What did you do after you left?"

"I went back to the main house and tried to pretend nothing was wrong."

"Did you visit Miss Donovan at all throughout the day?"

"No, I couldn't do that or it might have looked funny." She broke off as her father nodded agreement, then resumed. "So I called her a few times to check on her, to see if she was all right. I'd let it ring once, then dial again so she'd know it was me."

"And she was there each time?"

"Yes, of course."

"And what times did you call?"

Marian shrugged. "I don't know, after twelve and again at two and three."

"You were at home when you made these calls?"

"No, not for all of them. I went out shopping."

"Shopping?"

"Kitty didn't have any extra clothes or even a toothbrush. I couldn't loan her any of my clothes since they don't fit her, so I went to get her a few things and some groceries."

"When did you do this?"

"At about one. I left after lunch."

"And returned?"

"Around four, I think."

"Is that not a long time to be shopping?"

"You don't know my daughter, Mr. Escott," said Pierce. "A three-hour trip means she's only just started. Why are you so interested in the time?"

Escott held silent a moment. I found myself holding my breath, even though I don't usually breathe. "There's been a shooting," he finally said. "It may quite well be connected to McAlister's death."

A little ripple of surprise went through them and the usual questions came out. Not all of them were answered. Escott kept shut about who was shot and where she was now. He only said that the person was a friend of McAlister's and left it at that, which left them all highly dissatisfied.

"The police are still investigating. I cannot give out any more information than that."

"But how is it related to Stan's death?" asked Pierce.

"I'm not certain at this point, though considering the facts we have, one may come to a logical conclusion. The more immediate problem for us is that Miss Donovan does not have an alibi for the time of the shooting."

"What time was that?"

"The police think it happened between three-thirty and four, when the victim was discovered."

"Where did it happen?"

"At a city park less than a mile from this very house."

"Oh, good God."

"But I was *here*," said Kitty.

"Have you proof?" he shot back.

The girl went white around the lips and shrank back into the couch.

"Miss Donovan need not have even used her car; it's but a twenty-minute walk both ways . . ."

Kitty made a sound halfway between a moan and a whimper.

"Shut up, Escott," Pierce snapped.

Escott ignored him. "Have you an alibi for the time, Mr. Pierce?"

Pierce opened his mouth to say something and left it hanging that way as the implications sank in.

"Does Mr. Griffin have an alibi, or your daughter?"

"Me?" Marian's eyes went wide and she groped for her father's hand. Griffin's brow puckered.

Pierce shut his mouth, shaking his head. "All right, I see what you're getting at, not that I like it very much."

"Neither do I," said Marian. "Why are you talking to us? Shouldn't you be checking on this Leadfoot Sam or Shorty?"

"I expect I shall be doing just that after I've finished with things here. Miss Donovan, do you still have the gun that was in your possession last night?"

Kitty looked blank. "Gun?"

"Remember in the hotel lobby?" I prodded. "Or was that a dime-store toy?"

The memory reluctantly returned. "I guess it's still in my purse."

"Where's your purse?"

"Upstairs, in the first bedroom."

Pierce volunteered to go get it, but Escott said no and sent me. The stairs were just off the parlor and went straight up without any turns. The first door next to the landing stood open and the room beyond looked occupied. The bed had been made up, but the covers were all wrinkled, and feminine clothing lay scattered around. The wastebasket was overflowing with tissue wrap and a stack of empty boxes stood next to the dresser, evidence of Marian's shopping jaunt.

On the dresser was Kitty's purse. Inside the purse was her little automatic. It was the one I remembered from last night and it was a .22.

I filched a handkerchief to pick it up and sniffed the barrel. It hadn't been fired. She could have cleaned it, but there was no evidence of fresh gun oil. I searched the room and could find no cleaning kit, but something like that could be anywhere in the house or out in the garage with her car. Kitty hadn't killed McAlister, and though I couldn't see her gunning down Doreen, either, my vision might not count for much. I could be near-sighted.

I came back down to a silent room. None of them seemed too happy when I exhibited the gun in its cloth nest. Escott took a close look without touching it and sniffed the barrel as well, then dismissed it.

"Are there other guns in this house or the main house?"

Pierce nodded. "I've a couple of hunting rifles and a Luger."

"What caliber are the rifles?"

"They're both .30-30s."

"You should be safe enough, then, though I would advise you bring them to the attention of your lawyer when the time comes."

"This person who was shot . . . is he dead?"

Escott went quite still, studying each in turn. I hoped that he was reading more from them than I. "Yes, I'm sorry to say."

"Damn it. How does this tie in with McAlister?"

"The bracelet."

"Always that goddamned bracelet," he rumbled. He came to attention as a new thought hit him. "Did he have the bracelet? Was it . . . ?"

"The bracelet was not on the body." Escott bent his eye on Kitty again. "Miss Donovan, were you aware that McAlister might have stolen Miss Pierce's bracelet?"

"Not until Mr. Pierce told me about it tonight. I feel terrible that I was the one to bring Stan into the house."

"Do you believe he stole it?"

She faltered. "Well, that's what Mr. Pierce said. . . ." She looked at him for support and got it.

"Of course he stole it," he told her. "But there's no need to worry about that. It's over and done with. Whoever killed him probably got the bracelet, and I could care less."

"Do you, indeed?" queried Escott.

"What do you mean by that?"

"I cannot say, but may be able to tell you presently. What's needed now is to tell the police your side of things and make them believe it, something that's best done with experienced legal help."

Pierce took the hint with a heavy sigh. "All right. I'll phone and see if the old shyster's turned up a likely candidate."

He did some dialing, located his lawyer, and broke into a smile at the news he got. Arrangements were made for a meeting. Kitty would have to repeat her story, first to the new lawyer, and then to the police. I hoped that she had the stamina to last through the process. She had a long night ahead.

Escott was asked to come along, but declined. "Your lawyer is your best help there," he said. "Besides, you want the real criminal brought in, and I cannot work on the problem from the police station."

I also suspected he wanted to keep some distance between himself and Lieutenant Blair for the time being. Pierce accepted the point as it was given and didn't press things.

After we got our coats, Pierce excused himself and walked us out to the car.

"You don't really think that little girl did anything?" he asked Escott. Away from the others, his confident front wavered; his own private fears were more noticeable, now.

"No," he replied. "But I do believe she has been used and used wretchedly. Finding proof of it is quite another thing, though."

"Is that what you're going after?"

"I hope so." Escott got into the driver's side, started the motor and got us moving. It was at a snail's pace. His driving sometimes reflected his preoccupation with a problem: the busier his mind, the slower he drove.

"Good move back there," I said. "Were you hoping to find out something by making them think Doreen was dead?"

"I was, but not with any reasonable expectations. My primary purpose was to ensure some little safety for Miss Grey by assuring her attacker of her inability to talk."

"If he or she was there to hear it."

"Hmm."

"That bit about the key to the flat . . . McAlister didn't have one on him, did he?"

"No. His pockets had been turned out. His wallet was gone, and if he had been carrying his own key, it was also gone, no doubt taken by the murderer. Any prosecutor will hold that Miss

Donovan must have let him in herself. We've only her say-so that McAlister possessed one."

"Which he probably did, since we know she didn't do it."

"It's a pity we cannot bring Lieutenant Blair into our confidence on that point. . . ." He caught my look. "Never mind."

"Leaving Kitty out of it means that Stan let in the killer. He either answered the buzzer or met him outside and they walked in together."

"And in ten minutes or less he is lying dead on the kitchen floor and the killer gone."

"Fast worker," I said.

"Why the kitchen?" he mused.

"It's loaded with weapons."

"So are most rooms in a house. Your conclusion implies a degree of premeditation, and the attack on McAlister looked impulsive to me. It was cold; perhaps they went there to find something with which to warm themselves."

"They get to arguing, McAlister turns his back, gets clubbed with a frying pan, and stabbed for good measure to make sure he's really dead."

"Something that I have noted is that if a woman is murdered, the violence frequently occurs in the bedroom, but when a woman herself murders, she chooses the kitchen as her stage."

"You're thinking of Marian Pierce?"

"As a possibility."

"What's her motive?"

"Unknown at present. Perhaps later you might talk with her and ascertain if one exists."

I didn't like this turn of the conversation at all. I wasn't ready to start explaining to Escott that I had given up hypnotic interviews. I tried for a change of subject. "You said something about a logical conclusion. . . . Wanna share it?"

One of his eyebrows bounced. "Yes, well, it has to do with Miss Grey and the bracelet. I believe she had it all along."

I winced inside.

"And if she did have it, then perhaps she was shot for it."

He left unspoken the implication that if I'd bothered to ask an obvious question last night, she might never have been shot at all.

"It was not in her possession when she was found. One may presume either a passerby performed a bit of impromptu larceny and escaped, or that the theft was accomplished by the one who shot her."

"And you don't think it was Kyler?"

"I really haven't enough information one way or another concerning his complicity to be able to make any kind of a judgment. He is most certainly involved, but we must determine the degree of his involvement."

"And maybe get Kitty off the hook?"

"We may hope as much. Her information was not utterly devoid of interest." He pulled out a silver cigarette case and juggled with it. The Nash threatened to cut a fresh road over someone's yard. I put out a hand to steady the wheel. He took advantage of the break and quickly drew out a cigarette and put it in his mouth. If we were at home or at the office, it would have been his less portable pipe.

"Like the part about Shorty?" I asked.

"Hmm." He struck a match.

"You think you know him?"

"I believe I know of him, though I've never actually met the fellow."

"Who is he?"

"A dweller on the fringe, I expect."

I briefly wondered if his damned smoking set him off on a tangent or if he only used it as an excuse to do so. Either way, the effect was the same. "Want to explain that?"

"You've met his type before. They never seem to work, but somehow manage to get by. They bounce from one unpaid bill to another and are experts at the art of living off the charity of others."

"The crash made a lot of guys that way."

"People like Shorty have always been that way. Their prime concern in life is usually centered upon their next meal."

"Or their next drink."

"There's that, too, though I believe the addiction to drink is but a symptom, and not the problem itself. I've seen hundreds of them . . . sad faces, angry faces, lost faces, and faces with nothing left in them at all. One wonders where they've come from and where they will go and what ruined dreams may lie behind their empty eyes.''

''That's what I like about you, Charles . . . you're such cheerful company.''

''I'm in a cheerful mood,'' he said.

''So are we headed for this fringe to look for Shorty or are you planning to tackle Kyler?''

''Oh, we shall interview Shorty first.''

''Why? About all he can do is back up Kitty's story.''

''And perhaps a bit more—if he is what I think he is.''

''Some kind of stoolie?''

''An information salesman,'' he conceded, always one to put a polish on things. ''I'm hoping he will give us a line on Kyler— or rather sell us one and thus save us a bit of time.''

''So what was he doing giving stuff away free to Kitty?''

''I'm not so certain that it was intentional, but perhaps he was hoping his early warning might have generated some income from a grateful McAlister.''

''How many stoolies have you met who were that dumb?''

He decided not to answer and focused his attention on the road and his cigarette. It was still fairly early and the amount of traffic reflected the hour. You'd think they'd all be huddled by their firesides, still gloating over their Christmas presents. If any. The last eight years had been starvation lean for too many people, and the realities rarely matched up with the cozy ideals in the magazine ads. I stared out the passenger window and watched the neighborhoods change from ritzy to nice, to good, to downright hostile, and back again. Escott finally slowed and parked the Nash in a borderland area of good that was starting to lose out to hostile.

Across the street a series of low buildings crowded close to each other, as if for warmth. On one of them hung a painted sign advertising the Angel Bar and Grill. One side of the sign was lighted, the other, with its broken bulb, dark.

Borderland.

''Looks like just the sort of place a guy like Stan would bring his girl,'' I said.

''One way or another, it would be certain to leave an impression.''

A trace of rain hung in the air, just enough to dampen the streets and make us cautious of our footing as we crossed

over and went inside. The place wasn't that big, but it was
crowded and dim. Escott nodded once at me and went over
to the bar. I peeled away and made a circuit of the room,
looking for anyone who matched Kitty's description of
Shorty.

A lot of unfamiliar faces looked back, reminding me of the
ones Escott had spoken of earlier. I shook off the image and
concentrated on the job.

Someone tugged at my coat from behind. "Hey, Jack."

I turned, mindful of pickpockets, and wondering who
could possibly know me here. No pickpocket this time, just
Pony Jones with his curiosity up. Pony did enough bookie
business to keep himself, but not so much that he drew attention from the big boys. Escott had introduced us some
months back when we were doing some other job. Pony always looked drunk, but never forgot a face or a name except
as a dodge to trouble, then he became as vague as his ap-
pearance suggested.

Sitting next to him was his half-brother, Elmer, sometimes
known as Elmtree Elmer since he was tall and about as tough.
He had a brain deep inside that big body, but was lazy about
using it, and usually content to let Pony do his thinking for
him.

"What'ya doin' here?" asked Pony.

I could almost see all the ears swiveling in our direction.
There was space at their small table, so I slipped into a chair
opposite them. "Hi, Pony, Elmer. How's business?" As I drew
breath to speak, I got a strong whiff of stale smoke, beer, and
sweat.

"Good 'n' bad."

"Looks like the bad's winning."

Elmer didn't react at all, choosing to play dense tonight.
Pony's crab-apple face only crumpled a bit more. "Don't be a
wise ass. You still working for that limey bastard?"

"Yeah, he's here with me."

Elmer grimaced. He liked Escott about as much as I liked
sunbaths.

"Why are you sitting with your back to the door?" I asked.

" 'Cause my back can stand the draft better than my front.
Who ya lookin' for?" His dark little eyes were avid. He knew I
was off my usual track in coming to a place like the Angel.

"You wouldn't know him."

His mouth twisted. "C'mon, Jack, no need to dance around all night. Just say a name an' I'll let you know if I know 'um.'"

"Uh-huh."

"Flat fee, only a sawbuck."

"Try a buck, Pony." Over his shoulder, I saw Escott had finished talking with the bartender. I caught his eye and shook my head once so he wouldn't interrupt.

"Aw, c'mon, I got family to support."

"Fine, go get a regular job." I made to get up.

"Okay, a buck's fine, but only if I know 'em. Cost you more to find out more."

That always went without saying. "Guy named Shorty."

"My sweet Aunt Tilly, you know how many guys I know named Shorty? F'cryin' out loud, some jerkballs even call *me* Shorty."

I gave him my best and broadest grin. Though my canines were neatly retracted, it was more than effective. He tumbled right away.

"Aww, no, Jack . . ."

"Aww, yes, Pony."

Pony shrugged, flashed a yellow grin of his own, and rubbed his thumb against his fingers. I found a dollar and he made it vanish. He kept his hand out and tried to look like a hurt puppy.

"I said more will cost you more."

"This place is too crowded for talk."

He made a show of resignation. "Okay. We gotta flop close by, but I'd have to show you."

I caught Escott's eye again as I stood up. "Fine with me, Pony. I could use the exercise."

"What? Right now? It's cold out."

"Yeah, it'll probably be like that 'til spring."

Elmer was looking alert and damped it down when Pony shrugged at him. He'd accepted his fate and would go quietly. He stood, all five feet one of him a visible declaration of his least favorite moniker, and made a show of buttoning up his coat.

We walked to the door, Elmer leading, Pony behind him, and me ready for either of them to try anything. Escott was there ahead of us and held it open. Elmer paused to sneer at him and caused a minor bottleneck.

Pony Jones was nothing if not an opportunist. He slithered around Elmer and, true to his nickname, bolted.

8

I GOT MY arm out fast enough, but Pony dodged, and my fingers only brushed his collar. Without thinking, I went transparent and shot right through Elmer's intervening bulk. Maybe he'd attribute his rush of abrupt cold to the winter air. I only hoped that the Angel's other patrons would put the alarming vision of a ghost-man running through him down to morbid imagination and take care of it at the bar.

Pony was little and had some years against him, but he was on his home ground. Though only seconds behind him, I almost missed it as he ducked between buildings. Delayed as he was by having to go around, rather than through, Elmer, Escott was seconds more behind me. He'd just have to catch up when he could; I didn't dare wait.

Pony Jones's small form threaded out the other end of the alley and cut right. By the time I did the same he was out of view, but I heard the slap of his feet against concrete down another turning. When I'd made that one, he'd doubled back to another dank passage. A moment later his footsteps stopped.

I took note of that: they'd stopped, not faded into the distance. He was holding his breath somewhere, banking on the darkness to hide him. As far as I could judge the area was pitch dark—to human eyes.

I picked my way carefully down the alley, my footfalls as soft as I could make them. No doubt in his own ears Pony's heartbeat would drown out their minimal sound. At the far end was a disordered row of trash cans, the tumbled remains of a discarded armchair, and an unidentifiable bundle of odds and ends that might once have been clothes.

The bundle was breathing, very quietly, and its heart was racing. I reached into it, this time getting a good grip on the collar before hauling him up.

"Aww, Jack . . ." he whined, shedding rags and limp sheets of newspaper.

I got my bearings and found we'd all but circled back to the alley behind the Angel. Escott popped into sight less than fifty feet away. I called to him. He skidded to a halt, peering doubtfully in my general direction. It reminded me just how dark it was for him. I kept my grip on Pony's collar and marched him forward. Spill from a distant streetlight defined our figures as we emerged into view.

"Well, well," he said, straightening his hat. "Was there any reason behind your quick exit, Pony?"

Pony dropped into his first line of defense, which was to shuffle with a bowed head and mumble that he didn't know nothin'.

"I see. Then you aren't too terribly interested in increasing this evening's profits?"

Scenting more money, Pony raised his head.

Elmer trotted up, puffing. "Leggo a' Pony," he told me, expecting instant obedience.

Escott got in between us. "Hold off your rescue for just another moment, Elmer, we're conducting a business deal."

"Huh?"

"Deal?" said Pony at the same time.

"Money for information is the usual pattern, is it not?"

Elmer became surly as he cottoned onto the fact that Pony wouldn't allow him to beat up on a potential source of income. "Why'n'cha talk normal, so's a guy knows what you're sayin'?"

"I think we understand each other well enough, Elmer."

"Limey bastard," he muttered, echoing Pony's earlier comment. The last time Elmer had dealt with Escott, he'd spent a few days in jail. He wasn't the forgiving type.

Escott had a smile on his face—a rather serene one at that—when he abruptly hauled Elmer around by both shoulders and slammed him back first against a wall. Elmer yelped in surprise, shock, and pain, cramming it all into the same sound. The impact inspired him to fight back, and he brought a sudden fist up and threw a gut punch with as much force as he could muster. He missed the bulletproof vest by an inch, digging in just below the belt.

Escott hissed once through his teeth but kept his grip. He was still smiling when he bounced Elmer against the wall again. And again, very hard. The third time he let go, and Elmer slithered to the ground and stopped moving.

He'd startled me, because though I'd seen him angry before, I'd never seen Escott lose his temper.

He stared down at Elmer, immobile except for a slight tremor in his hands as the excess adrenaline wore off. His smile gradually disappeared, easing away by small degrees until nothing was left but an impassive mask. Considering the insult, his initial show of teeth was understandable, but the mask I saw now made me uneasy.

"Charles?"

He brought one hand up, fingers spread a little, the gesture a request for silence. I clamped my mouth shut and waited.

He turned slowly away from Elmer and faced Pony. The mask was still in place. If I was uneasy, Pony was definitely frightened. Escott plucked Pony away from me and pushed his back to the same wall, pinning his shoulders to it. Both glanced down at Elmer's semiconscious form and then at each other. They arrived at an obvious conclusion at the same time. Pony gulped unhappily.

"Why did you run?" Escott asked him, his tone dangerously reasonable.

Pony shook his head. "Just wanted to, that's all."

There was more behind it, but Escott let it pass. "Tell me what you said to Kitty Donovan."

"Who?"

"Stan McAlister's lady friend."

"But I don't know . . ."

Escott shook him once so that his teeth clicked, then leaned in close. "Jones, we got off on the wrong foot, though that situation may be easily corrected. What you must keep in mind is that *it can get worse.*" He let that sink in. "Do you wish that?"

Pony shook his head a lot. He'd never seen Escott like this before. His last bit of resistance faded.

Even in the dim light, Escott read it in his face and posture.

"Good man. Now tell me what you did and said last night concerning Stan McAlister."

"It wasn't much," he said, licking his lips. "I saw his little twist walk in and park. Thought I'd go over and tell her that that clown Leadfoot had a head of steam up about Stan's owing him."

"Out of the goodness of your heart?"

"Don't be a—ahh, no, I thought I could get something outta her for it, but the kid's green as grass. She din' know what I was gettin' at or that it was supposed to be for sale. By the time I dropped enough hints on her, she'd put things together herself and ran out on me." He raised his eyes, looking for approval. He was disappointed.

"Was there a hit out on McAlister?"

"I dunno."

"How did you find out about McAlister's troubles with Leadfoot?"

"I keep my ears open, as usual."

"Exact information, Pony."

"But there ain't any. You know how it is. The news just goes around. I maybe heard it at the Imperial."

"Which is . . . ?"

"A pool hall. Leadfoot's muscle hangs around there. Sometimes they talk."

"And who else was there?"

"I dunno what you—"

"Who else was looking for McAlister?"

Pony shut his mouth.

"Was it Vaughn Kyler? Was it one of his men?"

"No! I dunno."

Escott's smile threatened to return. "Will I be able to find Kyler there?"

Pony was breathing fast, then he brought it under sudden control. His little eyes lit up with new confidence. "Yeah, you'll find him there—or at the Satchel. He keeps on the move, but you ask around and you'll find him . . . or maybe he'll find you." That thought cheered him—a lot.

"Then I'll be sure to tell him you said hello."

Pony dropped his grin and went six different kinds of pale. He struggled and pushed away. Escott let him go. Pony vanished around the next corner, content to escape himself and leave Elmer to our tender mercies. Maybe he'd return later to pick him up, but I wouldn't want to bet on it. Not that it mattered much; Elmer was showing signs of waking and might be long gone before Pony got up enough courage to check on him.

"You fight dirty, you know that?" I said as we walked back to the car.

"Pah, the man was hardly worth the effort, but at least we got some names from him."

"Yeah. Which place do we start with?"

"The Satchel, unless you want to risk running into Leadfoot Sam again."

"Uh-uh. I've had enough of him for one lifetime."

"I daresay he might share the same opinion about you."

He drove to an unpretentious neighborhood with modest and respectable storefronts and stuffily closed businesses. The only lights showing at this hour came from an undistinguished two-story brick building in the middle of the block. Cars lined both sides of the street. One of them pulled away as we came up, and Escott pounced on the empty spot.

"You sure this is it?" I asked. "I don't see any sign out."

He set the brake. "An establishment like the Satchel hardly needs or wishes to call undue attention to itself."

That's when the dawn came and I sat up a little straighter. "How'd it get a name like that?"

"I believe it's related in some way to the satchel the collection man carries on his rounds. This particular place is used as a sort of bank; the various funds are added, divided, and dispatched from here."

"Where do they go?"

"My dear fellow, though this city is not very old when compared with others, it does have a quite lively and consistent history of corruption to make up for its relative youth. . . . Use your imagination."

I didn't have to use much, since I'd seen the same thing in other places. Vice flourishes best when it makes regular contributions in the right pockets. We went up the steps together and opened the double doors. Music was playing somewhere inside.

"Wait a sec," I said.

He paused and turned to look where I was looking. A new Cadillac with smoke-dark windows was parked not twenty feet from the entrance.

"I think we've come to the right place, Charles."

"His car?"

"Or one of his stooges. Keep your eyes open."

"With pleasure."

The foyer was conservative: simple white curtains, a plant in a big brass pot, and a square of carpet, but then this part of the house was visible from the street each time the door opened. Furniture was limited to a table holding up a lamp and a chair next to it holding up the bouncer. He had the kind of scar tissue you get from boxing, maybe a couple pounds' worth, and all the rest of him was hard muscle. He gave us a close and practiced look, nodded, and pressed a button on the little table. A buzzer buzzed and Escott opened the next door in.

The parlor was fancier. A big Christmas tree stood in front of the curtained window, buried under sheets of tinsel and glass ornament. A wire was strung across the wall on that side, loaded with dozens of Christmas cards. At first it seemed odd, but then I thought, Why not? There was no reason why working girls shouldn't celebrate the holidays like everyone else.

In one corner was a phonograph, in the other a radio. Both were on and trying to cancel each other out with competing tunes. A short girl with thin legs was busy sorting through the records and hardly troubled to glance up. Two more were bent over the radio trying to listen, and four others were draped or sprawled over the lush furniture, flipping through magazines or talking. I took a brief—in this case, an extremely brief—inventory of what they were almost wearing and wondered why they even bothered.

Escott removed his hat and assumed a bland smile. I tried to do the same. It didn't impress the girls. None of them took notice when an older woman walked in through a curtained-off archway. She was in her forties, plump, and motherly except for the heavy powder and lip color. She smiled and welcomed us, asking if we'd like a drink.

"No, thank you," said Escott. "We're here to see Mr. Vaughn Kyler."

She shook her head, a study in polite confusion. "There's no Mr. Kyler here, or if he is, then he gave a different name."

One of the girls snickered.

"A pity, since it is most important that I see him. To be more correct, it is most important that he should see us."

Two blonds lolling on the sofa stopped pretending with their magazines and listened in. They'd caught Escott's accent and it was having its usual effect. The closer one put a leg on the coffee table in front of her and made a business of straightening her stocking. I watched the show with interest.

"I'd like to help you, but it's been a slow night," said the madam. "No one's been in here but a few regulars."

"It's early yet. Perhaps if you made inquiries with the gentlemen after they've concluded their appointments . . ." He produced a ten-dollar bill folded to the size of a business card. If my estimate was correct, he'd just bought each of us a pretty good time, or one of us a very good time.

She smiled, still polite, but with more sincerity now that he was speaking her language. "I'll see what I can do. In the meantime, make yourselves to home." She slipped through the curtains, leaving us in the company of a wide range of grinning possibilities.

"How appropriate," he said, quirking one eyebrow and apparently referring to the past of his own home.

"What's your name, honey?" The blond had finished one stocking and was busy with the other.

"Charles," he replied.

"Well, Charles, how 'bout you sit next to me and make yourself to home, like the lady said? You must be gettin' awful hot in that coat."

Her friend giggled.

"How kind of you to be concerned," he responded. "And your name is . . . ?"

"Trudy."

"How do you do, Trudy?" He shook hands with her, which charmed her and the others to no end. He acted as though he were having high tea at the Vanderbilts, not in the middle of a brothel surrounded by half-naked women. The others closed in and insisted on introducing themselves as well. I suspected that they wanted to keep him talking. An English accent must have been quite a novelty to them.

I found myself outside the circle, though it didn't matter to me, I was enjoying the show too much to want to be a part of it. Escott went into high gear on the polish and manners. His eyes twinkled and the smile he displayed now was positively lupine in cast. The girls couldn't get enough of him and were visibly disappointed when the madam returned.

Her own smile had faded and her eyes were hard and humorless. "Up there," she said, jerking her head at the curtains. "Last door on the left."

Escott excused himself to the girls. The madam stepped out of the way at the last second and stayed in the parlor. Her eyes slid past me completely as I went by her into the next room.

It was a landing empty of people and short on decor. A table held a load of drinks and ice and a tray of sandwiches. It had one comfortable chair and a table with a phone and nothing else. Escott took it in with one glance and stalked up the stairs as directed.

The second-floor hall was lined with doors, some open, others closed. The varied activities going on behind the closed ones were quite audible, at least to me, and left nothing to my fertile imagination. It was very distracting.

Escott stopped at the last door as directed, raised a hand to knock, then thought better of it. He gave me an inquiring look and I nodded, taking his place. He may have been wearing the vest, but overall, I was far more bulletproof. I knocked twice and a man on the other side said to come in.

The room was bright and Spartan compared to the parlor. There was no bed, but a long table with a double row of plain chairs took up the middle of the floor. It was covered with some pencils, a ledger book, a phone, and several thousand dollars in small bills. Standing over it, with a gun out and covering us, was Kyler's man Hodge.

One side of his face was swollen and bruised up where I'd hit him last night. From the expression that came over him when he saw me, it was clear that he remembered the incident as well.

"So Hot Shit's come back for more?" All those bruises gave him an unpleasant grin. Hell, it'd been just as bad before I'd marked him up. His eye dropped to the slash on my overcoat. "Rimik said he'd cut you good. He's making plans to finish the job he started."

"We're here to see Kyler," I said.

"Yeah, that's what I heard. You got some news on that broad?"

"Maybe, but it's for Kyler."

"He don't have time to waste talking to punks. You give me your news and get out while you still got legs."

"Oh, stop it, you're scaring me to death."

His grin broadened. "Now, that's an idea."

"Lay off the crap, Hodge. We want to talk to your boss and he'll want to talk to us."

"He's busy."

"We can wait. The company downstairs is nice enough."

The muzzle of the gun twitched back and forth. "You and your pal get your butts in here."

"First tell your friend with the asthma to come out from behind the door."

He did no such thing, but his friend cautiously emerged. She had a pinched face, thick glasses, and wore galoshes. Between them and her baggy woolen clothes I could figure that she wasn't part of the house's regular entertainment staff. She scuttled over to Hodge to stare at us. She didn't look lethal, so we walked in. Escott's eyes were all over the place, cataloging it before finally settling on Hodge.

"You . . . shut the door."

Escott obliged.

"Stand over there and keep your hands out. Opal, call the boss."

The girl grabbed the phone and dialed. It took a long time before anyone answered and she sounded relieved when they did. In a breathy, little-kid voice she asked for Kyler and mentioned Hodge's name. I thought he might put the gun away to talk, but he and the girl worked around that one. He held the earpiece in his free hand while she held the mouthpiece up so he could speak into it.

His report to the other end was a brief statement of his situation, then he listened for a time. The longer he listened the more he smiled.

"Okay, honey, put it away." She hung up for him.

"Good news?" I asked.

"You just wait here and see. Opal, finish what you started."

Opal plainly wanted to know what was going on, but was too timid to come out and ask. She sat at the table and with a nudge from Hodge began counting money. She quickly went through the stacks, put them in order, and stretched rubber bands around the bundles she made. Each bundle was recorded into the ledger.

Escott was looking at that book in much the same way a starving man would view a steak dinner.

Opal finished counting and loaded all the money and the ledger into her huge purse. And I'd been expecting to see a satchel.

Hodge nodded approval. "Okay, now get downstairs and watch for him. Lemme know when he comes."

"By myself?" Her face hardened with indignation.

"How else?"

"But those women make fun of me."

"So sit in the kitchen. G'wan."

She wrinkled her lip and nose in distaste and left. Hodge covered his annoyance with a laugh.

"I swear, she's gotta be the only broad left in this town past the age of consent that ain't consented yet. One of these days 'll have to screw her just so she can start understanding all the jokes."

"Mr. Kyler's accountant, is she?" asked Escott with mild curiosity.

"No, his gardener. Who the hell are you?"

"An interested party."

"Gimme a name."

"Escott."

Hodge's eye flashed to me and back again. "So you're the one who belongs to the Nash. How'd you know to come here?"

"I knew where to ask the right questions."

"Then somebody's been talking too much."

"On the contrary, not nearly enough. Mr. Kyler's made quite an impression on the community hereabouts."

Hodge didn't know whether to take that as a compliment or not. Opal saved him the trouble by coming in.

"He just pulled up."

"Get the bag and stay behind me. You two go out first."

We paraded downstairs, but turned right instead of left and exited the building through the kitchen. It faced an alley and we waited there while Opal went ahead with the money. When she came back, her purse looked a lot lighter and thinner. Hodge told her to wait in his car, and she all but galloped away.

A Caddy rolled across the alley entrance. It looked identical to the one I'd spotted earlier, right down to the smoked-over windows. The front door opened. Chaven got out of the driver's side and came around to check that everything was clear. He joined Hodge and gave us each a quick slap-down search. He found Escott's gun right away and relieved him of it. He nodded to Hodge and we were urged forward.

The front passenger window facing us rolled down. Kyler was on the other side.

"What is it?" His hard brown eyes froze onto mine. My back hairs starting climbing.

"About Doreen Grey. Someone shot her."

If anything, his expression got even more remote. "I know. What about it?"

"Did you do it?"

Now he had no expression at all. I tried to focus down on him, to pin him fast with my own influence.

Nothing happened.

There was enough light for it to work, maybe I needed to concentrate more. I tried again. "Did you shoot her?"

"No." His eyes raked me, indifferent to the pressure I was putting on.

My muscles contracted all over. His response was completely wrong. He should have been slack jawed or dreamy or anything, but in control of himself. On the edge of sight, I noticed Escott glance quickly at me. He'd sensed that something was seriously off.

In the alley behind us, Hodge and Chaven shifted on their feet.

"This one's Escott, boss," said Hodge, pointing.

Kyler's eyes narrowed. "I know."

Escott nodded. "We appreciate your personal attention in this matter."

"I'm off your suspect list for the woman," Kyler told him.

"To be sure, she was under your protection, but we had to be certain. Were you at any point ever able to make contact with her?"

"No. Someone got to her first."

"Do you know who that person is?"

No answer.

"Have you any idea at all?"

He turned his head to look at something in the backseat. When he turned back, his face was a little more animated with something that was a very distant cousin to amusement.

"You figure it out yourself, Mr. Private Agent."

Escott's chin lifted.

"Yes, I do know who you are. You crossed Frankie Paco once and managed to survive the hit he had out on you. You even bumped Fred Sanderson and shifted the blame to his partner."

The inaccuracy of fact was heartening to me. I felt marginally better knowing that Kyler was fallible on some level. On the other hand, it put Escott on the spot.

"That stuff's over now. After tonight, you stay out of my way."

One corner of Escott's mouth twitched. I knew him well enough to interpret it and felt my insides shrink. "Thank you for the warning," he said evenly.

"It's the only one you'll get. I want you to understand that I'm a lot better at this than Paco ever was."

Escott's eyes glittered. "Of that I have no doubt."

Kyler could tell he wasn't getting the reaction he wanted and it annoyed him. "Chaven."

Chaven took one step forward and buried his fist into Escott in a spot not covered by his vest—in this case, his right kidney. Escott bit back a sharp grunt of pain, but couldn't stop himself form dropping down on one knee. I moved toward Chaven, but Hodge still had his gun out.

"You just try it, Hot Shit," he said. "Give me an excuse."

It was enough to make me think twice about starting something that we'd all regret. I kept my movements easy and knelt by Escott.

I hissed in his ear, "You're an actor, goddammit, pretend you're scared."

He gasped a few times. Fortunately his head was down so it wasn't obvious that he was stifling laughter. "It's a bit late for that; he'd never believe such a show now."

"Maybe he'll believe it from me—I don't have to pretend."

"What could you be . . ."

But I lost the rest of it when Hodge loomed close and rammed a knee into my side. The breath washed out of my lungs. My back hit the cold, damp pavement and my head almost followed. I tucked my chin down just in time.

"That's for last night," he said.

I looked up, disoriented by my sudden roll from vertical to horizontal. Hodge was grinning, enjoying his chance to pay me back. His ability to really do damage was limited; my internal

changes had toughened me up inside and out, but that didn
mean I was happy just to lie there and take it. In fact, I wa
pissed as hell and wanted to kill him. What held me back wa
Escott; I didn't want him getting caught in the middle, but h
was already struggling to stand.

"No," I told him urgently. "Stay there and lemme—"

Hodge interrupted again. My teeth clacked together, barel
missing my tongue. White light flashed behind my eyes. M
body jerked and lay flat.

Vulnerable.

"That's for tonight . . ."

He'd used his foot this time, and my head had been the foot
ball. I had to fight to stay conscious. If I blacked out for even
second or two, I'd vanish into nothingness for who knows ho
long. Hodge watched my efforts with hot interest. He was wait
ing until I'd recovered enough to fully appreciate his next trick

". . . and this is for tomorrow."

He raised his foot, this time to bash it straight down into m
groin.

I was tough, but not that tough. Terror and reflex took over
I didn't think about whether the place was dark enough for me
to get away with it, or about the problems that might emerge
this was pure instinct. I disappeared a bare instant before con
tact. His foot plowed through empty air and slammed the pave
ment. He made a short cry, either from surprise or sudden fear
I couldn't tell.

Now I fought to regain solidity and won, by a narrow margin
My anger helped. I'd vanished for one long second, but reap
peared in the same spot with my hips shifted well out of harm'
way. Hodge's foot was still down, his arms waving as he trie
to get his balance back. With such an opportunity presenting
itself, I didn't have to think twice about taking it—the only rul
in a gutter fight is to survive. Because of the awkward angle,
couldn't put much force into the punch, but it was enough to d
the job. My fist swung up and smashed solidly against his groin

His scream tore down both ends of the street and made fla
echoes up the walls of the alley. He fell and rolled away, leg
pulled in, hands cupping and cradling, his face twisted.

I got to my feet. Fast. Chaven had backed off a few steps and
drawn his gun. It wavered equally between me and Escott.

A car door snicked open behind me. Kyler was out and hold

ing a fistful of automatic. The expression on his face was a beaut: a cross between fear and anger. He'd obviously noticed my vanishing act and was trying to make sense of the impossibility of what he'd seen. He sure as hell hated the uncertainty.

The only defense I had now was to bluff it out and act normal—or as normal as possible given the circumstances. I hugged my side with an elbow, doubled over a little, and tenderly checked out my jaw, remembering to breathe heavily.

Chaven and Kyler didn't move, each waiting to see what happened next.

Escott understood what I was trying to do and made his own contribution to the illusion. "Are you hurt?"

"Yeah, I'm hurt," I snapped. "That son of a bitch went too far. I hope he's crippled."

Their attention shifted to Hodge, as I'd hoped. "Check on him," said Kyler.

Chaven crab-walked over, keeping us covered. Hodge's replies to his questions were pretty incoherent. Even with my hearing, I was only able to pick up "shit," "goddamn," and "kill 'em," spaced between pain-choked groans. I wasn't about to feel sorry for him, though. He was only going through what he'd had planned for me.

Escott was on his feet by now and cautiously joined me.

"Did Chaven see anything?" I whispered.

"I don't think so, I was in his way."

That was something.

Kyler moved abruptly and with an air of finality. For him, even a bad decision was better than no decision at all. His gun arm went straight and steadied, the muzzle sight aimed squarely at me. I stopped hugging bruises I no longer felt and shoved Escott away toward the possible cover of some trash cans. He was still too close to the line of fire, but if he ducked fast enough . . .

The kitchen door of the Satchel opened and the bouncer stuck his head out, investigating the noise. Curtains in the side window twitched and faces full of speculation peered out at us. Opal appeared in the alley entrance and stared, one gloved hand to her mouth.

Kyler saw them and hesitated. They were part of his organization to one degree or another, but witnesses all the same.

There was a subtle shift in his posture and I knew hell was not going to break loose—at least for the time being.

"Chaven . . . get him out of here."

With Opal's nervous and clucking help, Chaven helped Hodge limp to his Caddy out front. Kyler kept us pinned the whole time with his gun and his eyes. I don't think he blinked even once.

Escott's expression had since assumed more serious lines, which was what Kyler must have wanted in the first place. Once Hodge was out of the way he walked over to get one more good look at us. No one was smiling.

"No changes," he said. "Escott, you stay out of my way. Fleming, I don't ever want to see you again. You can leave town or you can die, it doesn't matter to me. You have until tomorrow."

I focused onto his eyes, memorizing them, trying once more to break through their stone-hard surface to get at the mind beneath.

Nothing.

Chaven circled around to the other side of the car and opened the rear driver's door. He bent over some task for a moment. I heard a soft thud and thump against the road surface.

Kyler heard it, too, and started backing away until he reached the car. He opened the passenger door and slipped inside. Chaven was already in the driver's seat and had the motor running. The big Caddy glided off in near silence. Its twin, driven by Opal, followed a moment later. Hodge was in the rear seat and struggled up to the window for one last glare at me.

Good riddance.

Escott had nerves after all, and released the pent-up sigh he'd been saving. "You know," he said irritably, "that rat-faced fellow still has my Webley."

I had to swallow down a laugh that was trying to bubble up. If it got away from me now, I might not be able to stop. As a distraction, I checked to see what all our lifeguards at the Satchel were doing. Even as I turned, the bouncer withdrew and locked the door. The faces in the window disappeared. The lights still glowed, but the shades and curtains were in place again. With men like Kyler, curiosity was a shortcut to bad luck.

"You wanna go home?" I asked.

"That's an excellent idea."

Escott's stride was a little stiff. He absently rubbed his sore kidney as we quit the alley.

In the road before us lay a large, immobile bundle. I couldn't make it out at first; not until we walked closer, and saw that it had arms and legs.

A man's body.

Kyler had left behind his rubbish for us to clean up.

Escott cautiously turned him over. I caught the bloodsmell, sharp in the cold, damp air. The man had been put through the grinder. Twice.

His face was covered with blood, puffed, badly marked . . . and recognizable.

"Jesus," I said. "It's Harry Summers."

9

ESCOTT'S HAND dipped and held still. "He's got a pulse." When he tried to peel back an eyelid, Summers flinched.

"G'way," he moaned.

"Easy now, Mr. Summers, we're friends. I'm Charles Escott, we met yesterday—"

"Lemme 'lone."

"Harry," I said. "It's me, Fleming. Remember from last night? At the Top Hat?"

"G'ta hell."

"Never mind that, just tell us where it hurts."

"All goddamn over."

We spent a few minutes checking him for broken bones and bullet holes. Summers's answers to questions concerning his health were brief and grudging. The only time he showed any energy was when Escott stated his intent to take him to the hospital.

"Uh-uh. I'm not hurt that bad."

"You could have internal injuries, Mr. Summers."

"I've been in fights before. I know when to go in. I don't need to go in."

Escott decided not to press things. "Are you able to walk?"

"What's the rush?"

"We're all rather visible here. Besides, my car is infinitely more comfortable than the street."

The offer of a better place to rest penetrated Summers's somewhat dented skull and he allowed us to stand him up for the short walk to the Nash. We put him in with more care than Chaven had taken hauling him out, not that he was in any condition to appreciate our efforts. Once installed in the backseat, he heeled over on his side to hug his gut.

"You sure about not taking him to the hospital?" I asked.

"Humoring him will be much less difficult at this point. I'd also like to avoid official scrutiny until we find out how and why he ended up in Kyler's company."

"Okay, but if he starts looking really bad, he's going in."

"Absolutely."

Escott drove home and made good time getting us there. He parked out front for a change; the steps were broader and safer than the ones to the back door. I was thankful to see that he'd had my own car picked up and returned from the Boswell. I had a stinking idea that I might need it later.

Summers was reluctant to move, but we somehow got him out and into the house. Escott started the hot water running in the kitchen sink, then went upstairs for medical supplies while I settled our reluctant guest at the table. I made a quick raid on the liquor cabinet in the dining room. Summers needed no persuasion to drink down the triple I offered him.

"What happened?" I asked.

He snorted once as though I was a complete idiot and shook his head. His eye caught on the sleeve of my coat. "What about you?"

"I trimmed my nails and the scissors slipped. Why'd Kyler do this to you?"

He stared into his drink.

"What do you know about McAlister's death?"

"G'ta hell."

"What about Marian's bracelet?"

He stared at the table.

Escott had returned with an armful of stuff and was watching quietly from the hall doorway. He raised a questioning eyebrow. I shrugged. He walked in and dropped a load of towels, bandaging, and iodine on the table.

The water was running hot now, and Summers eschewed further help as he staggered to the sink to clean himself up. I ducked back to the dining room to find him another drink. Escott followed.

"Want one?" I asked.

"Please. The usual, but leave out the tonic this time."

I opened the gin bottle and poured generously, feeling a strong tug of regret that I couldn't join him. Physically, I could no longer tolerate the stuff, but the emotional need was still there; it'd been a hell of a night and I wanted to get drunk. I handed Escott his glass and tried not to watch as he took his first sip.

He looked past the dining room door at Summers, who was sluggishly washing his face. "He's not going to be especially cooperative," he said.

"I've already noticed that."

"You may have to nudge him along."

Occupied with Summers, he didn't notice my hesitation. "I think we'll get more from him if he works up to talking on his own."

"Unless it takes him all night."

"You in a hurry?"

"Possibly. It's Kyler that I'm concerned about."

"Because of Harry?"

He took another sip. "Consider this: Kyler could have dropped him at any point in the city he wished. Why, then, should he leave him with us?"

"It's a spit in the eye. He's sure he's got us pinned. We're all supposed to be too scared now to go running to the cops."

"And are we?"

He was serious, so I gave him a serious answer. "I'm still thinking it over."

"Are you, now? What about the ultimatum for you to leave town?"

"Or die. Don't forget that."

"Doesn't give one much of a choice, does it?"

"Yeah, and they're both lousy. Kyler must have been scared himself when I went out like that."

"Not that I can blame you for your action. Hodge's last assault was motivation enough for any desperate measure, and you certainly looked desperate. I must compliment you on your decision to pay him back in kind."

"Thanks, I spent hours thinking it over."

"Hodge might well be doing the same thing," he said with meaning.

"You're just full of encouragement, Charles. Hodge I can

handle. I know his type: he's garbage, which means he's nothing—it's Kyler that's got me worried."

"Indeed?"

"I'd be a dunce not to be."

"Buy why? What have you to really worry about?"

He'd sliced right into it and wasn't going to be fobbed off with
a light excuse this time. Mindful of Summers in the next room,
I lowered my voice. "Last night I started showing off and pulled
a couple of fast ones with Leadfoot Sam. Mostly I scared the
shit out of him, because he didn't know what he was seeing—or
wasn't seeing. All he wanted was to get away from me and stay
there because he couldn't handle any of it."

"And Kyler is of a different sort than Leadfoot?"

"He's either smarter or dumber, depending how you want to
look at things. Smarter because he knows I'm different and could
be a threat, dumber because he hasn't the sense to leave it alone.
You were standing right there, you saw what was going on."

"Then you did try to hypnotize him?"

"Three times. Nothing happened. I was going up against a
brick wall and bouncing right off. The ball drops away and the
wall just sits there and doesn't notice a thing."

"The only time that's ever happened to you was with—"

"Yeah, another vampire. I know."

"Is Kyler . . . ?"

"No," I said with much relief. "That's one of the first things
I thought of, so you can bet your ass that I checked. He's got a
nice, steady heartbeat."

"There's one other possibility—also a rather unpleasant one."

"You've got my attention already."

"It concerns Kyler's mental state. Do you recall the problem
you had with Evan Robley a few months back?"

I did, and the memory of the experience was still uncomfortably clear.

"You tried to break through to the man and could not."

"Only because the poor guy went over the edge without a
rope. I see what you're getting at, but aren't the situations just
too different? Evan was going through a horrible emotional shock
and had lost control; Kyler's his exact opposite. I never met
anyone who was so totally sure of himself."

"Yes, each an extreme opposite to one another—but both able
to resist your influence. It's probably not a conscious resistance,

either. Mr. Robley was so affected by his grief that for a time he was simply unaware of your presence.''

"But that changed later," I pointed out.

"Because Mr. Robley was nearly recovered from his shock. He went over the edge, but managed to climb back. By contrast, Kyler is in a similar mental state, but able to function as though he were normal."

It sank in. Deep. And I didn't want it.

"I hasten to add that whatever is wrong with Kyler need not claim a severe emotional shock as its source, as in the case of Mr. Robley. Some people are born that way, or so it would seem."

"Charles, any way you look at it, Kyler's loony-bin material."

"Possibly. For now, all we may do is speculate, basing our speculations upon a single piece of negative evidence."

"What? That I can't influence him, so he has to be nuts? It sounds good to me."

"But there's also your personal reaction to the man, as well as my own. Earlier tonight you compared him to a snake. Having met him, I'm inclined to heartily agree with your assessment." He rubbed the spot on his back where he'd been punched.

"Which isn't exactly the kind of hard evidence you like."

"Ah, but I do set much store in instinctive reaction. We may have no conscious reason why certain individuals repel us but it is generally a good idea to give such inner reactions sober consideration. Time and again I have relied upon it and have thus far suffered no regrets."

Like the time he'd followed an amnesiac vampire around to see what made him tick. "Okay, no arguments from me there."

He finished off his gin. "No arguments, indeed. But you may yet end up having to do something to protect yourself from him."

"Are you trying to talk me into taking on Kyler?"

"I'm attempting to set out all the options in my own mind. Verbalizing them sometimes helps. As for having another direct confrontation with Kyler, that is your decision entirely."

I wasn't so sure about that. "I wouldn't even know where to find him."

"To quote our abbreviated friend Pony Jones, 'maybe he'll find you.' ''

"Yeah," I said glumly. Which was what I was really afraid of, and anyone standing next to me could get caught in the cross fire.

In the kitchen, Summers had shut off the water and was gingerly dabbing his face with a towel. I finished pouring out a second drink for him and we went in.

Once all the blood had been washed away, the damage looked only slightly less alarming. One eye was swollen shut; the other had a cut over the brow. The rest of his inventory included various bruises in tender spots, a split lip, and a broken nose.

"If you are still adverse to the idea of a hospital, I know of a doctor you may see," Escott offered. He put down his used glass and stepped over to the refrigerator, pulling out an ice tray.

"I'll be all right," Summers insisted, dropping back into his seat at the table. "What d'you want, anyway?"

"You may recall that I was engaged by Mr. Pierce to locate his daughter's missing bracelet. Have you seen it, by any chance?"

Summers gave him a go-to-hell look. Escott ignored it and took the tray to the sink. He produced an ice pick from a drawer and began chopping. "Two people have died over this business so far, Mr. Summers. Vaughn Kyler is involved and I believe you know to what extent and why. We want you to tell us—"

"And get another going-over? No, thanks."

Escott scraped the shards of ice onto a towel, bundled it up, and offered the makeshift ice bag to Summers. He accepted with some suspicion, then cautiously held it to his closed eye.

"I've no wish," said Escott, "to involve the police just yet. . . ."

"You leave them outta this, it's none of their business."

"If not, then it is most certainly mine, since Kyler was kind enough to drop you into my hands. He would not have done so if he were at all worried over the information you can give us."

"I don't know anything."

"Then you are at no risk in telling us about it. Why did Kyler do this to you? What did he want from you?"

Summers said nothing.

"Very well, then let's try it this way: Kyler was most interested in locating a friend of Stan McAlister's, and so, apparently, was someone else. That friend was shot today, Kyler claims he did not do it. Perhaps you did."

"I dunno what you're talking about."

Escott's lips thinned and we exchanged a look. Summers was a poor liar. "You know enough to have tried to keep it to yourself; otherwise he wouldn't have expended so much effort upon you. And whatever it is, it's quite important, or you wouldn't have put up so much resistance."

Summers fiddled with the towel to pack the ice into a smaller bundle. The crunch and click were loud in the quiet kitchen.

"What did you tell him?"

"I didn't say anything, not to him and not to you."

"I see. So Kyler did not get the information he needed; that or he knew it already and only wanted you to confirm it for him, which you did in some way or he would not have released you."

"I didn't say anything."

"There are forms of silence that may speak volumes to the right observer, and I've no doubt that Kyler is an observant man. What did he ask of you?"

"Nothing."

Escott raised one brow at me to let me know it was my turn. The tension that had turned my hands into fists now traveled up my arms and down my back. I was expected to give Summers the works, to put him under, and then steal from his mind. That had been our pattern in the past and I'd followed it freely enough and with little thought. A fast suggestion or a brief question for a simple answer wouldn't be good enough this time. Refusal would only prompt Escott to question me, and I'd either have to not answer or lie to him, and I didn't want to do either.

"If you're done, then I want to go home," Summers rumbled.

"Yeah, we're done," I told him.

Both of them looked surprised.

"We don't need him, Charles, any more than Kyler did."

Escott frowned for a long moment.

"Think about it," I said. "Kyler doesn't care who killed Stan McAlister or if Kitty gets the blame for it, that's not his business. All he seems to want is the bracelet. He puts out word that he wants to meet Stan's friend, who probably has it. He guarantees their safety and promises money at the end of things. But someone beat him to the meeting and the friend is shot. It makes him look bad, as though he went back on his word. He doesn't like looking bad. The bracelet's nothing to him now, he's going after the person who crossed him up. He can't get to Kitty, Pierce, or Marian; they're too well protected, so he picks up Harry to get some answers. It's easy enough to figure out just what Harry knows.''

Summers's bruised face got darker.

''Which takes us back to Stan McAlister. You *could* have killed him, Harry. You once took a swing at him for looking at Marian the wrong way.''

''How did—'' He clamped his mouth shut. He'd assumed, inaccurately, that Marian had told me all about it.

''Jealousy's a damn good motive. And though it's just possible that you could have talked him into letting you come up with him to Kitty's flat, Stan wouldn't have been dumb enough to turn his back on you. But you wouldn't have stood behind him and used an iron skillet and then a carving knife to make sure of the job, you'd have simply smashed his face in.

''But none of that happened. Someone else killed Stan. It wasn't Kitty, all she did was walk in and run out. Not smart, but the kid was too scared to think straight. The only others with a motive are the Pierces.''

Summers's heartbeat, already high, jumped higher.

''Sebastian Pierce wanted the bracelet back; he hired us to get it. That could have been a move to provide him the cover he needed to murder Stan and avoid being a suspect. But I don't think he's the type to try anything complicated. Besides, he's got enough money and connections to order up anything he pleases and have the job done right. If his goal had been to kill Stan he'd have been a lot more efficient about it. That leaves us with Marian—''

''No it doesn't. She didn't do anything.''

''Then it won't hurt if I speculate about it—just so we can eliminate her from things.''

Summers subsided, all but growling, and glared at something inside him. He wasn't going to like what I had to say but hadn't worked up to the point of stopping me before I said it.

''This started out as a theft, with us hired to recover the goods, but Stan was a blackmailer, not a thief. Suppose he didn't steal the bracelet, but that it was given to him? You said last night that she went with you because you did some time. Marian likes to break rules, and going out with tough guys is part of the thrill for her.

"Now, Stan had a nasty little blackmail racket going. While he got naked with any girl who had some money put aside, his partner was in the next room taking photos of all the fun and games. Later on, he'd show the results to the girl, making a convincing threat, and collect his living from them if they fell for it.

"He had a real talent for finding women who liked rubbing shoulders with his kind of lowlife. Maybe Kitty's one of 'em, I don't know, but he'd made friends with her and she had the kind of high-brow connections that took him straight to Marian Pierce.

"We'll leave out the details of how and when and just suppose that he started blackmailing Marian, but for once, instead of cash like before, he decides to go for something really big and demands her bracelet as payment. He gets it, but it's eventually missed. Her father suspects a straight theft, and we're brought in to recover it.

"But Marian's got her eyes open for trouble and spots us, picking me out to pump for information at the club. When she failed, she went to Stan and told him what was going on, and he ducked out. He didn't go straight back to his hotel, because he had a date with Kitty. I figure he went to the Angel Grill to find her."

"Could he have not broken his appointment and apologized later?" asked Escott. "The man must have surely been in too much of a hurry."

"You've got to include the stuff I got from his partner."

"What stuff is that, specifically?"

"That Stan had fallen in love with Kitty. As far as we've learned, she's the only one he didn't blackmail, though she certainly fits into the pattern he set with all the other women he's known."

"Negative evidence," he cautioned.

I shrugged. "Maybe so, but it accounts for why he didn't rush directly home to the Boswell to start packing. He went to the Angel, missed her or heard she'd left, then drove home. When he did arrive, Kitty warned him off, and he bolted for her place. Now he and Marian had their heads together at the club, but they didn't have much time for talk, and Marian probably had a lot to say. Stan could have let drop where he'd be and Marian decided to meet him there."

"Or Stan could have asked her to follow him."

"Yeah?"

"To obtain ready cash from her," he explained.

I nodded. If McAlister had wanted a quick exit from Chicago, he'd have had a hard time trading the bracelet for train tickets. "Okay, so when Stan turned up at Kitty's place, Marian was waiting for him. They go inside with Stan's key and eventually end up in the kitchen, probably looking for a drink. Now we've got two different things for them to talk about at this point: Stan could be demanding more money from Marian, or Marian could be wanting to get the bracelet back."

"Or both?"

"Either way it ends up in a fight. Stan makes the mistake of turning his back on her and she hits him with the first thing that comes to hand, which was an iron skillet. It must have killed him outright. She might not have known he was dead, but she was mad enough to kill him."

Escott shook his head once, not as a denial of what I was saying, but as a caution not to say it. Summers was hunched low over the table. He didn't need to hear the details of the knifing that had been done to make sure McAlister died.

"She searches the body and finds Stan's wallet and the gun his partner said he carried. She takes them and closes up afterward with his key, leaving Kitty to find Stan, and us to find Kitty. Then Marian runs like hell. She ran right to you, Harry, because she knew you'd give her an alibi. . . ."

Summers had at last worked up to his breaking point, only now he was far beyond just telling me off. He swung the ice-filled towel, using it like a cold, wet blackjack. I'd been expecting something like that and dodged. It hit my shoulder instead of my face. The towel came open and ice exploded across the kitchen. I made a grab for his arms, but he was too fast and, twisting the other way, made a lunge for the counter.

Correction: he made a lunge for the ice pick on the counter.

He got it.

He was too crazy to do much beyond blindly striking out at anything that moved, which included Escott. Escott aborted his attempt to grab at the ice pick and hauled himself back just in time to avoid a stab in the chest. Summers started after him.

"Harry!"

My shout got his attention. He turned and sliced air in my

direction. His expression was fixed midway between red-faced
fury and helpless frustration. With or without the bruising, he
was unrecognizable. My idea of calming him down and talking
him into dropping the ice pick was not going to work. He gave
me no time to try, anyway, and rushed toward me.

The kitchen wasn't that big a room and only got smaller with
the three of us playing tag around the table and chairs. The ice
pick made the place positively claustrophobic. I was too busy
watching it to see where my feet were going. My leg bumped a
chair over while I backed away. It toppled in the wrong direction
and I nearly fell on it. Summers turned my distraction into an
opportunity for himself and went in under what little guard I
had left.

The point of the damned thing missed the underside of my
chin only because Summers's foot skidded on a piece of ice. I
caught his arm just below the wrist, turned him fast so that I
was behind him, and grabbed his other arm. He shifted his
weight automatically like a dancer and rammed an elbow into
my stomach. It didn't do me any good, nor did his heel when
he raked it down my shin and onto my foot.

Escott cut in, fastening onto Summers's left arm. I let go and
put all my concentration on the hand with the ice pick, using
both of mine to slam it down hard against the old oak table.
Nearly an inch of the business end embedded itself into the
wood. Summers's hand shot past the handle. He let out with a
roar of outrage when it connected with a muffled crack against
the hard wood. The roar went up the scale, lost its force, and
died off. His knees abruptly gave way and he sank to the floor.
The knotted muscles in the arm I held went as limp as wet rope.

The incident hadn't lasted more than a few seconds. His encounter with Kyler had left him too sore to fight for long and he
was puffing like an Olympic runner. Between gasps, he called
us every name he could think of, and a few more besides before
finally winding down.

Escott was breathing hard through his teeth. It was more from
anger than from physical need. He wasn't used to having
homicidal maniacs tearing around his house. "At least we know
just what led up to his beating earlier tonight," he said.

"Yeah, he and Kyler both have short fuses."

"I cannot say that I'm terribly sorry over it."

"Is that how it happened, Harry?" I asked.

"G'ta hell," he moaned.

I let go of my grip and stood away from him. He continued to kneel, leaning on the table as though in awkward prayer. Escott released him, curling his lip disapprovingly at the ice pick. With a slight effort, he removed it from the table to put it away in a drawer. He'd forgotten his compulsive neatness for once and the omission had nearly cost us both. Knowing him, he was probably more embarrassed than anything else. I decided to forget about it, since it was a cinch that Escott wouldn't.

"You were saying something about Marian Pierce?" he asked.

"Yeah." I looked down at Summers's bowed back. He was going through hell and I knew exactly what he felt like. "She killed him, Harry. And she told you all about it, didn't she?"

"It's not her fault," he insisted. "None of it was her fault. He was coming after her. The son of a bitch was tryin' to rape her, for God's sake. It was self-defense."

Self-defense. I glanced at Escott and saw confirmation of my own disbelief. It was just remotely possible. Summers had accepted her story, but then he was in love with her; he needed his illusions.

"And she asked you for an alibi?"

"She didn't have to ask," he snarled.

"No, I guess she didn't." I looked at Escott. "My best guess is that when she couldn't find the bracelet she went to the Boswell, but too many people were there first, and she could figure they were all looking for it themselves."

"And from the hotel, she began to follow Miss—McAlister's partner." Escott was still throwing out a smoke screen to protect Doreen's identity. I was glad of that.

"Or me," I added, "until I finally ended up at the studio. While the partner and I were busy at the bar down the street, Marian broke in and searched the place. Again, she came up with a blank."

"And this is where Kyler comes in."

"She needed help, so she called in a professional. We don't know her connection to him yet, but I'm ready to start looking for it. What's Pierce's number?"

Escott gave it, his brows drawing together and his mouth falling into a hard, thin line.

I eventually got hold of the housekeeper, identified myself, and asked a few fast questions. The news was good. Pierce, his daughter, Kitty, and Griffin were with the police and had been for most of the evening. Lieutenant Blair was probably doing a thorough job on them, and for once I had reason to silently bless his zealous attitude.

Hanging up, I drew Escott back out of earshot and filled him in. "I'm going over to Pierce's. Can you meet me there later?"

"Certainly, but—"

I jerked a thumb toward Summers. "You'll have to take him in to the hospital, after all. I broke his arm, only he doesn't feel it yet."

Escott looked surprised again.

Excuses always sound self-conscious. I cut off the one I was about to make and stuck to cold fact. "It snapped when I slammed it on the table. I felt it go."

The situation was beyond reasonable comment, so he didn't make one. "Very well, I'll take him in. What are you planning to do at Pierce's?"

"A little illegal searching. Kyler's had a big head start, but maybe I'll get lucky. That's the other reason he dumped Harry with us—to keep us busy while he goes after the bracelet. Odds are he'll want to go after Marian, too, so you'll have to call Blair and fill him in so he can keep her safe."

"Arrest her, you mean."

Anger that I'd been unaware of and holding down flared quietly with that possibility. "Yes, goddammit. If she's the one who shot Doreen I want her put away."

Then his question was suddenly there again. It was the same one he'd wanted to ask a few scant hours ago in his office when he first knew something was wrong for me. Telepathy was not a part of my changed condition, but I could almost hear his "why?" bouncing between my ears. He was asking for something beyond the simple and obvious need for justice; what he wanted was an explanation of my personal motive.

There were dozens, but the top dog of them all was guilt. If I hadn't been curious or been made drunk and stupid by the easy power the hypnosis granted me, if I hadn't . . . hadn't . . .

The room seemed very closed up. The silence added to my discomfort. I tried to ease it with talk. "While you're at the hospital, would you check on her for me? See how she's doing?"

Then he face went neutral. I winced inside. That bland front meant he was making all kinds of connections now. Once he saw her, he'd have all the proof necessary to turn them into conclusions. I might as well have tied a ribbon around it as a late Christmas present.

"Certainly," he promised, his voice also carefully neutral.

He had pockets of privacy for himself and was perceptive enough to recognize and respect them in others, but this particular one touched too close to our work to be avoided. He wouldn't let it pass, not later, when there was time for talk.

He watched my face. God knows what he made of the expression there. Probably a lot more than I ever wanted to reveal. I could have stood there all night telling him how I'd lost control, how sheer appetite and self-indulgence had brought me that close to killing her. The words only clogged in my throat.

And the worst part was that as much as the experience had shaken and frightened me, the insistent desire was still there, and it was very, very strong.

It wanted—no, *I* wanted . . .

Doreen had provided only the merest sample of what the full sensual potential must be. I'd cut off far too soon. She wouldn't have minded if I'd gone on; she wouldn't have cared.

She hadn't *cared. The overwhelming pleasure had been there for her as well.*

I wanted . . . to finish what had been started. The craving for her blood was like an itch inside my mind, one that I could reach but didn't dare scratch. Dear God, it wasn't enough that I'd raped the woman, I was ready to do it again until she died from it.

I palmed my car key and walked out.

Quickly.

I don't remember the trip over to the Pierce estate. One moment I was just starting my car and the next I was rolling through a lush neighborhood of tall trees and large, rich houses. It was like the kind of travel that happens to you when you dream, except I was sure I didn't dream anymore, at least not in a way that could be remembered upon awakening. No real sleep, no more dreams. I wondered if the lack could make me go crazy. Or maybe it was like the liquor in Escott's cabinet, with no true need beyond what was generated in my own mind.

If I could only apply that to Doreen.

No. I don't want to think about her.

I managed to blank her and everything else out long enough to get to the right address, then my mind shifted over to safer and simpler areas, like how to sneak onto the estate unseen. Easy for me, not so easy for my car—I wasn't about to leave it someplace and hike.

The entrance to the front drive had big stone gateposts to punctuate the ends of a long brick wall, but no gates hung from them. I ignored the opening and went on to circle the rest of the block. This property took up the whole of it. The brick wall was unbroken until I made my second turning and found another, narrower driveway. Small blue and white tiles set into the cement of the curb spelled out Pierce Lane. A sign on a second, and less ostentatious, set of gateposts informed me that this was a private drive and to keep out. There were gates on this, the back door, but they'd been left wide open.

It was a mixed blessing: I was able to sail right in, but it left me wondering if anyone else had done the same or was about to do so. Kyler was very much on my mind and I was realistically expecting him to be here ahead of me, and if so . . . well, I'd think of something.

For starters, I cut off my headlights and coasted forward, going easy on the gas pedal. I was anticipating a quick walk up to the main house, getting inside, and locating Marian's room. Once there, I planned to quietly tear it apart until I found the bracelet. But that idea got tossed out as I rounded a gentle curve and saw lights on in the guest house.

Some member of the household staff could be doing a little late cleaning up after Kitty's invasion, but I was too suspicious to take that on faith. I swung the wheel over. The car had just enough momentum to run up the curve in the drive and slot itself next to the guest-house garage. At least it was out of view from the house. Anyone coming in by way of Pierce Lane would spot it, but cars and garages were a natural pair and hopefully the two blended together enough to be overlooked.

I remembered not to slam the door shut and took my time approaching the house.

The kitchen curtains were the kind that covered only the bottom half of the window. They were still effective, since the uncurtained top half was some eight feet from the ground. I got around the height problem by going transparent and floating up.

The lights inside were clinically bright to my night-conditioned eyes. It took a second to blink things into focus. I got a fast impression of the usual furnishings plus one guest sitting at the dining table.

Marian Pierce.

She was still in her collegiate costume; draped on the table was a dark overcoat and her purse. Next to them was an ashtray, and from the nervous way she was smoking, she'd have to empty it fairly soon. Everything about her tense, restless posture howled that she was waiting and impatient about it. As I looked on, she glanced twice at her watch, once to get the time, and again because she'd forgotten what she'd seen.

I could wait around outside until whomever she was expecting showed, but that course of inaction was dismissed as quickly as it came to mind. Instead, I went solid, dropped lightly to the ground, and knocked on the back door.

She probably jumped and froze for a few seconds; it took her about that long before her quick footsteps approached. A bolt scraped and the door opened a crack. I bulled in before she could see me and change her mind.

She backed up until she was stopped by the table and stared as though I were a new kind of fashion in unexploded bombs. "What are you doing here?" she demanded.

"Just checking up on things. What about yourself? I thought you were with the others talking to the cops."

She grabbed at the conversational opening with visible relief. "They finished with me. I got bored and took a cab home."

"So why are you here instead of home?"

"I'm just getting Kitty's things together."

"Uh-huh." I made no effort to sound like I believed her.

She bit back what promised to be a couple dozen sharp replies and decided to go for sympathy. "All right, if you must know, I'm here because this place feels less like a prison than the main house."

"Yeah, the poor-little-rich-girl problem. I know, I saw *My Man Godfrey*."

She ignored my mouth running off with itself and slid to one side until the table was between us. She tried to make it look like a casual movement and failed. She was a lousy actress.

The muscles in my neck went stiff when she dug into her coat pocket, but she only produced a pack of cigarettes and made a business of shaking one out and lighting it. "Carole Lombard had it easier. She was able to do whatever she liked."

"And you're not?"

"Not without everyone knowing about it."

"Everyone being your father?"

"Don't you have some secrets from your family?"

More than you could imagine.

She took a long drag on the cigarette and let the smoke flood upward. "You said you were checking up on things. What does that mean?"

"Driving around and thinking." Or not thinking, as the case had been. "I came up the back way and saw the lights."

"And found me," she concluded, with a stunning smile that put my back hairs up. Our last talk had ended on a decidedly sour note, and she wasn't the sort of person to forgive and forget. "Aren't you the lucky man?"

"That depends on whether or not you can come clean about you and Stan." My voice was going thick.

She didn't blink. She was a very good actress, after all, good enough to give me a serious twinge of doubt when I least needed it. "Stan?"

"You and Stan," I repeated.

No reaction. My doubt grew and shifted, like a large animal stuck in a small cage.

"Escott and I talked to Harry tonight. He told us everything."

"What about Harry?" she asked. Her tone held the perfect balance of puzzlement and irritation.

"Only that I had it right earlier. You got him to lie for you."

"I don't understand." Perfect again.

I was wrong and hating it. I needed to blame someone for Doreen, so I picked out a spoiled brat with bad manners instead of . . .

When I didn't reply, she broke away with a puzzled shrug. As she moved, her eyes swept past her wrist, checking the time again. Whoever was to meet her was overdue. We could be interrupted any moment.

I noticed her things on the table and gave myself a mental kick. She said nothing when I picked up her purse and turned it over, scattering its feminine clutter. The bag itself was still heavy. There was a pocket in the pale silk lining. From it I drew out a small .22 revolver. In the same pocket was a black velvet pouch. I shook it open. An explosion of red and silver sparks spilled into my hand.

Everything turned and returned. It happened that easily and quickly.

The bracelet felt heavy. One person was dead over it, maybe two, God forbid. The thing weighed a ton. I let it slip softly back into the velvet bag.

She'd almost stopped breathing. Her large eyes darted from it to my face.

I ignored the bracelet and opened the gun's cylinder. It held five shots. I pushed the rod. Two bullets and three empty shell casings dropped out, rolling a little.

That got a reaction, but not the kind you could see. It was as if a totally different person had dropped in and taken over her body. The change was sudden and complete; what was so frightening about it was that she still *looked* the same.

The floor seemed to swell under my feet, as though I were on a boat and the sea beneath it were fretful from an oncoming storm.

The doubt in me vanished forever.

I was staring at a killer.

10

"YOU BITCH," I said, my voice low and gentle.

Her chin jerked. "I don't know—"

"You *bitch*." And this time it cracked and cut like a whip.

She whirled and ran from the kitchen, trying to reach the front door. I went right through the table and caught up with her in the entry parlor. When my arm snaked around her waist she began screaming. I smothered it off with one hand. She kicked and scratched. A lamp crashed over, followed by the spindly table that held it.

Lifting her clear of the floor, I swung her around, dropping her hard into a chair. Every time she tried to jump up and run, I pushed her back. She got the idea and stopped fighting.

"Daddy will kill you for this," she gasped, out of breath from her one-sided fight.

"Forget him. You're on your own."

"I—"

"Can it."

She did and fell back in the chair to glare at me.

I wasn't impressed. "You're going to tell me the truth or I'll wring your neck. Take your pick."

Something in my face must have caught her attention, because I saw the first sign of real fear in hers.

"It's not that hard, Marian. You can start by telling me why you killed Stan."

"He tried to—"

"Not the crap you told Harry. The truth."

Fear won out over anger. "He had my bracelet," she muttered.

"Blackmail?"

"He had photos . . . of us. He was going to show them to Daddy at the Christmas party. He said he'd trade them for the bracelet. So I did."

"But did he give you the negatives?"

"He said he would."

"You're not that dumb."

"He *said* so," she insisted. "I believed him then."

"Was he going to give them to you last night?"

"Yes, but for cash instead."

"At the Top Hat Club?"

"Yes."

"Until you spotted me."

"He put it off when he thought you were after him. He said to meet him at Kitty's and we'd trade there."

"What went wrong?"

She shook her head.

"Tell me."

"I said I had to have the bracelet back."

"He must have laughed right in your face."

"He'd complained before that he couldn't get as much as he'd expected off the bracelet. I told him he could make more money if I paid him in cash out of my allowance."

"And he wanted both?"

"Yes. He wouldn't give it back. I thought if I just knocked him out, I could . . . so I did. It wasn't in his pockets. I couldn't stand it, I—I don't remember what happened afterward." Her eyes were all over the place. Her memory was fine, she just didn't want to talk about it. "I was so angry, I had to have the bracelet back."

"Why?"

"I can't—"

"Yes, you can. Why?"

"I owe money to . . . to . . ."

"Vaughn Kyler? Is that how he's connected to all this?"

She nodded fearfully.

"How'd you manage that? More blackmail?"

She swung a fast arm and slapped me. I blocked her next attempt as though waving off a fly.

"Come on, Marian."

"The tables," she hissed.

"What? Gambling?" So she had another little vice to add to her thrill list. "He let you run up a bill, right?"

"I didn't think it was that much, but added together . . ."

"And if you didn't pay it wasn't just showing photos to Daddy, it was things like broken legs and arms."

"That man with the knife . . . he said he'd skin my face."

"So you killed Stan to get the bracelet, only he didn't have it on him. Did you try his room?"

"I couldn't get to it. I had to wait, then I saw you talking with that red-haired woman outside the hotel. I remembered seeing her there before. Stan once said that she was a photographer and laughed about it. She looked scared when she left, so I followed her. I thought—"

"You figured right, she was Stan's personal photographer. What happened after you tore the studio apart? Is that when you called in Kyler?"

"I didn't. His men had been following me."

"You must have all made quite a parade."

"I told them that that woman had the bracelet. They said they'd get it."

"Except Doreen got away. How'd you find her again?"

"She called me. She said she'd trade the bracelet and the negatives for some cash."

"And you met in the park."

"But by then Kitty had come in, the papers were full of the story about . . . about Stan and the woman knew everything that had happened."

"Her name is Doreen," I said, almost to myself.

"I *had* the money, but sh-she was angry. She knew that I . . . I'd . . . that Stan—"

"Then you shot her."

"I—"

"No self-defense, no rape stories, you shot her, Marian."

"It *was* self-defense! She knew about me! She was going to take the money and tell the police no matter what. I could see that in her face. And the kind of person she was . . . the things she did . . . can you blame me? It's not as if she were . . . *she wasn't anybody important!*''

My hands spasmed into fists. A double dose of rage coursed through me like a jolt of electricity, half-aimed at her and half-turned upon myself. I backed away from her, fast. If I didn't, she'd be dead in seconds. To hear her mouth the same idiot's reason that I'd used to justify my own excess of appetite . . .

Not everyone likes a mirror; me, least of all.

In a burst of self-loathing I forced myself to stare at mine. Like all mirrors, she was unseeing and oblivious to what she reflected. With a terrible inner lurch, my rage transmuted into cold, sick horror. I looked at my mirror and understood perfectly all that was there.

"Yeah," I said at last, sounding lost in my own ears. "I guess she really wasn't, not to you."

The shift startled her, but she took it as a good sign, and was quick to land on her feet. "You have to help me, Jack. If you help me, I c-can give you anything you want. I mean that. I can give you anything. Tell me what you want and I'll give it to you."

She'd crawled up from the chair and stood before me, taking my silence for affirmation. I dimly felt the touch of her hands.

"Stop it, Marian."

"It's all right. Believe me. It'll be just fine. I want this, too."

I caught her hands and held them away from me. The action slowed the soothing flow of her promises. "But I don't."

"Maybe not yet, but I can—"

"No, Marian. It won't work this time."

First bafflement as she tried to understand, and then a flash flood of her own rage when she did. "You can't."

"I have to."

She shook away from me. "You won't."

"Get your coat, Marian."

Her initial response was incoherent, but I got the general idea. "I'm not helping you," she concluded. "You'll have to drag me out."

"If I have to."

"No one will believe you, anyway. I won't tell them anything."

"You won't need to once they match the bullets up with the gun."

"I'll fight them and so will Daddy. It won't happen."

My head drooped. I felt very tired. "Maybe not, but we're still going in."

She backed up a step. "If you touch me again I'll make sure it shows, and you know what I'll tell them about it. Daddy will kill you no matter what."

My eyes fastened onto hers. She broke off and began again, like a record-player needle skipping over a bad groove.

"No matter what . . ."

I said her name and swept into her mind like a winter wind. Its cold tug pulled me along as well, the blast twining us tightly together.

This wasn't safe. I had to stop before it took us too far— before *I* went too far.

Then Doreen's face seemed to overlay Marian's. We were standing across from one another in her studio. Time had slipped backward to repair broken equipment, to stitch up the torn floor cushions; everything was in its place again.

Doreen wore a shapeless white hospital gown and walked toward me, arms out and eyes closed. Her lips parted, silently breathing my name, anticipating my next touch—the touch that would kill her. The vision was so strong and clear that once more the red taste of her blood lay like fire upon my tongue.

Her body was solid and warm as she clung to me; I traced the smooth, taut skin of her neck. To be linked to this woman, to any woman, to take until nothing remained of them . . . The mere sound of the blood in their veins was enough to seduce me—a single scarlet drop of it enough to damn me.

I kissed and kissed deeply, savoring the beautiful taste of that damnation. It flattened and dispersed and ultimately vanished, leaving behind the soaring desire for more.

She was laughing. Harsh and low, it kept time with her heartbeat.

What to do when she died?

What to do later, when the hunger returned?

A single drop was not enough for the *hunger*.

Laughter—silent now.

Heartbeat—fading.

Gone.

A dead weight lay in my arms and upon my soul.

I let her fall and stared at the wreckage. The hunger would

return. It would always be there, ready to tear me apart, destroying others as it fed. An ocean of blood could not fulfill that insistent want. It would never be satisfied.

She was the first. She *had* to be the last.

"No," I murmured. "No more."

It could be controlled if I remembered to control myself. To do that, I had to close off this door forever and walk away.

The fire abruptly died and cooled. The ashes were bitter and dry but felt clean. Maybe I was damned myself, but I would drag no others down with me.

Marian's face jumped back into sharp focus. Her throat was unmarked, her eyes sharp and alert. Nothing had happened, at least not to her. We'd been under for only a few seconds, but time in a dream may be stretched to infinity's edge. I felt as though I'd been there and back again.

Dreams were not lost to me, after all, nor were the nightmares. They were somehow linked to the hypnosis. I'd driven two men insane and all but killed Doreen because of it. But no more. The door was shut, and I was walking away.

Marian's expression changed to a curious mix of fearful hope and suppressed excitement. She was looking not at me, but beyond me. The weight of my own waking dragged heavily; the dream memory of a false past left my mind too sluggish to react to the shifting situations of the present.

When I turned, I turned slowly, which was just as well. A sudden movement would have set him off.

Hodge was in the room and held his gun level with my stomach. Marian's overdue guest had arrived at last.

"You're gonna die, you shit," he told me. His voice shook from sheer joy at the idea.

I said nothing and didn't move. Marian was behind but well to one side of me, fairly safe. I could trust him to hit a target six feet away. He could kill me if he liked. Others had tried. I felt oddly calm about the whole business; must have been leftover shock from the dream.

"You hear me?"

He'd come for the bracelet. Once Marian had found a little time to herself she'd let Kyler know she was ready to pay off her debt. It was a convenient payment since it also got rid of a telling piece of evidence against her.

"It's in the kitchen," I said. "In a black bag on the table."

The lawyers could still make a case without it. Once the story hit the papers, though, Kyler might find the thing too hot to even break down to individual stones.

But Hodge didn't know what I was talking about. He was so wound up over me that he wasn't listening. His face was fever bright and slick with thin sweat. He was probably still feeling the aftereffects of my last punch. Maybe that was what had delayed his arrival.

Marian was moving, but I didn't look at her. It was best to keep Hodge's full attention on me.

"The bracelet's in the kitchen," I explained.

"You're dead."

"Kyler wants the bracelet, not me."

A chuckle twitched out of him. Kyler had nothing to do with this; Hodge was working on his own initiative. He raised the gun a little, just to dispel any doubts.

"He said I had until tomorrow, Hodge. Do you want to cross him on that?"

"Kyler ain't gonna find out."

"You don't want to take that chance."

Another twitch, this time without any humor behind it. He was thinking hard. I left him to it and wondered about Marian. I couldn't see her out of the corner of my eye anymore.

Hodge made his decision. He was going to chance things. The hard question for him now was where to put the bullet. A grin split his face up as he picked a target and lowered his aim. Considering that last punch, he was not only going to even the score between us, but permanently top it. I was awake now and ready. The timing involved for my vanishing would be close, but once he pulled the trigger, he was in for the surprise of his life. I'd worry about explanations later.

A crack and my head jerks forward.

Teeth rattle.

Darkness and light mix behind my eyes, canceling one another.

Knees strike the floor.

Arm hits something and twists out.

Face barks against the rough pile of the rug.

A spine-cracking thud.

This was wrong. It wasn't the quick, sharp pain of a bullet. It was far more deadly.

Another thud.

I try to crawl away from the agony.

Can't move.

God, my head.

Hodge yells something.

She keeps hitting me. Marian. With each strike, she gasps out some wordless sound. It's ugly, full of hatred and perhaps a lifetime of frustration.

I try to vanish.

Nothing. The pain is too much. I'm paralyzed from it.

Wood. She's using wood.

She's not stopping.

She won't stop until I'm dead.

Dead like Stan. She'd grabbed up a knife and struck out at him, venting God knows what fury onto his inert body when she couldn't get her way.

Dead.

Others had tried to kill me before.

Maybe this time would finally . . .

Finally . . .

"You crazy bitch!"

Hodge's voice. He seemed annoyed. I wasn't overly concerned. Marian's response was mumbled. "Yeah, he's dead, so lay off."

Bless you, my son. After that, pain distorted their voices past the point of understanding, and I drifted out of the conversation. I lay flat on my stomach with one arm awkwardly turned and the side of my face mashed against the rug. My left eye was partially open to a panoramic view of dark blue pile and a low slice of wall. Saliva oozed from my sagging mouth, making a wet place under my chin.

I'd had worse, but not recently, and past survivals give no comfort to current pains. For the time being all I could do was lie dormant until my nervous system decided to pull itself together. Too bad that Hodge had missed his chance at me; hit or miss, a metal bullet was nothing compared to wood. No wonder it was so popular for dispatching vampires.

Something dropped into my field of view with a clatter. I

eventually identified it as the small table we'd knocked over ea
lier—Marian's improvised murder weapon, now discarded. It ha
looked so fragile then, not the sort of thing I'd choose for suc
a job. Who'd have thought—

Shut up, you're babbling.

The better to distract me from the pain, my dear. Christ,
felt like an elephant had used my skull for a batting practice.

"Get ready to go," said Hodge.

"Why?"

"Because the boss wants to see you."

"I can't leave. Daddy and the others will be coming back.'

"And you want to wait here with the body?"

"Then get rid of it."

It. I'd been reduced to being an *it*. Coming from her, quit
understandable.

"I don't work that way, honey."

"But I can pay you. I've got some money with me. It's your
if you help me."

Hodge coughed out a brief, shaken laugh. "Yeah, that's how
it all works for you rich bitches. Wave some money and ge
someone else to clean up your garbage."

"Will you do it?"

He took his time answering and there was an edge to his voic
when he did. "I'll do it. Now, get your coat."

"Where are we going?"

"Place by the river. Wrap up good, honey, it's cold out there.

"I'll have to be back soon."

"Don't worry about it." His tone was preoccupied. He wa
busy figuring out just what to do with me. I expected to b
dragged to the trunk of his car, perhaps to wind up in the sam
spot as Willy Domax and Doolie Sanderson. Kyler probably ha
a regular assembly-line process for getting rid of troublemaker:
Hopefully, it would take time, and by then I'd be in better shap
to handle things. Hodge's big surprise would be only a littl
delayed.

As for Marian . . . she stirred up an army of black though
and feelings. Most of them were beyond voice, but not actior
God help us both when I saw her again.

If I ever moved again.

Marian was in the kitchen; her heels clacked on the linoleun

Hodge prowled the living room. Something thumped and hissed. Marian returned, attracted by the noise.

"What are you—oh, my God, what are you *doing*?"

"Cleaning up the garbage. Now let's get out."

She started to make another objection, but he must have grabbed her to hustle her along. They went out through the kitchen, not bothering to shut the back door.

Without them for distraction, the pain in the back of my skull blossomed. I tried once more to crawl away from it, but my body was still frozen in place. Vanishing was impossible, negated by the use of wood. Damn it, why couldn't she have hit me with the lamp?

The damage must have affected my ears; something like radio static filled the air. I should have been able to hear their car as it drove away, though if Hodge was using that Caddy with the smooth motor . . . I hadn't heard him arrive, but then I'd been occupied with other things.

What had he meant by "cleaning up the garbage"?

Nothing good; even Marian hadn't liked it.

After a solid minute of effort, I managed to blink one eye. The right one that lay hard against the rug remained shut. I must have looked like Charlie McCarthy on a bad day.

There was a dry, dusty tang in the air. Well, that's what happens when you fall on a rug with your mouth hanging open. I spent another minute messily trying to work it shut.

Stick to blinking, it's easier.

A few years ago, I'd once suffered the all-time mother of hangovers. Even if I'd blanked out the drunken journey, the memory of arrival was still uncomfortably clear. Just short of my bed, I'd collapsed on the floor, spending an oblivious night on its hard, cold surface. In the morning, my joints were stiff and unforgiving, but it turned out to be a good thing not to have made it to bed, after all. When I woke up, my stomach's reaction to the excess abuse was instantaneous and awful. In acute physical agony, since my head felt like a popped balloon, I'd cleaned it up myself, too embarrassed to call the janitor.

The pain had been just as terrible then, but unlike tonight's fiasco, self-inflicted. Oh, for the good old days when I was too smart to hook up with a private detective.

Agent, Escott's voice automatically corrected in my mind.

This wasn't tracing stolen goods to be returned in triumph to

the owner, it was destroying lives. McAlister dead, Doreen . .
maybe, and eventually, Marian.

Part of me was ready to kill her for doing this to me. I wasn
proud of that desire, but it was reassuringly human. No seductiv
draining of her blood figured in my mind, though. It would b
up close and personal, a toss-up between strangulation or break
ing her neck.

Babbling.

The radio static was louder.

I tried moving my fingers next. They were farther from m
damaged skull. Maybe the nerves there hadn't heard the news
like a snake that keeps wriggling after the head is chopped off

Queasy thought.

They felt like overstuffed sausages and were about as deft, bu
they faintly responded. As if in echo, my toes flexed a little
There was hope for me yet. Another month or so and I'd be tap
dancing on flagpoles. I'd embrace it as my new vocation. I
probably paid better than writing and was safer than being as
sistant to a private agent.

Where the hell was Escott, anyway? Surely he'd have take
care of Summers by this time, unless there'd been trouble at th
hospital. If something had happened to Doreen, he might b
reluctant to deliver the news.

The static had developed into an unmistakable crackling.

Fire.

Mind-numbing panic washed over me for a few uncontrolle
seconds before reason took hold. There *was* a fire, but in th
fireplace. It had been burning earlier, all during that interviev
with Kitty, and when Marian had returned, she'd merely—

Fire.

As if in confirmation, the electricity failed and the lights wen
out except for a soft glow reflecting off the slice of wall. My on
working eyelid blinked at it stupidly.

They'd left me to burn to death.

Not to death, my mind continued idiotically, they thought yo
were already dead.

Panic on top of panic as I tried to crawl out. A wave of hea
washed over the top of my head and down my body. I wa
pointed toward the living room, the direction I had to go to ge
to the door serving the kitchen. Behind me was the front door
a shorter distance, but it was closed and perhaps even locked

Hodge and Marian had left the one to the kitchen open. I had a
wonderful vision of myself slithering through it, tumbling to
cool safety.

It was countered with harsh memories of fires I'd covered for
the paper in New York: bodies burned black, limbs stiffened into
unlikely poses of death. Would my brain burn up as well, or
would it continue to live on, trapped and insane inside a charred,
grinning wreck?

My feet flinched but could not push me forward; my fingers
grasped but had no strength.

Vanish. Try to *vanish*.

Smoke flooded the room, dimming the firelight. Would anyone from the main house have noticed by now?

The desperation to wink out and swirl away was strong enough
to fool me into thinking I'd actually done it. I felt the familiar
disorientation take hold; the heated air of the room would lift
me to the ceiling, then with a swift mental push I'd melt through
it into the open air. . . .

Illusion. I might as well have been welded to the floor.

The place was oven hot and loud. I'd forgotten how deafening
a fire could be. Would anyone hear my screams? By the time the
flames reached me, I would, indeed, be screaming.

My legs trembled. If I could get my arms under me—my toes
caught on the rug, slipped, and caught again.

Move.

My arms spasmed, pushing me forward toward . . . oh, God,
I can't go in there.

I was just able to raise my head briefly, long enough to see
what hell looked like. Shifting, treacherous gleams of red, or-
ange, and yellow-white danced along the living-room walls. The
curtains were thick with flames; spinning clouds of smoke raced
from them to the ceiling, filling the house. A forgotten magazine
on the floor ignited and burned, the pages curling open one by
one as though an invisible hand were swiftly turning them.

Half cursing, half sobbing, I urged my inert body to move
before it was too late while begging for more time to recover.
Another minute. Just one more minute and I could crawl. Please,
God, give me that much.

I flopped and twisted, trying to roll away. The kitchen exit
was blocked by the growing fire and my own limitations. I'd
have to try for the front door and hope it wasn't locked.

Not enough time. The edge of the rug I lay upon was already being eaten away. The whole thing would soon catch and go up, enveloping my clothes . . . me . . .

If I could scream, I could move. Don't waste the energy on anything else.

Coordination was too slow to match my level of terror. I got a water-weak elbow under me and pushed. It slewed me to the right. The worst part was trying to lift my head; the neck muscles weren't up to holding it for more than a second or two. It dragged on the floor like an anchor.

Glass shattered somewhere, probably from the heat. I didn't really care; I was too busy.

Christ, the door was miles away. Maybe if I rolled toward it . . .

I writhed, thinking of that damned headless snake again.

Another glassy crash.

Air rushed in, feeding the fire.

Someone shouted. My name, I thought, but I couldn't tell. My imagination had fooled me before.

More air. A sea of it rolled in; smoke dense enough to cut rolled out.

My name.

Someone coughing.

My name.

Blinded by the smoke, he blundered into me. Frantic hands clawed, randomly seized one arm, and tugged. I pushed in the same direction. Inelegant, but it worked. He cursed and coughed and damn near tore my arm from its socket. We made progress. The door loomed close, gloriously close. My head thumped against the threshold, reminding me of the original injury, but didn't care anymore. We were out of the furnace. One last pull and he dragged me clear of the porch and onto the hard ground.

Inexplicably, he began beating on my ankles with his hat. I understood why when a whole new kind of pain shot up from them and blasted through the top of my skull. Stung to movement, my legs kicked and flailed and generally interfered with his efforts. In spite of this, he managed to smother the flames before they got out of hand.

He dropped next to me, doubled over with hoarse coughing.

God looks after fools, after all. Thanks, Boss.

"Are you talking to me?" Escott wheezed, his eyes streaming and red from the smoke.

I hadn't realized I'd spoken aloud. "Not exactly."

"Good God, what happened to you?"

Having no need to breathe regularly, I hadn't taken in the smoke and was better able to talk, only I didn't feel like doing much. "I was dumb enough to turn my back on Marian."

"Is she in there?" He made a half start toward the burning house.

"No," I said quickly, waving him down. "Got away."

"Where?"

Now was not the time for explanations. We had to be somewhere else and fast. "We gotta get outta here, Charles. Are you able to walk?"

"Are you?"

Details, details. "How far?"

He rubbed at his eyes and shook his head. I couldn't tell if he was coughing or laughing. "Hang about."

I wasn't in any condition to do much else. He staggered away, returning a short age later to improvise a new driveway over the grounds with his Nash. He parked a narrow yard from where I lay and opened the passenger door. After that, it was a simple matter of hoisting me inside.

"The Stockyards?" he asked, sliding behind the wheel. First aid for me always meant a long, healing drink.

"The river."

Which is full of water, he seemed to be saying. *Not your preferred draft, old man.*

"Just get us moving, Charles. I'll tell you about it."

He coughed again, but shifted gears and hauled the wheel around. As we passed the guest-house garage, I nearly choked on a suppressed growl of outrage.

"That screw-faced son of a bitch stole my car!" A ridiculous reaction, considering what we'd both just been through, but it was one way of draining off some of the built-up stress.

"Which screw-faced son of a bitch?" he asked, managing to sound dignified despite his cough.

"Hodge. He came here tonight. When he left with Marian, they must have taken my car."

His face was one big question mark.

Right. I owed him—among many other things now—an expla-

nation, or at least part of one. In a few short sentences I covere
the disaster, omitting only the details of what happened when
tried to hypnotize Marian. It left a noticeable gap open to ques
tioning, and Escott jumped straight into the middle of it.

"How on earth was Hodge able to sneak up on you?"

I shrugged, as though uncertain myself, and hoped that
looked convincing. "I was preoccupied with Marian, with get
ting her to talk."

He made a noise indicating that he understood and I belatedl.
realized that he thought I was referring to a hypnotic question
and-answer session. I let the misinterpretation stand. For th
moment, it was better than the truth.

"She knew that I knew too much and jumped the gun—
Hodge's gun, to be exact—by lambasting me with that table,"
continued. "She couldn't have been listening to him. She wen
crazy like she did with McAlister. Hodge stopped her. I think i
shook him up to see her like that."

"I daresay. Perhaps he even prevented her from inflicting mor
serious damage than she did."

"Or he was mad that she cheated him of the satisfaction o
doing it himself. It would have been so much simpler if she'
just waited and let him try to shoot me."

"Most unfortunate that she did not. Are you better? You soun
better."

I opened and closed my hands, evidence of my physical re
covery. My singed legs *hurt*, but I'd soon be able to take car
of them. The emotions would take longer, perhaps a lifetime
even by my changed standards. "I'm getting control again. I
takes a little time and I didn't have any before. How'd you knov
I was there?"

"I didn't, nor did I look for you since I did not see your car
That may have been why Hodge stole it. As for why he set fir
to the place . . ."

"To confuse and distract, like stirring an anthill with a stick
It leaves the ants running all over trying to put stuff back in
order, and in the meantime they forget about the stick."

"Or its possible return."

"Okay, so if you weren't looking for me, then how . . . ?"

"I heard you," he said in a muted tone that made me fee
quiet as well. My throat wasn't aching because of the smoke

"Then I saw you through the front window, which I had to break to open the door. I think you're aware of the rest."

"Thanks for pulling me out, Charles."

Shows of gratitude always made him uncomfortable. "Well, good help is hard to come by," he demurred. "I've but one request."

"Anything."

"Don't do that again."

I started to make a light reply, then for the first time noticed how tightly he gripped the steering wheel. His eyelids were jumping around and I could almost feel the nervous energy coming off him. He was putting up a calm front, but it was plain to me that I'd thoroughly scared the shit out of him.

"Scout's honor," I said humbly.

He nodded once, to close the subject, and switched to a new one. "You said the river. Do you think she's getting away via the facilities offered by the IFT warehouse?"

"That's my best guess. If she's not there, then I don't know where she'll be. And it's not a getaway or she wouldn't have questioned him. All she planned to do was to turn over the bracelet, then I showed up and threw a monkey wrench into the works. Hodge had orders to take her out. Since she didn't know what they'd done to Harry, she was just stupid enough to go with him."

"So Kyler could sort her out about shooting Doreen?"

"Yeah, only she might not survive the experience."

"Would he go so far?"

"What do you think?"

For an answer, Escott stepped on the gas.

11

THOUGH IT HAD been a solid and busy six months since his last visit to International Freshwater Transport's warehouse, Escott' memory needed no prodding on how to get there. He picked out the fastest possible route, pausing only to chafe at stop signals. At this hour most of the intersections were empty, so the wait was doubly hard, but he wasn't about to attract attention by running through them. A curious cop was the last thing we wanted.

I was having trouble deciding if the tightness in my gut was due to Marian's assault or the situation we were walking into. Maybe it was a bit of both. Now that I had time to rest and take inventory, more aches stood up to be counted, especially along my spine. My lower legs and head were still the worst; I'd have to tend to them before anything else.

Eyes shut to concentrate, I tried to vanish. Except for a faint shiver running over my skin, nothing happened. My head throbbed in protest.

Damned wood.

I waited a few more blocks and tried again, failed, and waited some more. Each attempt got me farther down the line; on the fourth try, I finally melted away into the air.

Escott made a choking sound and the car swerved. It startled me back into solidity.

"What's going on?" I grabbed the arm rest for balance.

"Would you mind giving a fellow a little warning before you

launch into that bloody Cheshire cat routine of yours?'' he complained, looking very put out.

He usually held things in, but events were also eating him up from the inside. I couldn't blame him for letting it show for once. "Sorry. I have to do it again. Consider yourself warned."

He grunted and kept his eyes on the road.

I faded into a wonderfully numbing nothingness better than any salve, and stayed there. The only problem was trying to hover in one spot: I tended to keep moving forward whenever the car braked. The windshield glass and metal body of the car helped to confine me inside; the trick was remembering to hold in place on my end of the seat. It wouldn't do to distract Escott further by bumping into him with an abrupt rush of cold.

"We're here," he announced, his voice made distant by my invisibility.

I was reluctant to return, but when I did, things didn't hurt nearly so much. The skin on my legs had stopped burning and my head felt only slightly tender. A day's rest, a stop at the Stockyards, and I'd be . . .

"They're not exactly secretive, are they?" he commented, drawing my attention to the front of the warehouse.

"The gang's all here," I agreed.

Parked along the street were two identical Caddies and my Buick. In this drab neighborhood they stuck out like birthday cakes at a funeral. A light was on in the warehouse office, the rest of the windows were dark. If my heart had still been working, it'd have been trying to thump its way out of my chest.

"Anything wrong?"

I nodded. "Not twenty minutes ago I wanted to kill her; now I'm here to play Douglas Fairbanks and rush to her rescue."

"After what you've been through, your reluctance is understandable." Escott had one hell of a gift for understatement.

"It's more than reluctance. I'm ready to say to hell with it and leave her there."

"And will you?"

That question demanded more thought than I had time to give it. "I want to, but if I stay, then you'll go in instead, won't you?"

He said nothing, though for him it made for an eloquent speech. He'd go, all right, with or without me, and I wasn't about to let him do anything so crazy.

I laughed once, and not because I was happy, then started shrugging out of my overcoat. Escott's borrowed suit coat went, too. The cold wouldn't bother me for some time yet, and I wanted to be free to move. I tore off my rumpled tie and tossed it on the pile.

"Are you sure you're in shape for this?" he asked.

"Why? What do I look like? No, don't answer that. Let's just say that I'm in better shape than they think I am. You got a gun?"

"Yes." In addition to the stolen Webley-Fosbury, he owned a much smaller snub-nosed Colt revolver, which he started to draw from his coat pocket.

"Hang on to it for yourself," I told him. "If any rats get past me, you'll need it."

He saw the logic and kept the gun. "Good hunting."

"Break a leg."

We got out at the same time, swinging the doors shut, but not letting them latch. The plan was for me to go in first and scout around for the best opportunity to get Marian out. If it didn't exist, then I'd have to make one. Escott was to back me up if it became necessary. Knowing how crazy Kyler and his stooges got when crossed, I was going to be damned careful.

Though they looked deserted, I checked each of the cars to make certain of the fact. Escott followed and we ended up crouched in the same patch of shadow cast by one of the Caddies.

"I'd like to cut off their lines of retreat," he whispered.

"As long as it's quiet."

He flashed a rare smile or a rictus grin, I couldn't really tell, and eased open the driver's door. He felt under the dashboard a moment and something snapped in his hand. He darted to the other Caddy, performed the same operation, and returned. "That should put them in the shop for a while," he said.

"What about my car?"

"I'm hoping we may simply drive it out. Have you the keys?"

"Still in my pocket. Hodge must have hot-wired it."

Ideally, we wanted a clean getaway without any legal fuss. Escott was ready to use his gun, but it'd be better for us if he didn't. It was up to me to make sure things stayed quiet.

I crept up to the front door of the warehouse, feeling rather vulnerable in the dim light thrown out by its overhead bulb. I listened for some time, my ear pressed to the crack between the door and jamb and heard nothing. Shrugging a negative back at Escott, I pointed to myself and then toward the door. He gave me a thumbs-up in acknowledgment, turned gray, and ceased to exist.

Filtering through the same narrow crack was easy enough, then I made a quick sweep of the small room. It was empty and hadn't changed much since my last visit, as I discovered after materializing. An extra layer of grime and an oil heater had been added, but nothing more interesting. The second door leading into the warehouse proper was shut. I listened there for a time and eventually caught the faint sound of voices. One of them seemed to be Hodge's, but I wasn't sure.

I quietly unlocked the front door for Escott, then slipped through the inner door myself. I stayed invisible and felt my way around to what I hoped was a concealed corner and faded in slowly, eyes wide, and ears straining.

The place was vast and dark and the high ceiling caused the voices to echo deceptively, though I eventually pinned down their direction. I took my time approaching, half of it in a semitransparent state to avoid making sound myself. This lasted until I got a third of the way into the warehouse and ran into a familiar obstacle. The place was built well out over the river to expedite the transfer of goods to and from cargo ships. It was fine for the ships, but lousy for me with my inherent problem with running water. I'd be able to vanish easily enough; coming back again was the hard part. To do that, I had to be over land.

I went solid and tiptoed forward, then had to dig my heels in and really work. The resistance was like trying to push a long, heavy curtain back from the bottom, hard to get started and reluctant to keep moving. Once I was well out over the river I was all right, but as they say, the first step's a lulu. At least now my hearing wouldn't be handicapped.

They were at the far end of the long line of crates, using only a single work light, the kind with a handle and cord at one end and a hook on the other. They'd hung it awkwardly onto the lip of an open crate. It made a harsh fan of localized glare; odds were, they'd be fairly night blind outside of it. I moved closer.

Chaven was busy digging through the crate; stray drifts of excelsior littered the floor around him. He strained and lifted out a hunk of new-looking metal. I didn't know what it was beyond the fact that it looked like the internal part of a large machine and that it was obviously heavy. He tossed it ponderously onto the floor with other, similar parts. The light on the crate shook as he worked. Shadows jostled one another.

"That enough?" he asked, straightening.

Kyler stood just behind the light and was difficult to see. "More."

"But that's over a hundred pounds."

"More. Those things get buoyant. I'm not risking a floater."

"Have a heart, my back's killin' me." But Chaven began digging again, pulling out piece after piece.

In the floor a couple of yards behind him gaped a trapdoor into darkness. Hodge sat on its edge, his legs resting on steps going down under the warehouse. I heard and smelled water.

"You can help," Chaven said to him.

"I've done my part." Hodge patted the spot under his left arm where his gun was holstered. I went very still and cold.

"If you want to stay here all night that's your business. There, that's two hundred pounds at least. Okay?"

"Take it down," said Kyler.

"Huh." Chaven bent, picked up a part in each hand, and walked up to Hodge. Hodge obligingly moved over to give him better access to the steps. Chaven grunted "huh" again and descended. He was gone for about two minutes, then returned empty-handed to take away two more parts.

I slipped back the way I came and made a fast and hopefully quiet round of the stacks. When I moved toward the light once more, I was behind Kyler, all but looking over his shoulder. The work light wasn't in my eyes so much from this angle. Now I could see Marian, a dark form in her long coat.

She wasn't moving. She lay on her side, huddled compactly at the foot of a tall packing case. It was the same one they'd backed me up against only last night. A ball of ice formed down in my stomach and rolled a little. Closing my eyes didn't help. She was still there when I opened them.

Hardly aware of it, I walked up to Kyler and gave him a solid punch in the kidney, one that Escott could appreciate. He dropped almost too fast for me to catch him, but I managed and held him up in front of me.

Hodge was alert enough to notice and react. He drew his gun and jumped to his feet, trying to squint past the light to his boss.

Kyler almost jabbed my gut with his elbow, but he didn't have enough force or follow through. In return, I slapped the side of his head. Once was all that was needed, then he had to have my full support to stand.

"Boss?" Hodge skirted the trapdoor. He saw me, or part of me. The light was still in his eyes, but he had enough of a target to aim at. He held the gun ready.

I made sure Kyler was entirely in his way. "Put it up, Hodge, not unless you think you can shoot through your boss."

"Who . . . ?"

"Besides, he said I had until tomorrow . . . remember?"

The stunned look on his face indicated that he did. "You go to hell," he said, but there was a crack in his voice. He was plenty scared.

"Not this time."

I pushed Kyler ahead of me. He tried to fight, but I had a solid grip on his arms and was practically holding him off the floor. Hodge took a better aim at me but Kyler stopped him.

"Get behind him, you jerk! Shoot him from cover!"

Hodge's reflexes were good. Two fast steps, and he was swallowed up in the shadows between the stacks. I dragged Kyler out of the fan of light and shook him the way a kid shakes a rag doll. He was too dazed to resist as I went through his pockets. Right away I found his gun and pulled it. I didn't have enough hands to use it and let it drop to the floor. In his inside pocket with his wallet was the black velvet bag. It still seemed to weigh a ton.

He recovered quickly and just enough to be inconvenient. I shoved the bracelet away and threw him toward the trapdoor. Arms flailing, he tumbled right into it with a brief yell. Another yell in another voice matched him for surprise and pain. Chaven must have been coming up the stairs when Kyler fell through onto him. They made a lot more noise rolling and crashing all the way to the bottom, and then they stopped making noise altogether.

I forgot them when Hodge fired his first shot at me. I was nearly deafened by the roar, but felt nothing. Seeing me come back from the dead must have left him with a bad case of the shakes. So much the better, since I wasn't ready to vanish just yet.

Gray smoke from the gun hung in the motionless air, giving

away his hiding place. I went low and scuttled over to Marian. He fired again, missing completely.

"Boss? Chaven? You okay?" He sounded very worried. I didn't think it was for their skins, but for his own. Armed or not, he didn't want to face me by himself.

Neither of us heard an answer from the trap.

I turned to Marian, checking for a pulse, but I was way too late. It was sad to say, but the only honest regret I felt was for her father.

"This is your work, Hodge," I heard myself shouting. The echoes filled the place, chasing each other into nothing.

"I did what I was told," he shouted back.

"Kyler gets his turn later."

Shot.

He'd moved. The bullet creased air next to my left ear and tore into the case behind me.

Shot.

But by that time I was moving as well and dropped flat.

Shot.

One in Marian's heart and five embedded in the crates. If he carried a round ready in the chamber, it meant he had at least two more bullets left, maybe a lot more if he had a spare magazine. Not that it mattered much to either of us in the long run. He could be packing a Thompson with a full drum and it wouldn't help him. But I couldn't afford to let myself be hit any more than a normal man could, not while I was over water.

No shot. He must have realized he was running short. Good. I didn't want to have to remind him and possibly tip my own hand.

Silence, except for his breathing, then came a stealthy step and a shifting of cloth. He was on the other side of the stack from me and creeping forward. He stopped for a long time to listen and perhaps puzzle out why I'd left Kyler's gun behind. I hadn't thought of it at the time, but now I could see that it was turning into an excellent piece of bait.

At the far end of the warehouse a door creaked open.

That had to be Escott, drawn in by the shooting.

Hodge jumped into the open, intent on Kyler's gun. I broke away from the stack and went after him.

He heard me charging up, whirled, and got off one more shot.

It went wild. Before he could trigger another, I tackled him, and we fell flat.

His head thumped against the floor and the whites of his eyes showed for a few seconds. He gagged, trying to recover his lost breath. He still had the gun, though, and enough presence of mind left not to use it until it could do him some good.

We were matched for weight, but I had him on raw strength and was able to immobilize him easily enough. His reaction was frustration, not surprise, as he kept struggling and got absolutely and utterly nowhere. I had one hand holding fast onto his gun arm. It'd be a simple matter to crush his wrist. . . .

Instead, I bent his hand around, forcing it in the direction I wanted. When he realized what I was doing, he thrashed and yelled, throwing all his desperate energy into a last scrabbling fight for life.

The gun was at half cock and as I found out when I pressed my finger on top of his trigger finger, had one round left. The sound was so loud I didn't really hear it, the muzzle flash blinded, the smoke burned.

I didn't know which I'd remember the longest: Hodge's terrified shriek, or the look on his face as it happened.

Limbs twitching and hands shaking, I stood away from him and swallowed back the laughter that surged up like a rush of bile in my throat. It helped when I turned my back to him. The exit wound was very bad and where most of the bloodsmell came from. Despite the evident and total finality of that wound, he still looked alive.

I will not regret this. If I had to, I'd do it again.

A few steps and I was leaning against a crate, hiding my eyes from it all. The laughter hung heavily in the back of my throat, threatening to either choke me or turn into a sob. It wasn't finished; more work remained to be done. There was yet one more suicide to arrange, maybe two.

First I groaned in protest, then, as though a switch had been thrown, everything shut down at once. The laughter died to nothing; the sickness forming in my gut faded away. I looked around with new eyes and found corners to be just a little sharper than they'd been before, and colors were brighter. The light from the lamp was both harsh and beautiful. I'd turned crazy cold— a mechanical man about to perform an unpleasant but necessary job. This wasn't vengeance—no more than a butcher is vengeful against the animal he carves up.

I drew a long breath and let it filter slowly out as I walked past Marian and Hodge and closed my hand over Kyler's gun.

"Jack?"

He'd come up softly. I was too wrapped in my own silent hell to have noticed his approach but was not surprised to see him. Escott was my friend and I could trust him to be sensible in an emergency. He saw Marian right away and went to her and learned what I had learned. He shook his head and said something, but I didn't quite catch it. Then he turned around and saw the rest of the place.

He stared at Hodge's body lying at the narrow end of a spray of blood and brains. The gun was loose in his hand now, but still pressed to his temple. That was wrong. I had to change the position slightly, to pull his hand back a bit to allow for the recoil of the shot.

"I'm taking care of it," I told Escott. "Don't worry about anything." In my own ears I sounded extraordinarily calm, as though I were doing a household chore for him.

Like taking out the garbage.

Now he stared at me; I nodded back reassuringly and stooped to adjust Hodge's gun and arm. There, that looked more natural.

"We have to leave, Jack." Escott did his best to match my calmness, but I knew better. His heart was racing fit to burst. My own was, or rather, my own wasn't. . . .

Never mind that.

I smiled at him. "In a minute. This won't take long."

Cheerful. Almost. That's what it sounded like. I wasn't feeling at all cheerful, but then I wasn't feeling, period.

I walked to the trapdoor and started down the stairs.

Below the reinforced flooring of the warehouse were the dozens of thick cement pillars that supported it. They marched away in even rows in every direction, their tops wrapped in dirty shadow, their bases sunk deep in the water. The river had left them stained and stinking. The stairs led to a broad wooden landing that rose and fell with the lap of water. Tied next to it was a sleek inboard; on its deck sat an open crate. It didn't take much genius work to figure out where Chaven had put the heavy machine parts. Once the lid was nailed down, they had only to take a quiet cruise out to deep water and Marian's body would disappear forever.

The closer I got to the water, the higher my back hairs rose. For a few seconds I had to fight to stay solid, so overwhelming was the instinctual urge to vanish and draw away to the safety of land.

Kyler and Chaven were still sprawled on the landing. Chaven was groggy but trying to pull himself together. Kyler bled from a cut over one eye and was rumpled all over, almost comic in his disarray. He squinted up at me without recognition. The light was bad here for human eyes. To him, I'd be a silhouette against a slightly lighter shadow.

"Hodge?" he asked, doubtful.

"Hodge shot himself." Not quite true, but details like that didn't matter now. "You're going to shoot yourself as well, Kyler."

"What the hell . . . ?" said Chaven.

I raised my hand high so they could see what was in it. "I brought your gun along to do the job." Had I been capable of laughter, I might have laughed at their expressions.

Chaven woke up very fast and clawed inside his coat. I centered Kyler's gun on him.

"Jack." Escott's voice.

"In a minute," I called back.

"You've no time left to make a proper job of it," he reasoned. "We have to go while we can."

That made a lot of sense, but I hated to leave the work half-done when only another minute was all I . . .

Chaven got his gun out and fired. His aim was off because of the darkness and his own fear. The slug sang through my arm. Negligible damage anywhere else, sheer disaster here. I dropped Kyler's gun, staggered back against the rail, and forgot about everything but the necessity of remaining solid.

Shadows grew lighter, threatening to turn gray and vanish altogether. My hand was going transparent; I willed it back, ordering it to *hold* on to the stair railing, and not to slide through.

"Do you see? Do you see?" Kyler's voice. What the hell was he talking about?

I flickered back and forth between pain-filled reality and numbing dream. Escott shouted my name but I couldn't break my concentration to answer. Kyler and Chaven were limping away, stumbling into their boat, and I was helpless to follow. While Kyler fumbled at the ropes, Chaven took aim for a second, more careful shot. He hit his target, but for him the timing was ill judged, catching me in a semitransparent phase. The bullet whizzed right through my chest and smacked into one of the steps.

Before he could fire again, another gun went off. The roar so close above almost buried me in sound. It was all I could do to just hold on to the flimsy stair rail. I'd lost sight of everything except the bottomless black water that seemed to swell closer. . . .

Escott grabbed my shirt collar and hauled me back. Kyler and Chaven swung into view once more. They were both in the boat now and blue smoke belched from it as Kyler got the motor started. He was doing all the work; Chaven was hanging on to the box and not doing much of anything besides cursing.

Kyler gunned the boat and it glided rapidly away from the landing. He held a straight course between the tall pillars until he was free of them, then turned onto the river and was gone.

"You had time for another clear shot, Charles," I said. "Why didn't you take them?"

Escott gave no direct answer to my question. "We have to go, Jack."

The searing heat in my arm dissipated and with it the imminent threat of vanishing. Still sensitive to the pressure of the water all around, I was unable to do more than crouch on the stairs. Escott eased past me and retrieved Kyler's gun. He slipped on the safety and dropped it in his pocket. Coming back up, he held his hand out to me.

"Come along, old man. It's very cold down here or have you even noticed it yet?"

With his help, I found my feet and we trudged up and emerged from the trapdoor. He steered me well around the awful tableau framed by the work light, and we headed toward the distant front door.

"Are the cops coming?" I asked.

"It's best that we leave before we find out," he said, not really answering again. What was the matter with him?

The inner door was open and he left it that way. He did the same thing with the outside door, leaving it wide. We stopped

t his car and he had me put on my overcoat. As he'd guessed,
I hadn't noticed the cold. I felt nothing at all.

He took me to my own car and asked if I could drive it. It
seemed an odd question, but I said yes and got in. He told me
to go straight home and promised that he'd be following right
behind if I needed anything. I shook my head, a little puzzled,
but strangely touched by his obvious concern.

We drove off quietly, obeying all the speed laws and traffic
stops. For me it was another dream ride like the trip I'd taken
earlier over to the Pierce house. I pulled up to my usual curbside
spot in front of Escott's old three-story brick house. Escott broke
away to park in the narrow garage behind the building. He re-
appeared quickly enough to walk with me up the steps and unlock the door.

The place was warm and, after the fresh outside air, stuffy
with the smell of his favorite pipe tobacco. We shrugged out of
our coats; I draped mine on the hall tree, he put his on a hanger,
and then put the hanger on an empty peg. After that we went
into the parlor. I sat in the leather chair by the radio and noticed
my hands for the first time. They were very dirty and smelled
all at once of wood smoke, cordite, and blood. A sickening
combination, but I did not feel sick.

Escott went into the kitchen and dialed a number on the phone.
His call was very short and he'd swapped his English accent for
a German one. He gave the address of the warehouse and in a
frightened voice complained of hearing gunfire, then hung up.
He made a brief stop in the dining room before coming in to sit
on the couch opposite. He must have poured half the contents
of his bottle of good brandy into the glass in his hand.

"I wish you could have some as well," he said. "If anyone
needed it . . ."

"Is something wrong?"

"No, Jack." His answer was easy and reassuring. After a
drink and a minute for the stuff to work into him, he said, "I
expect what you really need is a very hot bath and some kip
time."

I blinked a little, thinking it over. "That sounds good to me."

He must have been holding his breath, for he visibly relaxed.
"You go on up and do that, then."

He seemed anxious for me to go, so I went to my room upstairs and peeled slowly out of my clothes as though shedding

an old skin. Another layer came off in the hot water of the tu
and yet another as I shaved. When I came downstairs again, m
body felt better, but still strangely detached from my mind.

He was on the kitchen phone speaking in a low voice with
hushed shock that was only partly assumed. On the other end o
the line it must have sounded sincere enough.

"I'm terribly sorry to hear that. . . . They do? . . . Oh, there
no question about it, I shall come over immediately. Yes, o
course . . ."

And so on, until he hung up.

"Pierce?" I asked.

He nodded. "Letting me know about the arson on his gues
house. He thinks it's connected with his case and wants me t
look at things. I don't know when I'll be back. Will you be al
right?"

Again with the questions. "You want me along?"

"Not this time. Besides, you need the rest."

Maybe he had a point there. "Does he know about Marian?"

His face grew longer. "Not yet. The police may not have ha
time to sort it out yet. Anonymous calls don't always send then
bolting off to an immediate investigation."

He left to get his coat. I noticed that he'd tidied the kitche
up from Harry Summers's visit. The empty brandy glass stoo
rinsed and drying with the others on the sink drain board. H
wouldn't have wasted good brandy and I had no doubt that he'
properly finished it off, but his manner so far was stone-col
sober.

"I found this," I said when he returned to leave by the back
door. I drew out the black velvet bag from my bathrobe pocke
and put it on the table.

"Dear me." He arrested his move to put on his hat and opene
the little bag instead. He studied the bracelet for a while, turning
it over and over in his long fingers. I wondered if it felt as heav
to him as it had to me.

"I thought you'd want to give it back to Pierce."

He pursed his lips, managing to look thoughtful and horrifie
all at once. "No, I couldn't possibly—not at this point, at an
rate."

"The warehouse, then. Plant it on Marian, where it belongs."

"We can't take that chance. As soon as the police get there
they'll be all over the place with their notes and cameras. It'

be impossible to smuggle it in, especially if Blair conducts the investigation.''

''Then mail it to Pierce. We sure as hell can't hang on to it.''

He balled the thing up in his fist, then poured it into the bag. ''For the moment, we shall do exactly that.'' He sounded like a man with an idea, but wasn't ready to share it yet. ''You keep it for now until I have time to put it in the safe. It'll be all right in that vault of yours below stairs.''

It'd be just fine, but I didn't want to have any part of it. I also didn't have the energy left to tell him, so I meekly stuffed the bag back in my pocket.

He locked the back door behind him and soon had the Nash out of the garage and was gone. The house loomed huge and empty about me. The place must have been warm enough, but I suppressed a shiver.

Without thinking much about it, I vanished and seeped through the floor to the walled-off alcove directly below the kitchen. It was so much faster than using the basement stairs and had the added attraction of taking me out of the world for a few moments. It was some time before I returned to solidity.

The room was hot and still. The lamp was on, just as I'd left it when I'd walked through the wall to find out why Escott wanted to interrupt my writing. Had that happened only last night? I squinted at the neatly typed sheets as though they were someone else's property. They were. I felt quite different from the earnest would-be writer that had typed them, different in that I wasn't feeling anything at all.

A tremor ran up my spine in the hot little room.

Bobbi's photo smiled at me from the makeshift desk. It was a studio portrait, done by the best in the city and glamoured up, though with Bobbi they didn't have to work very hard. She had one of those faces that the camera practically makes love to; all she ever had to do for a drop-dead photo was to smile.

I started to pick it up for a closer look and noticed my hand was trembling. I gripped it with the other, but it was just as out of control.

No regrets, remember?

The trembling spread from my hands to my arms and joined up with the tremor in my back. I couldn't seem to hold it down or stretch out of it.

No regrets, so why was every nerve in my body starting to scream? I rolled onto the cot and its layer of earth and shook and shook and shook and never once stopped until the sun came up at last and released me from the night's terrors.

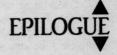

EPILOGUE

THE FACT THAT it was a whole different night when I awoke was of absolutely no comfort. It was still night, and some can be darker than others, as I'd come to learn, and I was starting this one with my equivalent of a hangover. My head and spine held fast to a residual ache and my muscles were cramped and tired and stiff as a . . .

Go on and say it, since it's true.

. . . corpse's.

I thought of a lot of unpleasant replies for that nagging voice in my head, but it hardly seemed worth the effort. If I felt bad, then no one could blame me for wanting to groan.

When I finally dragged myself upstairs to the parlor, I found Escott stretched out as usual on the couch smoking his pipe.

"Are you all right?" he asked in his most neutral tone, but studying me closely.

"Yes. I think I am, anyway."

"You sound better."

"How bad was I?"

"You were in some sort of shock. Last night your eyes looked like black pits with nothing in them. Most disconcerting."

Understatement was his specialty, but I didn't want to spend any time going over my troubles. Too much rehashing and they might come back on me. I dropped into the leather chair by the radio and asked a few questions about the events of the day and got an earful.

Soon after his arrival to view the smoking remains of Pierce's guest house, the cops came by with the bad news about Marian. Escott had gone with Pierce to identify her body.

"How's Mr. Pierce doing?"

"As can be expected, he's carrying a heavy load of grief. It's very hard for him, since he doesn't know all the details and I can hardly tell him. He will find full enlightenment, perhaps, to be of little comfort."

I couldn't help but agree.

The warehouse murders had opened up a whole new line for Lieutenant Blair to follow and he was good at his job. My efforts notwithstanding, he'd figured that Hodge's suicide had been a complete fake and was looking for the third party who'd arranged it. Escott suggested burning the clothes I'd been wearing at the time, especially the shoes. I'd left a fairly clear footprint behind. That they might trace it to me was unlikely, but why take chances?

"What do they call it? Accessory after the fact, or aiding and abetting?" I asked.

"I call it keeping a friend out of trouble."

The back of my neck prickled. "Charles, I murdered the man. I had a choice, and I chose to kill him."

"And we've been down this road before and survived. Would you do it again under the same circumstances?"

I dropped my eyes, giving him his answer.

"We may argue the fine distinctions between murder and execution if you like, but it will eventually come out that you no more wish to turn yourself in over this particular business than I do."

"It's just . . . just knowing that that kind of thing is inside me."

"It's in all of us, not just you. Last night you asked me why I did not take that second shot at them. Believe me, I truly wanted to."

"But you didn't."

"The idea was to get you out of there as quickly as possible. That was much more important than killing Kyler. Perhaps I should have risked complications at the time and done so, because there are sure to be more problems to come from it."

"Good God, he's going to be coming after you with an army."

"When he gets the time. At the moment he is far too occupied with avoiding the authorities."

The police had quickly traced the ownership of Kyler's Cadillacs and were trying to locate him to get an explanation of why they were parked in front of a murder site. Blair was also starting to turn up connections between Marian Pierce and Kyler and the gambling clubs he ran.

"I doubt much shall come of it, though." Escott sighed. "Kyler wields a great deal of power in this city, whether the city wants to admit it or not, and he's inherited some influential political allies from Frank Paco. There are threads to connect him to Marian Pierce, but I fear they are not plentiful enough or strong enough to twist into a rope for his neck."

"We're talking stalemate."

"For the moment." But he looked thoughtful.

"You thinking about the bracelet, Charles?"

"Hmm."

"Of using it somehow to nail him?"

"Somehow. But I haven't quite decided just how. It will come in time. I'm sure of it."

Doreen was far from well, but the doctor was more optimistic than he'd been last night. She'd regained consciousness long enough to state in no uncertain terms who had shot her—and why. Though they couldn't prove by paperwork that the gun found in Marian's purse had belonged to Stan McAlister, his fingerprints were still on the bullets. The bullets taken from Doreen by the surgeons were matched to the same gun. Since Blair's original case against Kitty Donovan was too flimsy to hold up, he was dropping it altogether and backtracking Marian Pierce. His talk with Harry Summers more or less clinched things.

Sebastian Pierce's load of grief was proving to be very heavy, indeed.

Some of my own load lifted, though, at the news about Doreen. While he lighted a pipe, I trotted upstairs and dressed. It didn't take long and I was coming down again, in my best suit and another pair of shoes. Last night's clothes were tied up in a bundle under my arm. I'd snipped off the laundry marks and anything else I could think of and had stuffed those into a pocket.

On the way to the hospital I made several stops, twice at gas stations to flush away labels, then I detoured over a bridge to scatter the buttons in the river. The latter was the most difficult because of the water; the physical discomfort reminded me of the warehouse, and the warehouse reminded me of Hodge. I was glad to leave.

It was more luck than looking, but I found an incinerator still going at full blast in a backyard junk pile close to the Stockyards. The air stank of burning rubber and meat, but I was able to slip in and out without being spotted. Invisibility has its advantages. Shoes and clothes safely disposed of, I stopped next at the Stockyards and hoped that the drink I took there would clear away the last of the aches.

Visiting hours weren't quite over when I reached the hospital, but Doreen was isolated from the other patients and the nurse was reluctant to let me do more than look through a window set in the door. Dr. Rosinski was with Doreen and I cornered him as he came out.

"She's doing as well as can be expected," he told me, which wasn't saying much. "So far there's no infection, which is a very good sign, but it will be awhile before she's past all the risks."

"Is she awake?"

"Partially. If you went in there, I doubt that she would really notice."

"Then it's all right if I go in?"

He could see that it was important to me, but the casual way he ordered up a mask and gown left me with a bad feeling. Perhaps he was taking all the precautions he could to help her, but he still didn't think much of her chances. He told me five minutes and repeated the same to the nurse.

Doreen looked smaller, more crushed somehow. Even the color of her hair was muted. I said her name a few times and touched a limp, cold hand. She stirred a little and her eyelids shivered open to half mast.

"Remember me, honey?"

The corner of her mouth curled slightly.

"No need to talk, I just came in to see how you were doing."

I suddenly felt incredibly awkward. There was no way I could say all I needed to say. I wanted to apologize to her like crazy, to tell her anything that would make it all better again, but it was impossible. The disappointment was a jolt; so much of a jolt that I finally realized why I was there. Sick as she was, I'd come to her to get comfort, not give it; to try to clear my own conscience at her expense.

The self-disgust I felt almost made me turn away, but I sat next to her and held her hand and smiled, though she couldn't see it through the gauze mask.

I kept up a one-sided conversation for another minute or so. Inane stuff, but she seemed to be listening. That, or I was fooling myself again.

"You . . ."

Her whisper was so soft I had to bend close.

". . . got away."

"From Leadfoot Sam? Yeah, I got away. He won't be bothering you, either."

"Yeah?"

"Promise. He's leaving you alone now. I made sure of it."

"Thas' good." Her eyes closed and opened. "Cops get her?"

It took me a second to work out that she was referring to Marian. "Yeah, she won't be causing you any more trouble. You're home free." God, I hoped that was true.

"What's your name again?"

That threw me until I remembered I'd given her one name and Sam another. "Jack."

"Then thanks, Jack."

I said you're welcome and left it at that.

"You got a nice girl home?"

"Yeah, you could say that."

She smiled a little. "Treat her good, huh? You . . . you're good people."

"I'm glad you think so, honey."

"Don' tell 'er 'bout us," she slurred out, her eyes drifting shut. "You're the kind to c'fess, you don' wanna do that. Not to her."

"Doreen—"

"Lissen to me, I been there m'self. You tell her an' it'll change things. I know. If you got somethin' good, don' screw it up."

I wondered just how much she did know or remember about those few moments in her cold studio. Apparently it was a pleasant memory.

"Yeah, honey, I promise. You just rest for now and I'll take care of things for you."

And so on, until she was asleep again.

* * *

I'd gone in for comfort, decided against seeking it, and got it anyway. Doreen was some woman and I'd keep my promise to her. Not all confessions are good for the soul; some can even tear them apart. The last thing I ever wanted to do was to bring more grief to Bobbi's life, so I would be silent. I knew now that I could visit her tonight and feel comfortable about it.

The hospital parking lot was fairly empty as I walked out into the brisk air. In a few more minutes I'd trade it for the lot at the Top Hat Club and sneak in once again by the stage entrance to her dressing room. After that, I'd try resuming my life again.

I pulled into the street and stepped on the gas. In the rearview mirror, I chanced to look back, and saw a silent Cadillac with smoke-dark windows doing the same.

Snake, I thought, and my hands began to tremble.

CLASSIC SCIENCE FICTION
AND FANTASY

279